FRACTURED INTENTIONS

J.A. OWENBY

GIVEAWAYS AND MORE

Enjoy giveaways, the inside scoop about J.A. Owenby, and never miss a new release again! Sign up today at https://www.authorjaowenby.com/newsletter

1

———

"**D**ad!" I yelled as a black truck barreled through the red light and directly toward us at top speed.

Our tires screeched as the Porsche 911 Carrera 4S fishtailed, and the inertia from the impact shoved my head against my headrest. A scream shot from my throat as a loud boom filled my ears, and the pickup sped away.

Terror dug its fingernails into me, sending shockwaves through my system while I fumbled around, trying to comprehend what the hell had just happened.

The deflated white airbag caught my attention, and I struggled to wrap my brain around the wreckage I was sitting in.

"Dad."

My voice cracked with anxiety, and tears pricked my eyes while I stared at him. Blood oozed from his slightly open mouth, and his neck bent toward me at an awkward angle. The windshield had sprayed pieces of glass in every direction, slicing his face and arms. I assumed I had cuts as well, but I didn't have time to check.

I patted his cheek gently. "Dad. Dad!" My heart rate spiked with each unresponsive second, and I hoped like hell he was only unconscious. "Hang on. I'll figure this out."

Fear clawed its way up my throat. I attempted to open the passenger door, but it wouldn't budge. Somehow my window was still intact, and I wasn't able to crawl through it. I leaned back toward my dad's seat, pulled up my leg, and rammed my foot into the side of the car, forcing the door open.

A dark curl of smoke snaked in through the open space, and the sickening scent of burnt rubber assaulted my nostrils. I tugged the collar of my top over my nose, attempting to block out the foul smell, and offered a silent prayer to the universe that nothing would explode —not with my dad still inside.

Pieces of glass from the front windshield fell from my lavender silk blouse and designer jeans, pinging off the concrete, as I stood on shaky legs. The shards crunched beneath my heels as I hurried to the other side of the vehicle. My ears perked up at the wail of approaching sirens.

"Daddy," I whispered, reaching through the remains of the driver's-side window.

A whimper escaped me as I reached through the opening and placed my trembling fingers on the side of his neck. My hand flew to my mouth, and a small wave of relief washed over me. He was alive.

Stepping back, I examined his door, but I would never be able to pry it open. I wasn't even sure how I'd managed to get out of the passenger's side or how I was in one piece, and I had no doubt in my mind that my dad would have to be cut out. His beautiful Miami-blue Porsche he loved so much was totaled, resembling a crushed soda can.

"Ma'am."

I turned toward the dark-haired, muscular EMT who'd hopped out of an ambulance and rushed toward me. I raised my arm, pointing at my father's still body.

"My dad. Please."

"Hi, my name is Neil. A full crew is here to help. What's your name?"

"Avery. He has a pulse. It's light, but it's there."

"I promise he's in incredibly capable hands. I need you to let me take a look at you."

My mind buzzed while men and women ran around the scene of the accident, shouting orders at each other.

"I don't know how this happened. It's all a blur," I said softly, my focus darting around the intersection of Division Street.

"By the looks of it, you were in a hit-and-run accident. Avery, can you follow my finger?"

"Neil," I whispered as a chill skated across my skin, making it clammy, and I began to tremble violently.

"Abe! Stretcher, please. I think she's going into shock," Neil yelled over his shoulder.

Before I could object, I was lying down, staring at the crystal-blue September sky. The bright sunlight assaulted my eyes, and I blinked rapidly while floaters clouded my vision, then I slipped away into darkness.

EVERY FIBER in my body hurt like a son of a bitch. I rubbed my forehead with the heel of my hand, glancing around the hospital room as the memories of the accident rushed over me. My stomach twisted into knots.

Dad. Is he all right?

I struggled to sit up and clear my thoughts.

"Dad," I called softly, tears stinging my eyes.

"Hi, beautiful. We don't know anything yet."

I twisted my neck gingerly toward the familiar voice, wincing at the shooting pain in my head and shoulders. A smile eased across my face when my attention landed on a blonde hottie. He looked stunning in his red polo shirt and denim shorts. Benji never looked bad. He was always GQ ready.

"Hey, Benji." I sank back into the pillow, relieved to see one of the most important people in my life next to me.

"Hi, hon," Tensley said, tucking a lock of her long blonde hair behind her ear while she approached me. She ran her hands down her light-blue shirt and rubbed them against her skinny jeans, her fingers splaying out, a telltale sign that she was stressed.

No matter how shitty life was, I had the best friends in the world. They'd both been through hell and back, and I had so much love and respect for them.

Benji leaned over and lightly kissed my forehead.

"How did you know where I was?" I asked, my focus bouncing between them.

"I'm one of your emergency contacts if they can't reach your mom, remember?" Tensley sat down on the edge of my bed and squeezed my hand. Her blue eyes assessed me carefully.

I assumed I looked like a total mess, and every square inch of my body was screaming at me.

"You're banged up pretty badly, but you didn't break anything." Benji sat on the other side of me, his expression softening with concern. "You went into shock. That's why you're here. The doctors want to monitor you for a bit."

I blew out a big breath. "I'm lucky." I stared at the ceiling, unblinking. "The truck came out of nowhere."

Tensley offered me a reassuring smile. Although I loved her for trying, it wasn't helping me feel any better.

"Can you get an update on Dad?" A part of me wasn't sure I wanted to know. Once the words were released into the air, there was no turning back. If he didn't live, it would fucking gut me. Images of his bloodied and battered body hammered my overloaded mind, and I struggled to breathe from the suffocating weight bearing down relentlessly on my chest.

"My mom and dad are trying to reach your mom, but the hospital won't talk to us, since we're not related," Benji explained.

"I guess I hadn't thought about that. I'm awake now, so I'll find a doctor and ask."

"Let me find someone for you," Tensley offered, standing. "You rest. I'm hoping you can go home soon."

"I'll keep her company," Benji said.

Ten left the room, and I squirmed on the firm mattress, attempting to find a comfortable position, but found none.

"Layne is in the hallway, waiting to see you. He wanted to allow Ten and me to talk to you first."

"That's sweet. I'm so glad Tensley has him."

"Girl, me too. It does *not* hurt my feelings to have eye candy around on a consistent basis either." Benji winked at me and grinned.

"*You're* my eye candy," I said, squeezing his knee.

Benji chuckled and patted my hand. "If only I liked vaginas."

"Can't blame a girl for trying." I flashed him the best smile I could muster.

A shriek broke through my thoughts.

"You little bitch! How could you?" My usually well-kempt mother flew into the room toward me, her expression twisting with savage anger. Her shoulder-length dark hair flew around her face as she barreled toward me.

Benji darted around my bed and blocked her with his body. "Mrs. Davenport, you need to calm down," he commanded.

Mom smacked Benji in the side of his head with her overstuffed Louis Vuitton bag.

"Dammit!" Benji howled, grabbing his head.

Before Mom could move past him, Layne flew into the hospital room and wrapped his arms around her from behind. Mom bucked against him, but he continued to restrain her.

"Ma'am, you need to calm down. Why don't we go into the hall and talk?" Layne's voice sounded like soothing honey as he continued to speak to her in a low tone and walk backward, inching out of my room.

"This is your fault," Mom spat. "You killed him!" Her large brown eyes were bloodshot, and her black slacks were horribly wrinkled. I suspected the midafternoon call concerning the accident had woken her up.

"Is he…" My voice shook. "Dead?" I covered my face with my hands, tears spilling down my cheeks.

"I hope you rot in hell!" Mom yelled.

"Get her out, Layne," Benji said, his anger-fueled gaze narrowing at my mother.

"Yup, I got it." Layne disappeared, my mother's shrill accusations echoing through the hallway.

Benji hurried across the room and closed the door. "Jesus, Avery. What was that?" He ran his hands over his short blonde hair and heaved a sigh. "Fuck this. You need to find out about your dad, but I don't want to leave you alone."

The door cracked open, and Tensley poked her head in. "I have the doctor with me, Avery. We're coming in."

I nodded, unable to find my voice. Benji crawled into the bed next to me and wrapped his arms around my shoulders. I leaned my head on his chest, craving the safety he was offering.

"Avery, I'm Dr. Conner. How are you feeling?"

"I'm not what's important right now. I need to know if my dad … died." My words hung in the air, thick and heavy with fear.

Dr. Conner shoved his hands into his white coat. He cleared his throat, his expression growing grimmer by the second. "He's alive, Avery."

"But?" My body went rigid with sickening dread, my stomach churning as bile swam up my throat.

"He has swelling to the brain, two broken legs, and a broken collar bone. We've had to induce a coma to see if it will help his body heal."

"Can I see him? Will … will he recover?" My hands shook as I wrung them together, terrified of what the doctor would say next.

"It's too soon to know if he can pull through, Avery. You can see him, but first, I need to take a look at you. I can send you home with some Tylenol #3 if everything checks out. With the number of cuts and bruises you're sporting, I can only assume you're in a great deal of pain. Honestly, I saw pictures of the car from the EMT report, and I'm not sure how you or your father are alive. We'll count our blessings, though."

"Avery," Tensley whispered, tears dampening her cheeks. "I'm so glad you're okay." She crossed the room and embraced me gently.

Ten minutes later, the doctor had released me. Before the nurse returned with a wheelchair, I reached behind me and attempted to untie my god-awful hospital gown.

"I've got it," Benji offered softly.

"Here. With all the excitement, somehow, I had a moment of sanity and grabbed you some clean clothes you left at my place." Ten held out a duffel bag.

"Thank you. My clothes are torn and dirty. I doubt I'll ever get it all out. I'll have to toss them into the trash when I get home."

"Ten, I'll let you help her get dressed. I'll wait in the hall." Benji excused himself and closed the door behind him.

"Is Layne back yet?" I asked while I slipped into the jeans Ten had brought me.

Ten reached her arm toward me and helped with my balance as I dressed. "I was going to ask you where he was, but I figured he'd gone to the bathroom or something."

"Nope. My mother came in here and caused a scene."

Tensley's brows knitted. "What do you mean?"

I tugged a pastel-pink polo shirt over my head and pulled my long, straight black hair from beneath the collar. "She barged in here, screaming that I killed Dad." A messy combination of fear and anger wedged itself into my throat. *How could she have lied to me?* He wasn't dead.

Tensley placed her hands on her slender hips, exasperation sparking to life in her blue eyes. "What the hell?"

"Poor Benji intersected her before she could reach me, but she whopped his head with her purse. God only knows what she keeps in there."

I actually knew what she kept in there—a dozen kinds of medication and a full vial of cocaine. Mother never left home without a snort or her pills. I was thankful that we had a driver, or I would never leave the house with her. That was just another secret I kept to myself, but no matter how much I attempted to hide it, the shadows always whispered around me, leaving me feeling exposed.

"He didn't mention it, but I would think her attacking him brought back some shitty memories." I shook my head. My mother had balls.

"He's come a long way since that night. We both have." Ten nervously glanced at the floor then looked back at me. The color had drained from her cheeks.

I suspected she was reliving that horrible night as well. At least the cops had arrested the men behind the hate crime, but it didn't erase the dark scars.

"What in God's name is wrong with your mother, Avery? I mean, no disrespect, but she's pulling shit now?" Tensley shook her head, disbelief dancing across her features. "Scratch that question. We need to get you to your dad. Are you ready?"

"Yeah, thank you for being here with me." I reached for my bestie and embraced her. "I'm not sure how I'm going to make it through this without you."

"You know Benji and I are here for you. Layne too." Tensley grabbed my hand and smiled sadly. "Your gorgeous face is bruised. Try not to be startled when you look in a mirror."

"Thanks for the warning." I inhaled deeply, summoning the courage to see my mother, if she was waiting for me again. "I need to see Dad now."

Ten nodded, and we left the room in silence. Apparently, the hospital was busy, because a nurse with a wheelchair hadn't shown up yet. It didn't matter. My only focus was to visit my father. A loud buzz sounded in my head as my anxiety climbed to an obnoxious level.

Ten minutes later I left Ten, Benji, and Layne in the ICU waiting area while I walked down the hall and searched for Dad's room number. The stench of death hung in the air, waiting to claim its next victim and devastate the family that was left behind. I wondered if we were next on the list. Chastising myself for even considering that Dad wouldn't make it, I shoved the thoughts into the cellar of my mind and threw away the key.

Identifying my dad's room, I came to an abrupt stop. If Mom was in there, I wasn't sure how I would be able to spend any time with him. I poked my head through the crack of the door, my attention landing on my pale and broken father. I gasped and hurried toward him, thanking God that his wife wasn't there.

"Daddy," I whispered, taking his hand. I wrapped his long, slender fingers around mine. "I'm here. You're going to be all right. I know it. You're a fighter." I leaned over and smoothed his dark hair, which was threaded with streaks of gray. "They say when someone is in a coma, they're still aware of their surroundings. I hope it's true. I'll do everything in my power to find out who ran into us, then we're going to sue them for every last penny on top of them serving time. I give you my word, and Davenports always... *you and I* always follow through on our promises."

Mom didn't even know what those words meant anymore. She'd lost the ability to be truthful years ago when she developed her drug addiction. At one time, Dad had talked her into seeing a therapist, but she'd backed out when they had arrived at the office door.

I dragged a chair up to Dad's bed, the metal legs scraping against the tile floor. Wearily, I sank into it, never letting go of his hand.

My brain kicked into high gear. I needed to call Dad's best friend, Patrick Goldman, who was my friend Ramsey's father. I needed his help to make sure Dad had the best medical care money could buy. Patrick had been a longtime family friend, and I would have to lean on him in order to navigate the muddy and unfamiliar waters while Dad was recovering.

Thankfully Dad had signed over power of attorney to me after I'd turned eighteen. He'd sat me down once a week, teaching me enough about the business, our bills, medical care, and everything I would need to know to manage life without him.

Obviously, neither of us had seen the accident coming, and we had scheduled a time to meet that weekend for dinner. Apparently, he had some new business we needed to discuss. I had no idea what it was, and I might not ever find out. Grief wrapped its frigid fingers around my heart, and I grabbed the bedrail in front of me as tightly as I could in a feeble attempt to ground myself.

After an hour ticked by, the machines whirring and humming, I realized I would need to slip out before my mother returned—*if* she'd show up at all. I would schedule a time to see him the next day.

It gutted me to leave, but even though Mom and I despised each other, I wasn't mean enough to keep her from her husband, even if she was snorting coke in his hospital bathroom.

My body cracked and popped, shooting daggers of pain through me as I stood. "I'll see you tomorrow. I love you, Daddy." I kissed his forehead and squeezed his hand, then silently slipped out of his room and walked to the waiting area.

"Are you guys ready? And ... shit." My shoulders slumped. "I completely forgot. I need a ride to the house."

The shrill sound of my mother's voice scraped across my last nerve. I couldn't see her, but I was sure every patient on the floor knew she was there. Apparently, she didn't understand what an inside voice meant.

"That's my cue to get the hell out of here before the banshee locates me and disrupts the healing of every patient on the floor even more."

"Let's go before she sees us. We can take you," Layne offered, threading his fingers through Tensley's.

"I'll follow. You're not going to be alone tonight. Besides, if your mom comes home, then you might need someone to intervene if she goes ballistic again," Benji added, shaking his head.

"Thank you. I can find it on my own," Mom said, her voice floating down the hall. She was close.

"There's no time like the present." I bit my lip and hurried in the opposite direction as fast as my bruised body would allow me to move.

2

The last golden rays of sunshine dipped behind the hills, leaving tangerine and indigo hues intertwining across the sky. I punched in the alarm code and opened the heavy dark-gray front door of my house.

"I'm so ready to find my own place again, but if Dad pulls through, I'll want to be here until he's better." I waved Benji, Tensley, and Layne into the foyer while a rush of cool air from the air conditioning greeted us. My heels clacked against the white marble floor as I led them inside.

"He'll make it," Layne assured me, his forehead creasing.

If anyone understood loss, it was Layne. He'd moved from Arkansas to Washington in order to start over after losing members of his family. Little did he know that his past was waiting for him ... Tensley. Once he was able to talk to her and set the record straight about who had been behind the bullying she'd faced in high school, their relationship blossomed, and they were engaged.

"Welcome to the abode." I motioned toward the living room.

Mom had remodeled the previous year, and the best way to describe our seven-thousand-square-foot house was modern contemporary. It had, clean lines, walls of windows, and marble everything—floors, countertops, and vases.

At one time, it was a comfortable, happy home, but now it was rigid and cold, without feeling—just like Mom, unless she was amped up on drugs and alcohol. Then her mood swings were extreme and sometimes violent.

The main color scheme was white, gray, and black. Dad and I had finally selected some art pieces with splashes of bright colors to hang on the walls. I'd threatened to finger-paint all the boring statues in the living room and formal dining area if he didn't do something to bring the shared spaces to life. He'd chuckled at me. It wasn't like I would have done any damage other than pissing off mom, but he'd gotten the point and took me shopping that afternoon.

Pain hit my chest, and I attempted to rub the ache away. I wondered if Dad and I would ever have our business meetings or shop together again.

"Wow," Layne said, his eyes widening as he looked around.

"Explore all you want. We're the only ones here. If I didn't feel like shit, we could take a swim, but I'm not up to it. However, we have a selection of brand-new swimsuits for guests if you guys want to take a dip. I'll pop some Advil instead of the Tylenol #3 and join you outside, at least." I led them into the living room, slipped off my heels, and tossed them into the corner. It pissed Mom off when I left my belongings downstairs instead of taking them to my room, but I thought, *Fuck her for scaring me so badly.* Dad wasn't dead, and it wasn't my fault.

I dug my toes into the Safavid silk and wool black rug that spanned half of the room. The iron-and-glass coffee table rested in the middle of the space, complementing the gray Italian leather couch and matching chairs. My favorite part of the room was the windows. I had watched some breathtaking sunsets over the years.

"What about the hot tub? Would that help your muscles?" Tensley asked, slipping off her teal-and-black Nikes.

"I'm sure it would help, but unless someone wants to carry me upstairs and tuck me in, then I'd better not. I'm physically exhausted but mentally wound the hell up." I winced as I placed my hands on my hips, attempting to dial in the pain that was pulsing through my body.

"If that's what you need, then I'll be happy to take care of you." Benji lightly rubbed my arm. "Man, it's been a while since we've been here." He gave me a chaste peck on the cheek then made a beeline for the kitchen. "I'm happy to make us all something to eat. You need to sit and allow us to take care of you."

"I'll help," Layne said, following Benji and winking at his fiancée before he left the room.

Tensley gave me a lopsided grin. "I love you. I'm so relieved you're going to be all right." She smoothed my hair, her expression darkening with emotion. "Your dad is going to pull through this."

Tears welled in my eyes and clung to my lower eyelashes. "I hope so. I can't …" I shook my head, unable to complete my thought.

Ten pulled me into a gentle hug. "We're all staying here tonight. I don't want to take a chance on your mom trying to attack you again."

I stepped away, wiping the moisture from my cheeks. "Thanks. I don't know what to expect right now." I curled up on the couch, wincing. Dragging my fingertips along the buttery material, I thought of Dad and the gravity of his situation. Panic bubbled inside me, but I refused to let it get to me. He was a fighter. It ran in our blood.

Tensley sat down next to me and tucked her legs beneath her. "Do you think she might have been scared about your dad? I mean … does she normally treat you like that, Avery?"

Pursing my lips, I inhaled deeply. Only Dad and I knew what it was like with her. Her addiction and behavior had escalated over the years, but it was our family secret to deal with.

"I do my best to stay out of her way." I stifled a yawn. My body was settling down, but my mind was still racing. "I should be at the hospital instead of home."

"Hon, I don't think you being there would be helpful right now. It sounds like your mom has a short fuse at the moment. The hospital will call if there's any change. The best thing you can do for him right now is to take care of yourself." She flipped her long blonde hair behind her shoulder, then propped her arm on the back of the couch, her gaze staring straight through me. I wondered what she saw and whether she could see the dark stains on my soul that I'd attempted to hide most of my life.

"Here's some Advil I found in the cabinet and some water," Layne said, approaching us from the kitchen.

"Thank you." I washed down the pain meds and handed the glass back to him.

"Benji popped some pizzas into the oven, so we'll eat soon," Layne added.

"Thanks, babe," Tensley said.

Layne kissed the top of her head then left the room.

"Now that you're safe, what happened? I mean, I know you were in a car accident, but was the other person hurt?" Tensley asked.

I propped my legs up on her lap and leaned back against the arm of the sofa. "I don't know. It was a black pickup truck. The driver ran through the intersection, hit us, then sped off. After I saw the car, I'm shocked we're alive." I choked on my words, overwhelming emotions clogging my throat as the image of my broken and bleeding father flashed before me.

"You are, so let's focus on that." Tensley patted my leg and offered a gentle smile.

"Is that how you got through being kidnapped?"

Tensley was the strongest woman I knew and a hero in my eyes. Six months ago, she'd been abducted by one of the most dangerous men in the country. The FBI had been tracking Jack for months without any success until Tensley.

She cleared her throat, her expression darkening briefly. "I remember telling Jack that for years, I'd wanted to die. Then when I wasn't sure I would make it out alive, all I could think of was Layne, Benji, and you. You all gave me something to live for. I held on to how much I love you and wanted to hug everyone again."

"We love you too. Obvi." I cracked a grin and pointed at her diamond engagement ring.

Light pink bloomed on her cheeks. Layne had been Ten's first and forever love. They had the real thing, and their relationship gave me hope that I would find the same one day. At least that was what I told myself.

Once again, my thoughts tormented me with a million different scenarios of what might happen to Dad.

The guys returned with plates and drinks fifteen minutes later.

"Thank you," I said and nodded at Benji and Layne as I took a bite.

"Do you want a real drink?" Tensley asked, arching an eyebrow at me. "You've only had Advil, and if you're not going to take the Tylenol three, then you're fine."

"I was thinking about that, but what if the hospital calls and I need to get back there?" My throat tightened. *Dad needs to make it through the night, so a phone call would mean ...* I shut the dark thought down and gave it a swift kick in the ass. I refused to entertain the idea that he wouldn't pull through.

"Girl, please. If they call, one of us will drive, or we'll call an Uber, but we're all going." Benji waved me off and grinned. "From your expression, it's obvi you're in pain, so have a drink or two. We won't get crazy. Not tonight, anyway."

Tensley giggled and gave me a gentle nudge in the leg with her elbow. "I think we could all use a drink, but one of us needs to have only one just in case."

Layne raised his hand. "I'll take a beer, but that's it. I'm happy to volunteer as the designated driver, if we need to go anywhere."

"You're the best," I said, giving him a lopsided grin. It was the only way my face didn't shoot daggers of pain through me. I realized I would eventually have to look in the mirror, but I was a little scared to see the damage.

The rest of the evening was filled with light conversation. I must have nodded off, only to be woken up as Layne scooped me off the couch and into his muscular arms.

Even through the grogginess, I hoped it wasn't awkward for Tensley as her boyfriend carried me upstairs. But we both knew Benji hadn't fully recovered from the brutal attack he had suffered the previous year.

Benji opened my bedroom door, and Layne gently placed me on

top of the plush lavender comforter. When Mom had started the remodel, I made her swear she wouldn't touch my room. I loved it as it was. Purple was my favorite color, so I'd chosen layered white-and-lavender curtains over blackout shades. Although I loved the summer, the sun rose before five in the morning, which interrupted my sleep and tanked any possibility of waking up in a good mood.

I had also painted a mural on one of my walls during my artistic years in high school. Two people were sitting on the edge of a cliff, the ocean waves crashing against the rocks below them. One person was me, but I wasn't sure who the guy was. I'd simply relaxed and ridden the artistic flow. They were sitting next to each other, facing the water. My long black hair flowed down my back against my pale-yellow shirt.

Whenever my world was turned upside down, I would spend time in front of my wall. It always soothed me as I imagined the smell of the salty air rolling off the water and the cold droplets of the ocean spray clinging to my skin.

"Ten and Layne are using the guest room on the main floor. They thought it would be better for someone to keep an eye out in case your mom came home," Benji said, interrupting my thoughts.

"Thank you, Layne. For being here with me."

"No problem. Get some sleep," Layne said, then left the room.

I stifled a yawn. "My mother is crazy," I muttered, sleep beckoning me at the edges of my mind. "Stay with me tonight?"

"Of course." Benji slipped off his loafers and crawled into the other side of the bed. He fluffed up the white pillows and rolled over on his side, facing me.

I heaved a sigh. "I love you, Benji Parker."

A low chuckle rumbled through his chest. "Love you, too, Avery Davenport."

Unable to roll over comfortably, I tilted my head and stared at him. "I sound like I'm a big chicken, but every time I close my eyes, I see images of Dad's bloody and mangled body. If he …" Fear, grief, and anxiety suppressed the rest of my words.

Benji reached for my hand. "Avery, we've known each other for several years now, and you're well aware that I'm not a bullshitter. I won't blow sunshine up your ass just to make you feel better, but regardless of what happens, I'll be right by your side." His smile turned a little devious. "And so will Laynsley."

I barked out a laugh. "You did not just give them a portmanteau nickname!"

Benji snickered, obviously proud of himself. "Girl, I can't wait to see her face."

I struggled not to break into a full-on fit of laughter while I imagined Tensley's expression morphing from surprise to "Oh, hell no." "I want to be there the first time you use it."

"Are you sure? I'm not sure you can duck fast enough when she throws something. Maybe wait until you're feeling better." Benji's cheeks reddened as he continued to laugh.

"I'll make sure I'm not standing anywhere around you." I winced and grabbed my side. "Fuck."

"Do you need some more Advil?" Benji asked. "Hang on." He bounded off the mattress before I could respond and disappeared into the hallway.

A few minutes later, he returned with the entire container of pain reliever and three bottled waters.

"Thank you."

"Get some sleep if you can." Benji slipped back in next to me.

For a moment, his friendship and presence offered some peace, and I drifted off into a fitful sleep.

3

Mother and I avoided each other at all costs over the next few weeks. When she came home, I slipped out and visited Dad at the hospital. Although he hadn't worsened, he hadn't improved yet either.

Anxiety hummed beneath my skin, an itch I wasn't able to scratch. I was restless, angry, and scared. At least my body had mostly healed from the assault of cuts and marks. The majority, I could hide, except the fading yellow bruises under my eye and cheek from the airbag. I'd gasped when I'd first peered into the mirror at the damage from the accident. Black and purple had taken over my tan face, and my freckles were barely visible.

Other than visits to the hospital, I hadn't ventured out much. Tensley, Benji, and Layne typically came over when my mother wasn't at the house. I'd attempted to keep myself busy with laps in the pool or a run, but no matter how hard I tried, I couldn't push the thoughts of Dad from my mind even for a few minutes. Everywhere I looked, his presence was with me.

I jumped off my bed and collected my laptop. I needed something to take my mind off the shitstorm that refused to settle down, even if it was only for a few hours.

My fingers flew over the keys, and I logged onto the hidden website of The Lily. I chewed my nail while I viewed the room choices, then the men. When I was finished, I opted to let the algorithm select my guy for the afternoon. The only criteria I chose was no talking, and I would wear a beautiful rose-gold-and-pink venetian butterfly mask that covered the majority of my face in order to hide the marks, which only reminded me that Dad was hanging on to his life by a thread.

After logging out and closing the browser, I shut down my computer. I checked my appearance in the mirror. My green eyes were usually more alert, but under the circumstances, I wasn't expecting anything different.

I slipped on my Gucci sandals, grabbed my purse, then hauled ass out of the house.

I ENTERED THE STORE, my Lily charm bracelet dangling from my narrow wrist. To everyone else, The Lily was an upscale women's clothing store but not to me. It was freedom from my life on the other side of the door.

I strolled past the water fountain in the middle of the store, which flowed and bubbled quietly, creating a relaxing atmosphere. A dark-haired young lady offered me a flute of champagne from a tray, but I declined. I located the new fall section and sauntered over to the racks. I wanted to replace my lavender top that had been ruined in the car accident. I began to flip through several silk blouses, noting the abundance of colors.

"The emerald green would look stunning on you," someone with a soft female voice said behind me.

"You think so?" I asked, removing it from the rack and holding it up for her to see. My attention landed on Skyler Grey, the manager of The Lily and one of the most stunning women I'd ever met.

Her sandy-blonde hair was piled into a tight bun on the top of her head, and her soft brown eyes held flecks of gold around the pupils.

Her gentle gaze could melt any cold-hearted human within seconds. She pushed her black-rimmed glasses up her slender nose and smiled at me.

"It's good to see you, Avery. I was thinking about you yesterday." Skyler cleared her throat, her attention landing on my battered cheek. "I don't mean to pry, but what …" She pointed at my bruised face.

I returned the top and sighed. "You should have seen me a few weeks ago. I've already healed a lot. I was in a car accident, and although I'm fine now, my dad is in a coma."

"What?" Skyler whisper-yelled. She quickly collected three blouses for me, then gently grabbed my arm. The fabric of her black linen pencil skirt swished as she swiftly led me into a dressing room and closed the door behind us.

She hung the tops on the metal bar and pulled me into a warm hug. "What do you need? How can I help?"

Tears stung my eyes when I looked at her. Skyler and I had developed a friendship since I had joined The Lily. "I just need … this." I pointed upstairs.

She took my hands in hers, her expression sincere. "I understand. You let me know if there's anything else I can help with, and I mean anything."

"Thank you. I will." I released a breath, attempting to collect myself.

"On another note, the software chose our brand-new guy. You're his first client," she said in a hushed tone. "I would love your feedback afterward, if you're comfortable with the idea."

"Sure, I don't mind. It will give me something else to think about."

"I'll have some champagne waiting for you in the VIP room after your session."

"Perfect."

One thing about me—I wasn't shy about sex, nudity, or discussing it. However, one of the conditions for membership was that we couldn't talk about what happened there unless it was with the staff. Plus, I wasn't sure how Tensley and Benji would react if I told them I paid for sex.

She smoothed her skirt, a genuine smile lighting up her face. "What blouse do you want?"

"I like the green one, if you think it will work. It's hard to tell right now, with my cheeks all banged up." I avoided the mirror, unwilling to engage in the pain I was trying to hide from.

"I'll have it wrapped and ready for you to pick up at the front desk. It's a gift. Take a deep breath and relax this afternoon, okay?"

"Skyler, I can pay for the blouse."

"Of course you can, but sometimes a gift from a friend helps a little bit." She winked at me, collected the other tops, then slipped out of the dressing room.

I leaned against the wall and inhaled deeply before I opened the full-length mirror and stepped into the hallway behind it then closed the door softly. Even though that dressing room was for clients only and allowed us to discreetly enter the members-only area, I still didn't want to draw any unwanted attention.

I removed my phone from my handbag and checked my confirmation for the room number. I barely had enough time to take the elevator to the third floor and settle in before my appointment began.

My gaze darted around the room, which was staged as a living room with a plush beige leather couch and matching chair. Thick white carpet caressed my bare feet. I laughed softly, remembering the session when I'd ended up with rug burn all over my back.

No matter how many times I went to The Lily, my heart pounded against my ribcage, nerves and excitement mixing together. But that day, and though I wasn't sure why, for some reason, I was extra nervous.

Since Justin and I had broken up four months ago, I'd ditched the dating scene. I wasn't in the mood to get played again. Sex, on the other hand, was a different story. As long as I was safe, I splurged a few times a week. What the public saw was an expensive women's store, which it was. But to its members, it was every female's forbidden desire. It was tailored specifically to women. No male clients were permitted, which promoted a sense of freedom.

Once I'd passed the intense screening and was approved to join, I simply entered a hidden website, chose a fantasy, then showed up for my appointment and played it out. I even had the option to choose from a group of incredibly sexy men or allow the algorithm to select one for me based on my past visits. Not only did I love the excitement and intrigue of not knowing what my partner would look like, but nothing was off-limits. I could select my playroom according to whatever mood I was in, including threesomes, role play, toys, anything you could possibly imagine. But it was my little secret. I'd never even shared it with my best friends.

I adjusted the dark-purple satin robe I had exchanged for my clothes. Cool air rushed between my thighs, and my anticipation grew. I slipped a blindfold behind the mask, then slid it into place. Part of the intrigue was not being able to see, which heightened my other senses. We also wouldn't be speaking to each other—touch only. Waves of desire rippled through me at the mere thought.

I rolled my shoulders back, attempting to minimize the stress twisting my muscles into thick knots. In minutes, I would meet a total stranger, and for just a little while, I would shut out the world below me. Inside those walls, I could simply enjoy myself, free of judgment.

I stood in the middle of the room and imagined a stranger's hands roaming my body. God, I was so damned ready.

The click of the door opening and closing reached my ears, and I stilled.

A strong arm slid around my waist, and a solid body melded to my back. I traced his hand with my nails, then trailed up the corded muscles of his forearm and biceps. His minty breath warmed my cheek as his lips brushed against my neck. Goosebumps dotted my skin as his hand wandered over my lower stomach, my hip, and around to my ass. His fingertips touched lightly, stirring a fire deep inside me.

The heat of his body left my back, and I shivered. A slight rustling sound reached my ears as he shifted, and I sensed him in front of me.

The calloused pads of his fingers skimmed over my collar bone, then between my robe-covered breasts. My nipples hardened against the silk fabric before he slipped the material off my shoulders, and it fell to the floor near my ankles.

He released a soft whistle, and I grinned. He liked what he saw. Even though I'd paid him to worship every inch of me, it still stroked my ego to be viewed as a beautiful woman. I might hate my mother, but I looked a lot like her when she was my age. I shared her long dark hair, freckles, and the right balance of curves. She was breathtakingly gorgeous, and she used it to her advantage. I hadn't, not like she had.

Hot kisses covered every inch of my body, and I allowed myself to get lost in his skillful caress.

I was guided toward a piece of furniture and bent over, my ass tipping up in the air.

A low groan escaped his throat as he parted my slick folds, and his mouth teased my core. A finger eased its way into me and pumped my pussy a few times, then he slid it into my puckered hole while he tongue-fucked me. I pushed against him, urging him for more. His other hand grabbed my thigh, digging into my skin. Pain shot through me, and I welcomed it. It was nothing to what I'd done before, and if he played his cards right, I had more delicious afternoons planned for him.

I moaned, my nerves tingling with the sweet sensation building inside me. I held on to what I suspected was the couch, my legs growing weak, my core becoming needier and needier. *Jesus, where did they find this guy?* He was doing things to me with his mouth I'd never felt before.

My body trembled, bringing me to the edge, then he stopped. I whimpered as he withdrew.

The rustling of a condom wrapper filled the room, then he was at my entrance. I slammed against him, shoving him deep inside me. My eyes shot wide open behind the mask. Although the male companions were available in multiple sizes to accommodate different needs, he was larger than what I was used to. I bit my lip hard in order not to cry out. With a few more thrusts, my body had adjusted, and the plea-sure began to build inside me again.

Our bodies slapped together, our heavy breathing and sounds of raw lust filling the small space. His hands dug into my hips as his pace quickened, sending shivers of ecstasy rippling through me. My core clenched around his big cock, and my body began to shudder as an intense orgasm ripped through me.

A guttural growl escaped him as his body tensed, then he stilled.

I attempted to slow my breathing as a smile eased across my face. I would be happy to provide Skyler with feedback, not to mention that I definitely wanted him again. My mind began playing with all the scenarios we could explore together.

He eased out of me, and I straightened slowly while I savored the delectable moments I'd just experienced.

"Shit. The condom broke," he said.

4

The blood in my veins ran cold. The condom was a huge fucking deal, but members and employees had to be tested for every health concern and screened over a period of weeks before they were even hired. I knew they were clean, and I was on birth control. *But that voice ...* I jerked my mask off and spun around, my mouth gaping open.

"Ramsey! What the hell?" Dread knotted inside my gut while our gazes connected.

Ramsey's blue eyes widened. "A-Avery?" he sputtered, sounding perplexed while the color drained from his tanned cheeks. "Shit!" He rubbed the back of his neck and stared at the floor briefly. "The mask hid your face," he whispered. "I had no idea it was you."

My stomach plummeted to my toes. "What are you doing here?" My pitch rose with each word. "How are you in this room right now?" I waved my arms like a crazy woman.

"I … I." Ramsey reached for me, confusion flickering across his handsome features. "Avery, your face. Are the bruises from the car accident? Are you all right? How's your dad?"

I stared at him in disbelief. *How can he ask about my dad when we've just fucked each other's brains out?*

"Do you not realize what happened less than sixty seconds ago? I can't do this with you. Goddammit, Ramsey, we had sex." I clenched my hands into fists, shoving down the scream that threatened to erupt.

Ramsey flinched at my words, his expression registering the gravity of the situation. "Please, Avery … don't tell anyone that I work here. I could lose my football scholarship and my chance at the NFL." He ran his hand over his dark hair, his blue eyes pleading for mercy.

My nostrils flared. "*I* was your first client at an exclusive sex club, the condom broke, and you're worried about your scholarship? Unbelievable." Not only was I stunned beyond belief, but I was furious. Apparently, my attention had another agenda, though, because I assessed every muscle, ripple, smooth surface, and his long now-deflated dick. And that cock was attached to my childhood friend.

We stared at each other like two stupid teenagers that hadn't seen someone naked before.

"I'm so sorry. I'm …" Ramsey tossed the condom into the small trash can, grabbed a long white robe, and slipped it on.

"I'll call my doctor and get the morning-after pill. I'm on birth control, but I can't afford to take any chances," I said, snapping out of my daze. "That can be taken care of way more easily than what just happened." My jaw clenched as I gathered my robe off the floor and put it on. His attention followed every move I made. "I won't tell anyone you work here, but you have to keep my secret as well."

He tossed his hands up in surrender—the same hands that had touched every inch of my body. His features sagged in relief. "I promise."

I gathered my clothes and purse while tears pricked my eyes, and I swallowed, willing them away. My tummy squeezed tight, and I was pretty sure I was ready to vomit the club sandwich I'd eaten hours ago.

Ramsey and I would never be the same again. Not only was my father's life hanging in the balance, but one of the people I cherished most in the world had breached every boundary I had. There was no coming back from it.

"Goodbye, Ramsey." My throat tightened as grief welled up in my chest.

His feelings were trapped inside his tense stare as our gazes locked. "Avery, wait. Let's talk about what happened. Please," he begged, his voice deep and raspy.

Ramsey reached for me, but I dodged him and darted out the door.

I bit my bottom lip, holding the tumultuous swell of feelings inside the best I could. My bare feet smacked against the cool wood floors as I ran to the elevator and lost the battle with my brimming emotions. A strangled cry escaped me while I stabbed the lobby button repeatedly. *How did this happen?*

I gasped for air, realizing it was my fault. If I hadn't worn a mask that hid my face, we would have seen each other, then probably laughed at the crazy situation and planned to meet for dinner later.

The doors whooshed open, and I pushed the VIP button. It was the only place to change clothes before I left the store. I sure as hell couldn't run to my car wearing no shoes and a robe that barely covered my butt.

I wiped my cheeks, but plump, hot tears gave me a big "Fuck you" and continued to fall. I clutched my clothes to my chest as my shoulders shook.

A soft ding alerted me that I'd reached my floor. Prepared to run straight to the dressing area as soon as the doors opened, I planted a foot in front of me, ready to haul ass.

The door slid open, and I stuck my head out, eyeing the path to my destination. I had no idea how many ladies would be in the lounge, drinking and enjoying the afternoon.

Laughter filled the air as I walked into the hallway, attempting to be discreet.

The VIP section was breathtaking, soothing, and came with free alcohol and hors d'oeuvres. I often indulged after working up an appetite but not that day.

"Avery, how did it go?" Skyler asked, approaching me. "Oh, hon." Her expression clouded with concern the second she saw me.

For the second time, Skyler took my arm and led me somewhere more private. It had completely escaped my mind that I was supposed to meet with her.

"What happened?" she asked under her breath.

"I … I need to change first." I peeked at her, hoping she would give me a few minutes to try to pull myself together.

"Of course. I'm sorry. I saw how distraught you were, and that's all I was thinking about."

Skyler pushed an "Employees Only" door open and led me into her office.

Soft lighting set the calm mood of the room, which I desperately needed. I eyed the chaise lounge near a small bar.

"Use my bathroom." She pointed me in its direction, and I scurried off like a little mouse, seeking a safe place to hide from the ever-growing storm that I referred to as my life swirling around me.

I locked the door and clutched my belongings against my stomach as I struggled to breathe against the suffocating weight that had settled on my chest.

Brushing the moisture from my eyes, I set my clothes and purse on the black marble countertop. I placed my palms against my cheeks and inhaled slowly. My pulse kicked up a notch when I realized I couldn't talk to Tensley or Benji about what had transpired between Ramsey and me. It was just one more secret I would have to tuck away and pretend that I was all right.

Five minutes later, I emerged from Skyler's bathroom.

"Here." Skyler handed me a glass of red wine. "Sit." She motioned to the black leather chaise.

I sipped my drink as I settled into my seat, tucking my hair behind my ear.

"What happened? Was he rude? Did he hurt you? You know I take care of my clients. I'll fire him as soon as we're done talking if I need to." Her tone was firm and protective.

I shook my head. "No, it's nothing like that." My chin trembled as I scrambled for the right words. "The condom broke, which wasn't anyone's fault."

Skyler reached over to her executive desk and grabbed her phone.

"I can make a call to get the morning-after pill for you. I promise you that all our employees are tested before they're hired."

I waved at her to put the phone down. "I remember the testing policy, but thank you for the reminder. I'm on the pill, but I will call my doctor and ask for the morning-after pill just in case. Thank you, though."

Skyler's perfectly shaped light-brown eyebrow arched as she waited for me to continue.

"I know him." My heart thudded louder, a steady, persistent drumbeat in my ears. *Oh God, how did this happen?*

"Shit," Skyler said, tapping her manicured fingernails on the arm of her chair. "Tell me everything."

I glanced up at the ceiling and closed my eyes against the water works that were once again threatening to escape.

"I …" I gulped down part of my wine then set it down on the glass end table next to me. "Our parents grew up together." I swallowed repeatedly, attempting to clear the lump in my throat. "From the time we were in diapers until age seventeen, we spent every summer in the Hamptons together. With Ramsey."

"Are you two close?" Skyler asked, her voice filled with compassion.

"Yes. Even when I stopped attending family vacations because I wanted to do other things, we texted and talked several times a week. He visited a few months ago to check out a college he wanted to transfer to that's located here in Spokane." I rubbed my clammy palm along my jeaned thigh. "He received a football scholarship, so we'll be at the same school."

"Did you know he was already in Spokane?" Skyler crossed her legs and leaned back into the chair.

"No. He called me a few nights ago, but I hadn't … I figured he was calling about Dad, and I couldn't talk about it yet."

"I see. If your families are close, I assume he knows about the accident."

"Yeah, he asked about Dad after we …" I covered my face with my hands. Ramsey had been inside me. His tongue … his dick. His fingers had roamed every curve and crevice of my body, and I'd loved every minute of it. I swallowed again, still attempting to clear the lump in my throat. "As I said, I've dodged his calls lately." I shook my head in disbelief. "I don't know if my dad is going to pull through, and I just fucked my childhood friend," I said, my voice hovering above a whisper.

"I can't imagine how you feel right now, but I need to make sure I understand correctly. He in no way shamed or harmed you, correct?"

"Correct. It ... he was amazing, actually." I slapped my forehead with the palm of my hand. "Dear God, what am I saying?"

A smile twitched at the corner of Skyler's mouth. "Maybe this is a good thing. I'm sure your friendship will move to a whole new level."

"No. Our friendship is over. I'm embarrassed that he knows I'm a member, not to mention he works here." My pitch rose along with my anxiety.

"Avery," Skyler said softly. "Hon, you need all the friends you have right now. Try to put it to the side as a fun afternoon romp, and let it go. But do *not* let *him* go. You two have a long history, and lifetime friends are difficult to come by. Don't throw it away over sex. It's not worth it."

"Thank you. I appreciate your input. And for the record, he will make a lot of your members very happy." I attempted a smile, but a sharp pang of jealousy stabbed me in the chest.

Hell no. No way would I allow myself to feel possessive of him. Ramsey had always been his own man and done whatever he wanted to, and I loved that about him. If he wanted to work there, then that was his business. *Who gives a flying fuck if he's paid for sex and touches other women?*

"I should go. I think moving forward, it will be best if I don't allow the software to choose a guy for me."

"As the manager, I have access to your file, including your likes and dislikes. What I find interesting, Avery, is that the algorithm matches you with someone compatible in the bedroom. I realize you normally choose your guys, but out of the twenty men we have available here,

Ramsey was your match. Not only a match, but a ninety-seven-point-nine-percent match. I've never seen that before."

My lips pursed. That information wasn't helping one damned bit.

"FUCK MY LIFE," I muttered, pulling into my driveway half an hour later. Mother's car was parked in my space, which wasn't a big deal, but she was home. I wondered whether she was asleep, or if I would have to deal with her finally.

I hurried up the walkway and let myself in the front door. Pausing, I listened for any signs that she was downstairs.

"There you are."

My head whipped around at the sound of her shrewd voice. She looked more put together than she had the last time I'd seen her a week ago. Her long dark hair flowed over her slender shoulders. Her white sweater hugged her ample chest and slim waist, and her bright-pink fingernails tapped against a tumbler full of whiskey.

"I'll stay out of your way, if you stay out of mine," I snapped.

"That won't be happening, I'm afraid." She walked toward me, her red-rimmed eyes swollen from crying.

"What do you mean?" My pulse skyrocketed, as I was afraid of her next words.

"I've tried to call you for the last few hours. Where have you been?"

I frowned and rummaged around in my purse for my phone. When I tapped the screen, a message with three missed calls popped up—one from the hospital and two from Mom. Text after text had also come through. In all the excitement at The Lily, I hadn't heard my phone.

I peered at her, my legs trembling. "What happened?" I whispered.

"Your father died an hour and a half ago." She took a drink, the ice tinkling in her glass as tears streamed down her freshly Botox-injected face.

The world blurred, and my stomach churned. "Tell me you're lying." I walked toward her, clutching my phone until my knuckles turned white. "Tell me it's not true." Her horrifying words sliced through me, and I struggled to breathe. Digging my fingernails into the palm of my other hand, I welcomed the distraction. It had to be a nightmare, and if I inflicted enough pain on myself, I would wake up.

"I wish I could, but it is." She lifted the tumbler to her lips, and I slapped it out of her hand. The sharp sound of glass breaking filled the space between us. Shards covered our feet, but I didn't give a shit. She'd ripped my heart out of my chest and stomped all over it.

"How can you *drink* right now?" I screamed. "I hate you! I hate you! You're nothing but an embarrassing drunk and a drug addict."

The sting of her palm connecting with my cheek broke my hysteria. Dad was dead—gone. He'd left me with Satan herself.

I tried to walk around her, but she grabbed my wrist and dug her fingers into one of my bruises. "Get cleaned up and act like a civil human being for once," she hissed. "I called the Goldmans. They'll be here later today."

I wrenched my arm free and glared at her. "Fine." We could argue later. We would have plenty of time for that, since Dad was gone and no longer playing referee between us.

I shook the remnants of her fake grief off my shoe as the doorbell rang. "I'll get it." Leaving my mother standing in shattered glass and expensive whiskey, I hurried toward the door.

"Gladys!" Mom screeched at the housekeeper. "Clean this mess up, for God's sake. We have company."

I ground my molars together but kept walking. Then I flung the door open and wished like hell I hadn't.

"Hey," Ramsey said, his eyes misty as he held my gaze. "I'm sorry about your Dad. Mom called and asked me to come over until they could fuel up the plane and get here."

"Oh." I stepped back, allowing him to enter the foyer. After the news about Dad, I didn't have the emotional capacity to be upset that he was there.

"How are you doing?" He shoved his hands into his designer jeans, his biceps flexing beneath his long-sleeved, red-and-blue-striped shirt.

"Numb. Shocked. Furious. It depends on what moment it is."

"Avery," Ramsey's deep voice cascaded over me, soothing my inner turmoil. "I'm so sorry. I tried to reach out earlier this week, but you didn't answer my calls."

I held my finger up to silence him. "What are you apologizing for? This afternoon or that I lost my dad?" I folded my arms over my chest, attempting to keep him at a distance.

"Both." He cleared his throat, pain flickering across his features. "He was like a father to me, and I'm fucking gutted. I can't imagine how you feel. Please, we've known each other since we were in diapers. Don't push me away."

Regardless of how I felt about our romp at The Lily, I needed him. I trusted him.

"I don't know what to do," I said, my shoulders shaking as the death of my father crashed down on me. I sank to my knees, but before I hit the marble floor, Ramsey pulled me to him and kissed the top of my head.

"We'll figure it out, okay?" Ramsey caressed the back of my neck while he held me, and I clutched at the soft material of his shirt for dear life.

If he let me go, I wasn't sure I would be strong enough to pick myself up again. *How will I make it without Dad?* He had been my entire world—my protector and my hero. In the blink of an eye, my life had changed.

"Avery, why don't you give me your phone, and I'll call Benji and Tensley. I know they'll want to be here with you. I'll even keep your mom company while you go shower. She's always liked me. Maybe it will help."

Peeking up at him through swollen eyes, I said, "Thank you. I desperately need a few minutes to myself."

I hurried toward the stairs before my mother could say another word to me, and I took the steps two at a time. I closed my bedroom door as sobs wracked my body, and I collapsed to my knees, my shoulders shaking with grief.

Not only was Dad gone, but I owned a highly successful business without my mentor to guide me through the transition. My hands-on experience had been with him sitting next to me or talking through scenarios. Now, I was alone.

I wiped my eyes, my body shuddering as I inhaled deeply. Obviously, Dad had thought I was capable of running the company, but I was still scared shitless. Even when my future had been planned out for me, I always had a nagging feeling in the pit of my stomach. I had always felt incomplete. Maybe stepping into a new role in my life was what I needed. Maybe it would fill the hole inside of me.

Half an hour later, I finished with my shower. Red blotches dotted my skin from the intense scrubbing I'd given myself under the steaming-hot water. No matter how hard I tried, I couldn't remove the devastation of my mother's words. If she hadn't been crying, I would have thought she was happy to get rid of him.

Numbness crept into every crack and crevice of my heart, and I welcomed it while I dressed in boyfriend jeans and a clean, burgundy V-neck top. I brushed through my wet hair and stared at the reflection in the mirror over my dresser. My expression was vacant. My entire world had just been ripped away from me, and I was powerless to do anything about it.

I sank my teeth into my bottom lip, trying to locate enough courage to reappear downstairs. Ramsey's parents would be there in a few hours, which would take Mommy Dearest off my hands for a while.

Closing my eyes briefly, I recalled my last afternoon with Dad, eating sushi and going shopping. "Shit!"

My body trembled as I recalled Dad's instructions on what to do if he were to ever pass away due to an untimely death. Rifling through my underwear drawer, I located a key and shoved it into the front pocket of my jeans.

I whirled around and opened my door. Poking my head out, I checked the hallway for my mother. She wasn't anywhere to be seen. *Thank God.*

I crept down the stairs then took a hard left once I was on the main floor. Ramsey's deep voice was the only sound I heard, and I imagined he was attempting to console the ice queen.

My feet landed softly on the floor as I made my way to Dad's office toward the back of the house. He usually kept it locked, but he had given me a key on my eighteenth birthday. I was never the kid who wanted to snoop in his belongings, and even after he trusted me with access to his safe and business files, I had always respected the fact that he believed in me. I'd never broken his trust. He knew I was his daughter through and through. We were so similar in our thought processes, and even mannerisms, that it had started to drive my mother insane.

Once, when I was thirteen, I'd overheard her accusing Dad of loving me more than her. I had no idea of how Dad had responded, but I suspected it wasn't what my mother had wanted to hear. Her drinking and drug use had escalated shortly after.

I slid the key into the doorknob, then slipped inside and locked the door behind me.

"Keep her busy for me, Ramsey," I whispered. Flipping on the light switch, I drew in a sharp breath, my brain reminding me that Dad would never again sit in his office chair. Pain sliced through my chest, and a small cry escaped me. My hand flew to my mouth, muffling the sounds of despair that I couldn't control. I moved away from the door and silently approached one of the bookshelves.

When I'd identified the financial book he had told me to locate, I removed it from the shelf. Wedged between the pages was a thin, unmarked envelope. I removed it and tucked it into the waistband of my jeans. Uncertain of the contents, I didn't want to take a chance of ruining it by shoving it into my pocket.

The chime of the doorbell sent my pulse racing. I replaced the book, then slipped out of the office undetected and hurried toward the front of the house. Rounding the corner into the foyer, I blew out a heavy sigh as Ramsey opened the front door. He hadn't seen me leave the office, but even if he had, he wouldn't question it.

The familiar voices of my best friends brought me a little bit of relief.

"Avery," Tensley said, hurrying toward me. "I'm so sorry."

She wrapped her arms around me, and I buried my face in her hair, crying once again.

"We're here, hon." Tensley patted my back.

"Thank you for coming over," I whispered as we released each other. I spotted Benji speaking quietly with Ramsey. They had briefly met when Ramsey had visited a few months ago, but this would be the first time we would all hang out for any length of time.

My eyes wandered to Ramsey's. Grief filled his expression. I swallowed over the tightness in my throat. He was devastated as well. Patrick, Dad, and Ramsey had started an annual men's camping-and-hunting trip nearly ten years ago. When Patrick and Ramsey had drifted apart, it was Dad that helped Ramsey navigate through some difficult teen years.

My mind drifted to our interaction at The Lily, and my stomach twisted into knots. We had tabled the issue in order to be there for each other, but when the dust settled, I worried what would happen. *Can we overlook what we did and continue to be friends? Or will it eventually tear us apart?* I bit my bottom lip as another option occurred to me, and Skyler's comment appeared front and center in my brain. *Ramsey was your match.* I couldn't analyze it right now. It would have to wait for another time.

"Do you want us to go upstairs, or are you more comfortable down here?" Tensley's voice broke through my thoughts.

"Let's raid the bar, then we can talk in the game room."

"Hey, gorgeous," Benji said, approaching me. He wrapped me in a tight hug and kissed the top of my head. "One hell of a day. I'm so sorry."

I nodded, afraid I would fall apart if I spoke. My head was already pounding from all the tears that I'd shed.

"Let's grab some booze and snacks and head upstairs," I said finally.

Maybe I should have felt guilty for leaving my mother on her own, but I didn't give a rat's ass. Patrick and Olivia would arrive in another hour, anyway, and she could be their problem. Besides, I had a letter to open as soon as I had a few minutes alone.

6

My friends stuck close to me the rest of the evening, and they finally drifted off to sleep around four in the morning. Ramsey and I had reminisced about Dad and our summers spent together. Ten and Benji had only met Dad a few times, but they knew we were close.

Even though I was grateful to be surrounded by friends, my mind had continued to wander to the letter Dad had left me in the office. I'd discreetly deposited it in my dresser drawer when I'd taken a trip to the bathroom. Until I knew more, I didn't want to mention it to anyone.

Quietly, I walked to my room, located the envelope along with a blanket, and headed outside for some fresh air. I flipped the pool lights on, then settled into a lounge chair.

A crisp cool breeze picked up, and goosebumps pebbled my skin. Shivering, I snuggled beneath the cover and switched my phone's flashlight on. Other than the soft chirp of an occasional cricket, the early morning was eerily quiet.

I bit my lip, my anxiety climbing a notch as I stared at the night sky. The earlier clouds had cleared, and I gazed at the stars, wishing

Dad were next to me. For the moment, I would have to take solace in the idea that he was above and watching over me.

My pulse hummed in my ears as I returned to the task at hand. Carefully, I opened the envelope, then I gingerly removed the letter, which was on Dad's personal stationery.

Dear Avery,

If you're reading this, I've left you early. I'm so sorry.

There will never be enough words in the English language to express how proud I am of you and all that you've accomplished. You, Avery, are the beat of my heart. Even after I'm gone, I promise I'll be guiding you every step of the way. I will never leave you.

I know the last several years have been difficult with your mother. As the attorneys review my will, you will learn more about her and eventually her secrets. My secrets. You will finally understand the fragile thread that held our marriage together and why I never left her. It was to protect you. It was always to protect you.

I was far from perfect, and although I've left you a fortune and a company to run, I failed in other ways. In the last six months, some unforeseen events have transpired. I've managed to piss some people off, and I'm afraid they might retaliate. I hope I'm just paranoid, but if I'm right, I'll be gone, and you'll be reading this.

My mouth gaped. *Is he insinuating that he might have been murdered?* My forehead creased while I struggled to piece his words together. I had been in the car accident with him, and the cops didn't think there had been foul play, other than a hit-and-run.

Avery, at one time, Vincent was a good man, and there are very few people you can trust right now. I've hired another attorney to counsel you as you take the majority share of Davenport and McCade Financials. His name is Larry Townsend, and he was referred to me by Franklin Harrington. Speaking of Franklin, if you find yourself in trouble, reach out to him. He's definitely trustworthy.

Honey, I know you'll be emotionally vulnerable. Listen to your intuition and question everything. People aren't who they say they are—even me.

There is one person you can trust, Avery. Over the years, I've watched you and Ramsey become close. Lean on him. Confide in him, if you need to. He's a stand-up young man, and he will do right by you.

I slammed my eyes closed. The memories and images of Ramsey and me together the previous day flooded my mind, and no matter how much I willed it not to, my body reacted.

Shoving the longing to the side, I focused on Dad's note again. I flipped to the second page and swore a blue streak.

This next part is going to hurt you, and all I can hope is that down the road, you'll be able to forgive me. Avery, you

The ink had been smudged across the rest of the page, leaving it illegible. My shoulders sagged with frustration. I flipped over the envelope, eyeing it carefully. Part of the glue had warped where it had been sealed. Someone had tampered with it.

I leaned back in the chair, clutching the note tightly. *Who else has a key to Dad's office?* I realized the possibilities of where he had written the letter were endless, and anyone could have tampered with it.

The soft creak of the kitchen door opening caught my attention, and I quickly folded the note and shoved it under the blanket.

"Hey," Ramsey said softly, approaching me. "Are you up for some company?"

His shirt was wrinkled from his passing out on the couch. He'd looked so innocent while he had slept. His full lips had parted slightly, and his arm had draped over his forehead. I had found myself wanting to cover him with a blanket and tuck him in, but I didn't want to risk waking him.

"Sure." I nodded toward the lounge chair next to me.

My eyes traveled over his short messy hair and down his broad, muscular chest and long legs.

He yawned then plopped down next to me. "Have you slept at all?" Concern flickered across his face.

"No." I held his gaze, wondering what he was thinking. "When did you arrive in Spokane?" I bit my lip, wishing I could withdraw my accusatory tone.

Ramsey cracked a smile. "There's the Avery I know. Direct and to the point."

"Sorry, it came out wrong. We haven't had time to talk, and so much is going through my mind right now."

"I get it. I got here last week. I wanted to settle in and get a bit more familiar with my new surroundings before football practice started."

"And start your job." There, I'd said it.

"Yeah." Guilt threaded through his tone. "I had no idea you were a member. I would have told you I was working there. No one else knows, especially not my parents."

"I know the confidentiality is in place to protect everyone, but this …" I pointed at him then me. "Ramsey, I—" I shook my head, unsure of what to say next.

"Nothing has to change, but please don't walk away from our friendship. I don't know what I would do without you."

Ramsey reached for my hand, and I let him take it. His skin warmed me, shooting an electric current through my exhausted body.

"How long are you planning on working at The Lily?" I inwardly grimaced, wondering if he had caught the jealousy in my voice. Grief was making me feel weird shit toward him.

He shrugged. "I'm not sure I'm cut out for it. I took the job to have my own money while I was here, and I thought it would be fun." His shoulders sagged.

I giggled. "What guy wouldn't love getting laid several times a day? Plus, I see the members. Ramsey, they're stunning. There are no strings attached. It's just wildly wicked fantasies." I wiggled my eyebrows at him, enjoying the reprieve from the gut-wrenching sadness swirling inside me.

Ramsey's low chuckle rumbled through his chest. "The room selection and fantasy options the women can choose from are …" He cleared his throat, his cheeks slightly reddening as he stared out over the swimming pool.

I shifted, the lounger creaking beneath me. "It's the one place I feel free. There's no one to judge me, write me out of the will, or make me feel like a whore. I've always been comfortable with my body and sex. If I'm not in a committed relationship, then I see no harm in indulging a few times a week." Everything I'd said was true, except for the time my choice was wrenched away from me.

"I'm not judging you at all. I was shocked that you were a member, but more than that …" He leaned his head back on his chair then stared at me. "Jesus Christ, touching you … tasting you." He gulped. "I've never experienced anything so sensual," he said softly.

Dumbfounded, I stared at him. My first reaction to hooking up with Ramsey had been anger and to push him away. I hadn't had time to process what had happened before I learned that Dad had died.

"I don't know what to say. We've known each other all our lives, and even though I told you goodbye, I can't lose our friendship. Especially now." I folded my hands in my lap beneath the blanket, a chill creeping down my spine.

Ramsey nodded. "Me too. It would devastate me if you weren't in my life. I've decided I'm going to give notice at The Lily tomorrow. I would like to help you with your Dad's business, and someone needs to manage your mom. She's a fucking mess, and I suspect she'll disappear into a bottle anytime now." Compassion filled his handsome face.

I chose to ignore his comment about Mom. Our families had been close enough that Ramsey had seen plenty of vacations to piece it all together. A part of me had just hoped he hadn't.

"Are you sure? You can make good money. Not that you need it, but still. It would belong to you, not your family." My forehead creased. "Don't quit because your first day was weird."

"It's not that. I need time right now. Football starts soon, and this will give me time to focus on what's in front of me." He squeezed my hand.

"If that's what you really want, I'll support your decision." Relief flooded over me. The mere thought of him touching other women the way he had touched me flipped my possessive-bitch-mode dial to full throttle.

Ramsey loved girls. As a promising football star, he never went without a female hanging all over him. Even during our summers at the Hamptons, the ladies would flock to him, and he would sneak out at night to screw them. All the little rich girls fawned over him like he was Liam Hemsworth. But not me—we loved each other as family. He was my male equal in so many ways, including being ambitious and a rule breaker when he wanted to be.

"I do." He ran his free hand through his hair then looked up at the sky.

"I'm glad you're here," I admitted, emotion thick in my voice. "So much happened today, and I've not had time to wrap my head around it."

Ramsey's eyes softened. "I'm glad I'm here too."

His words danced over my skin, and butterflies ran amok in my chest. *What in the hell is happening to me?*

"Look," Ramsey pointed to the east. "The sun is peeking over the horizon."

Silence descended on us as we watched the world come to life in brilliant streaks of red and yellow. The hint of fall hung in the air, with the promise of pumpkin patches and cozy evenings in front of crackling fireplaces.

Anguish stabbed me in the chest, the ache taking my breath away. Dad and I loved fall—the yellow and red leaves, the Starbucks coffee flavors, muffins, the crisp, fresh air that carried a cool undercurrent in it. It was our favorite time, and he was gone. Tears spilled down my cheeks, and I hurriedly wiped them away.

I glanced at Ramsey, the words from the letter returning to me. Dad had said I could trust him. If I was about to walk into murky waters blindfolded, I needed someone in my life that could throw me a rope and pull me back out if I started to drown.

If I shared the contents of the note with Ten or Benji, it would drag them into God knew what. My heart thundered inside my chest. I'd read enough of the letter to know that stepping into the business was going to cause waves, but there was something more, information that Dad was going to tell me about that, apparently, someone else didn't want me to learn. At least Ramsey knew things I'd never told anyone else, and he'd always had my back.

"Avery." His gaze bored into mine, and I immediately recognized that our conversation was taking a dark turn.

"Did you ever tell your dad about Vincent?" His tone was gentle, but his jaw clenched as his thumb stroked the back of my hand he was still holding.

I shook my head. "No. You're the only one that knows what happened."

"What are you going to do? You're about to take over the majority share of the business." Ramsey sat up straighter, his shoulders tensing.

Mental images of Vincent pinning me down over his desk against my will ripped through me, and I shuddered. My skin crawled with the memory of his mouth being on mine and him slamming himself into me. Dryness seized my throat and I swallowed, shoving the fear back down.

At least I had been old enough to know it wasn't my fault. Even if I'd worn shirts with my tits hanging out and bootie shorts, the bastard never had a right to touch me. At the time, I'd felt like I needed to keep it secret from Dad. I couldn't take a chance of what it would do to the business, or worse. My father would have buried Vincent alive, which would have put him in prison, and I needed him at home with me. It wasn't worth the risk of losing him.

Tightening my other hand into a fist, I refused to let it get to me. It was my time to get even. That simple fact would keep me going when I stared the son of a bitch in the eye and wanted to puke all over his Berluti dress shoes. "He won't mess with me. I'm not seventeen anymore. Besides, I have something else in mind."

"Hey, I'm here to support you. I get why you never told your dad, but he's … gone. You could deal with Vincent raping you if you want to. You can still press charges and talk to the board."

"Ramsey, it's over. I can handle it on my own. For now, I have to work with him, but I'll make sure he gets his in the end. He has to answer to me now. Dad groomed me for this. And I can't tell you what it is, but I have major dirt on him. Dad shared some things with me a few weeks ago. I'm going to be okay." I hoped I sounded convincing, because even though I had the upper hand, Vincent was smart, and I suspected he wouldn't go down without a fight.

Our gazes connected, and a lump of messy emotions clogged my throat. My heart was broken, and I was terrified of the changes, but I understood how important it was not to show any signs of weakness.

"I know your parents thought you wanted to stop hanging out over the summer because you were older, but you scared the shit out of me after what he did to you. I thought you were going to end your life. No way in hell will I allow that fucker to mess with you again. Please promise me you'll keep me in the loop." Ramsey swung his long legs to the side of the chair and pinned me with his intense stare.

"I will. You have my word." I tucked a strand of hair behind my ear and changed the conversation. "I'm sorry I panicked earlier today when I said we couldn't be friends anymore after our incident at The Lily. You're a huge piece of my life, and I guess it threw me off."

Ramsey rubbed his chin, and the corner of his lips slanted up slightly. "Yeah, it did me too. When I saw it was you ..." He shook his head, then leaned back in his chair.

I relaxed a little, realizing he wasn't going to say anything else.

A sexy-as-hell smile eased across his face as he shifted in the lounger, and I couldn't help but grin. I would give almost anything to have access to where his mind was.

The best thing about Ramsey was that conversation wasn't always necessary. We were comfortable merely hanging out together, and it was exactly what I needed right then.

7

Over the next few days, Patrick and Olivia helped me sift through Dad's funeral arrangements. I wasn't sure I would have made it through the planning and sorting of bills and insurance policies without them. Mom hid in her bedroom and refused to make an appearance. I assumed she'd loaded up on every pill possible, along with a stash of coke.

I stared at myself in the bathroom vanity mirror. During the remodel, Mom had insisted I have one. She went on and on about how she couldn't live without hers, and it would add value to the room, blah blah blah. Finally, I'd agreed to simply shut her the hell up.

As much as I hated to admit it, I loved the special makeup lights and the drawers. The beige top matched the marble counters, and the lighting was amazing. It also helped me keep all my makeup in one space instead of scattered all over the place like when Benji, Tensley, and I had roomed together. At least I'd been out from under her thumb when I lived with them. It had been worth losing all the amenities of the house.

The dark circles under my eyes were more prevalent than a few days ago. They matched my black dress and heels. A clap of thunder filled the air while I applied the finishing touches of my eyeshadow.

Numbness had flowed into every crack and crevice of my broken heart. Three weeks ago, Dad and I were discussing business over lunch before the car accident. Today, I was burying him.

Tears streamed down my face, and I swore under my breath. I grabbed a tissue from the small box and blotted the moisture from my lashes and cheeks, thanking God for waterproof mascara. I blew out a big sigh, stood, and slid the chair back into place. Clearing my throat, I squared my shoulders. It was time.

I located my handbag in the closet, then headed downstairs. I glanced around the kitchen and living area but saw no sign of Mother. I wasn't surprised. She knew when the driver was scheduled to pick us up. I wasn't going to search for her or wait. After Dad had died, I made a promise to myself that if she wasn't going to get clean and sober, I was no longer willing to take care of her, lie for her, or make excuses. *Let her snort her life away.*

My phone buzzed with a text message, and I removed it from my purse. The car was ready for us. "Mom!" The sound of my voice reverberated through the house, reminding me of how alone I really was. "Mom! We have to go." Only silence responded to me.

A whirlwind of feelings surged through me. *Where is she?* I didn't have time or energy to hunt her down. She would have to find another way to get there. Anger coursed through me as I left without her.

Our driver, Gregory, opened the door for me, and I slid into the back seat. Rain pattered against the windshield, and the soft whoosh of the wipers filled the otherwise silent Mercedes.

Gregory hopped in the front and wiped the water off his black jacket. "Miss Avery." He nodded, his gentle gaze brimmed with grief and compassion. "Will your mother be joining us?"

I shrugged. "No. You might need to drop me off at the funeral then come back to get her if she calls."

"Understood." Gregory shifted into drive, and we navigated out of the circular driveway.

The dark-gray sky continued to grieve with me, the tears from heaven falling freely. I leaned my head against the seat and imagined

Dad next to me—the smell of his spicy cologne, the stubble on his chin he grew on the weekends, and his mischievous expression when he was discussing the upcoming football season. He'd been thrilled that Ramsey was joining us in Washington. Other than Patrick, Dad was Ramsey's biggest fan.

My chest tightened with the raw ache of not attending games with Dad anymore. I placed my hand over my eyes, shielding the unwanted tears from Gregory. A cry escaped my lips, and my shoulders began to shake uncontrollably. I was never going to make it through his funeral intact. No matter how well I hid my feelings on a day-to-day basis, it wasn't the same. Losing Dad had unraveled me from the inside out. I was scrambling to find any sense of normalcy and reassurance that life would go on.

"Miss Avery." Gregory handed me a Kleenex box. "I know I can't change anything, but if you need to talk today or any other day, I'm always here. Your father was a good man, and he loved you very much. On the days you think it's too much to keep going, remember that he wanted you to live a good life. He wanted you to graduate and fall in love. All those plans you made with him, carry them out. He's watching and guiding you from above. You'll never be alone. Ever."

I nodded, unable to speak. Gregory was right, and I knew I had to hold my chin up and move forward, but that day, I needed to give myself permission to fall apart.

The car pulled into a parking space at the front of the funeral home. I carefully blotted my eyes and cheeks with the tissue then wadded it up into a little ball and shoved it into my purse.

"I'll grab the umbrella." Gregory turned off the Mercedes and hopped out into the downpour.

He opened my door, popped open the bright-red Davenport and McCade Financials umbrella, and helped me out of the car. The click of the lock filled my ears as Gregory held out his arm for me. I slipped mine through his and we approached the building together.

Gregory and I entered through the double glass doors and my stomach lurched. I prayed I could keep myself together, because I didn't think I could bury Dad.

Gregory gave me a kind smile. "I'll be toward the back of the room in case your mother calls." He collapsed the umbrella and gave it a gentle shake, droplets of water falling to the large black welcome mat.

"Okay. I'll see you after the service." I gave him a quick peck on the cheek and left him by the entrance.

A faint sterile smell greeted me while I entered the sanctuary of the funeral home. I glanced around, searching for my best friends, but I didn't see them. So far, I was the only one there. I smoothed my fitted dress as my anxiety kicked up a notch.

Red and white roses filled the front of the room along with more flower arrangements than I could count. Candles flickered near the lectern where the pastor would speak. It was beautiful. Dad would have approved. Two picture collages were on easels to the right of the coffin. I'd picked out all of the images, and Olivia had placed and framed them.

My focus landed on the closed casket, which was covered with every color of tulip possible, and I stood still. The intensity of the situation had finally slapped me full force, and I struggled to breathe. I needed some air. Spinning around on my heel and ready to run, I came face-to-face with Ramsey. A waterfall of emotions washed over me, and I threw my arms around him and hung on to him with everything inside me.

"You look lovely. Your dad would be so proud of you," he said quietly in my ear as he enveloped me in the safety of his arms.

"You look amazing yourself. I like the red tie." I backed away, then looked up at him. Amazing wasn't even the right word to describe how good Ramsey looked. The black suit jacket accentuated his broad shoulders and muscular arms. I'd only seen him in a suit a few times, but he'd always looked like he'd strolled right off a magazine cover. A small curl fell onto his forehead, and I resisted the urge to smooth it away. Maybe it was an excuse to touch him more. "I'm so glad you're here." I felt the thump of my heart in my ears, and I prayed I wasn't going to pass out.

"Are you all right? You look a little pale. Why don't we sit down?" Ramsey's large hand rested on the small of my back, and the warmth of his touch soothed me immediately. He guided me toward the first row, and we sat down together.

He cleared his throat. "I won't ask if you're doing okay."

"Thanks. I'm not, but I would think that's a given."

Ramsey nodded. "Mom and Dad are here too. They should be in shortly." He stretched his long legs out in front of him and laid his arm on the back of the pew. "I don't want you to worry about Vincent today. I'll keep him away from you."

"I appreciate it, but I have other things to deal with. I have no idea where my mom is. If she misses his funeral …" I pressed my lips into a thin line, holding back the scream I so badly wanted to release. "I've been thinking that after the will is finalized, I'm going to sell the house then buy another place. I know Dad left it to me."

"That's a big move right now."

"Probably. I'll take my time looking, though. I'm ready, Ramsey. Unless something significant changes between Mom and me … I'm done. I'm walking away. I have to find my new normal without Dad, and I have a company to focus on while I finish my degree. All she will do is cause chaos and drama for me." I leaned back against the uncomfortable seat.

"If it gets to be too much, you can always stay with me."

My eyebrows shot up. "I couldn't do that. You have your entire career in front of you. All I'll do is distract you. Besides, if things get shitty, I can live at the Davenport Hotel for a while. I'm not going to become someone's burden."

"I get what you're saying, but I have a nice two-bedroom apartment and no roomie. You're welcome there anytime. Besides, between football practice and games, I won't be there much. Plus, you're taking over the business. We probably wouldn't even see each other most of the time. You'd have the space and quiet you would need." Ramsey rubbed his hand on his suit slacks and offered me a kind smile. "At least I would know you're all right. I worry your mom is going to lose her shit one night while you're sleeping."

"You and me both. Over the years, you've seen her drunk and a bit unruly, but she hid most of it from you and your parents. It's bad,

Ramsey." I stared at the dark-brown carpet and wished I could allow the fibers to absorb me until I was nonexistent.

Ramsey cupped my chin and tilted it toward him. "How bad?" He pinned me with troubled eyes.

"I lost Dad a few days ago. I lost my mother years ago." The corner of my lips twitched with the confession. "I'm tired of covering for her, like buying new dishes and vases when she shatters them. She's a mess and refuses to go to rehab. When Dad was traveling, it wasn't uncommon for her to wake me up in the middle of the night. She would scream and hit me, and sometimes all I could do was curl up in a ball to protect myself. After a few times of coming home and seeing my face and arms bruised up, Dad refused to travel. Now … I don't know what to expect."

Ramsey balled his hand into a fist, his knuckles turning white. "You're not staying there anymore."

I shook my head. "I'll be fine." Even though the words came out of my mouth, I knew better. On the nights I'd locked my door, if she was coked out of her skull, she had broken it down or removed the doorknob with whatever tool she'd found.

"If you'll give me your phone, I'll add my address so that you have it. Come by anytime."

"Thank you." I handed him my iPhone and waited while he entered the information. "But, Ramsey, promise me you won't tell anyone. This is my problem, and I don't want a pity party. It's just how she is. I can leave, and I will."

"This isn't up for discussion. Mom and Dad will be heading back home tomorrow, which means your mom won't be chaperoned." His voice was hard, and his eyes were tight with indignation. "You deserve so much more."

"Hey, babe," Benji said, sliding down the bench behind me. He leaned over and kissed the side of my head. "Ramsey. Good to see you again."

"Hey, hon. Sorry we didn't get here sooner," Tensley said, kissing my cheek.

Layne patted my shoulder then leaned closer to me. "Avery, this is the hardest part. Hang in there. We're all here for you."

"Thanks," I said, taking his hand. "I'm glad all of you showed up."

"Avery, you're family. Where else would we be?" Benji asked, flipping open the button of his black suit jacket, then sitting down.

Tensley looked stunning with her long blonde hair flowing down her back. Her three-quarter-sleeved black dress fit her in all the right places. I was sure Layne also appreciated it. He slipped his arm around her shoulders and smiled at her. The guy had it so bad for her, and I adored him for loving her.

Patrick and Olivia joined Ramsey and me in the front row, and we quietly chatted about the plans for the rest of the day. Everyone would come back to the house and most likely bring enough food to feed me for a year. I would freeze what I could and send some with Ramsey to his new place. I suspected that after football practice, he could eat his weight in carbs.

During the service, I continued to peer over my shoulder toward the door, hoping Mom was going to show. She didn't, but Vincent did. A surge of anger boiled beneath the surface. I wasn't sure which was worse, that Mom didn't show or that Vincent did and played the doting friend and business partner.

My head buzzed with my churning emotions. If I didn't focus on something else, I would find myself back at the house, slapping my mother senseless. She wasn't worth it, though. All she had proved was that she was a worthless piece of shit who didn't even love her husband.

In order to keep myself together during the funeral, my mind played with the idea of what it would be like to have Ramsey as a roomie. He'd always been a constant in my life, but I wondered if I could live with him. I was almost as much of a mess as Mom was, but in a different way. It would take a long time for me to land on my feet again, and I couldn't suck him into the darkness with me. He deserved better, but my heart was disagreeing with my logic. Maybe my heart needed him more than I realized.

THE REST of the day was filled with an abundance of hugs, food, and well wishes, which Mom missed, since she was nonexistent when we arrived at the house. I'd eventually tuned out all the "Your dad was a wonderful man" sentiments. All I wanted was for everyone to stop. Nothing anyone said would bring him back.

After the last guest left at nearly ten that evening, Patrick, Olivia, and Ramsey headed toward the kitchen. I slipped off my heels and followed them, exhaustion sinking deep into my bones.

Olivia grabbed the freshly brewed pot of coffee and poured us each a cup.

"Do you need us to stay longer, Avery?" She set a steaming mug on the table in front of me.

"No. Thank you, though. I'm so grateful to both of you."

"I'll be around now if she needs anything," Ramsey added, then sipped his drink.

It was probably too late at night to have caffeine, but I doubted I would sleep, anyway.

"When will you start at Davenport and McCade?" Patrick asked as he crossed his legs and smoothed his slacks.

"Next week I'll meet with the board, clean Dad's office out, and settle in a little bit. I have two more classes to finish this term, then I'll have my degree and work there full-time."

Concern clouded Ramsey's expression. I suspected he was worried about Vincent. At first, I was, too, but he wouldn't want to ruin his reputation and lose his wife. A rape accusation, no matter how long ago it was, would hold a lot of weight, especially coming from Steven Davenport's daughter. Most of the people who'd worked there the summer of my seventeenth birthday were still employed. A few of them had even waved goodbye to us while I was seated in his office that fateful night. I was pretty sure I could jog their memories and encourage them to speak to the board of directors.

"Has anyone heard from Mom?" I massaged my temple wearily.

"No. She's not answering her phone." Olivia played with the

diamond pendant around her slim neck. "I have to admit that I'm shocked she didn't attend Steven's funeral." Even when Olivia was exhausted, she was pretty. She'd swept her shoulder-length brown hair into an updo and had opted for a neutral nail color.

Ramsey looked more like Patrick, with his expressive blue eyes and short dark hair. Patrick was taller, but Ramsey was thicker in the chest and shoulders.

"I'm not. Whatever you think you know about her isn't the half of it." I folded my arms on the table and placed my head down. "She'll show up eventually. She always does."

"This has happened before?" Patrick asked, his tone full of dismay. "Steven never mentioned anything."

I raised my head slightly and stared at Patrick, then Olivia. "Would you mention your wife was on a bender and didn't come home for a week at a time?"

"Avery, we're family. I realize you inherited the business and have major responsibility now, but you're still young. We are only a call away, and we can be here in a few hours. On the long weekends, you can fly home with Ramsey, as well as for the holidays, if you don't have anyone to spend them with here. You're always welcome. Just show up."

The compassion in Patrick's face nearly overwhelmed me, and I struggled to maintain my composure over the messy ball of gratitude mixed with despair that threatened to erupt.

"Thank you. I have my best friends here too. Benji and Tensley will make sure I don't spend a single holiday alone." I chanced a glance at Ramsey, wondering what his thoughts were on the matter, but he seemed miles away from our conversation.

Twenty minutes later, I excused myself to my bedroom. I couldn't wait to get into more comfortable clothes.

I unzipped the side zipper and wiggled out of my dress, letting the fabric float to the floor around my feet.

A soft rap on the door startled me. I grabbed my floral silk robe out of my closet and slipped it on.

"Who is it?" I asked.

"Ramsey."

"It's open." I finished tying the belt while he entered.

He'd changed out of his suit into gray sweats and a black T-shirt. Ramsey had the ability to look good in anything. Even naked. I swatted the thought away and returned my attention to him. Since we were alone, and I'd had some time to process it, I realized I had to talk to him about the letter.

"I wasn't sure whether you wanted any more company today, but I figured I would try." A gentle smile eased across his handsome features.

"It's fine." I strolled over to my dresser, opened the drawer, and located the envelope. The paper felt cool to the touch, and I inhaled deeply, attempting to clear my head. Once I shared the information with Ramsey, I couldn't turn back. He would want to insert himself even more into my life—protect me.

I faced him. "I need to tell you something. You should probably sit down for this."

Ramsey frowned but did as I suggested. "What's wrong?" His brows knitted together, his telltale sign that he was worried.

"I'm not sure." I crossed the room and sat on the end of my bed next to him then tucked a leg beneath me. "Promise me. Promise me, Ramsey, that you won't share this with anyone. I'm so serious."

"Avery, I've always kept our secrets. Even the ones I shouldn't have, but I won't bring up that sorry bastard right now." Guilt flickered through his eyes.

"About a year ago, Dad told me if anything happened to him, and he died early …" I was rooted in a haze of uncertainty, and my focus drifted to the floor.

"Take your time." His shoulders tensed slightly.

"He told me there would be a letter for me and where to find it." I handed him the envelope. "I want you to read it. But this stays between us. You can't tell anyone else. I've not even decided whether I should tell Benji and Tensley yet."

"I won't say a word." He carefully pulled the pieces of paper out and unfolded them.

Silently, I waited for him to read it and flip to the second page.

"Shit." He looked on the back of the pages then laid the letter on the mattress between us. He scrubbed his face with his hands, then his attention landed on me. "This isn't good. He no longer trusts his business partner, and he was about to tell you something else. I mean, we already know what a fucking scum Vincent is."

I folded my arms over my stomach. "He thought I could trust you, so I am."

Ramsey reached out and grabbed my hands. "You can. I won't let anything happen to you, but I need you closer. With me at the apartment and you living here, I won't be able to make sure you're okay. Please, move in with me. I promise I'll stay out of your way."

My heart swelled with gratitude. "I can't say it has ever crossed my mind that you'd ask me to move in with you." I cracked a grin. "I can crash with Tensley and Benji too. For now. I need to tread carefully, which means not making any decisions lightly. Involving other people isn't a good idea."

"Too late. I already am. I know you're broken up right now, but promise me you won't dismiss the idea. Please, Avery … think about it. This letter brings up way more concerns than I initially had."

"You've always wanted to protect me from the world, Ramsey."

His thumb stroked the back of my hand. "Do you remember the summer at the Hamptons when we were eleven, and a big storm had us cooped up in the house all day? We played every game known to man, but all we wanted to do was play on the beach." A chuckle rumbled through his chest. "Finally, you grabbed your sketch pad, sat in the window seat in your bedroom, and drew the devastation you thought was happening outside. The wind rattled the shutters on the windows, and your eyes got so big. You put on this brave-girl front, but I knew you well enough to realize you were scared."

"I do. My drawing was pretty accurate too. The next day we spent the better part of the morning locating our outdoor furniture."

"Do you recall what I said to you that night while you were sketching?" His voice was low and gentle.

His words rattled around in my head. "You sat down next to me and wrapped me in a big hug. Then you promised me you'd never allow anything or anyone to hurt me." Our eyes connected, and my heart pitter-pattered. "You said you loved me, and you always would. Whether I knew it yet or not, we belonged together. I was yours forever."

Electricity swirled around us, igniting the air and taking my breath away. *How could I have forgotten what he said that night?* I had dismissed it as preteen hormones. But since our encounter at The Lily, our friendship had taken a turn. To where I wasn't sure. Maybe the guy I had always dreamed of had always been right in front of me. My emotions bounced around inside me like kernels of corn in a popcorn maker on the fritz.

"Those weren't the words of a horny kid?" I offered him a smile, teasing him.

"No." His fingertips traced my cheek. "I'm not asking for anything now, Avery. I wanted to remind you that I love you. I'm always here."

He leaned forward, his lips hovering over mine. Then he pressed a gentle kiss to my mouth.

With one touch, he reached the broken pieces inside my soul and breathed life back into me.

He pulled away and leaned his forehead against mine.

"I love you too. I'm just not sure in what capacity. My entire world is upside down. Can you …" My voice hovered above a whisper. "Can you hold me tonight?"

If I spoke my thoughts out loud, they would become reality, and I couldn't afford to fall apart any more than I already had. But I was scared, and I recognized that I would naturally gravitate toward the one man who had always been there for me.

"Yeah. I'd love to." He flipped down the lavender comforter, then we nestled underneath the covers.

He wrapped an arm around me, and I placed my head on his chest. Snuggling with him should have felt strange, but it didn't. It was the most natural thing I'd allowed myself to do in a long time. As his heart beat in my ears, I hoped his presence would chase all the nightmares away.

8

The chill of autumn had arrived almost overnight, and I had opted for dark slacks and the green silk blouse Skyler had given me. Anxiety hummed through me while I stood outside the eleventh-floor office of Davenport and McCade. I had just finished a meeting with the board of directors, and I was eager to show my presence.

I adjusted my bag on my shoulder and pushed through the doors. Rubbing my chilled hands together, I plastered a smile on my face as I entered the reception area.

"Good morning, Miss Davenport." The young receptionist smiled politely.

"Hello, Janine. I'm going to clean out my father's office and set mine up today."

"I'm so sorry about your dad. He was always kind to me … unlike some." She looked over her shoulder, a paranoid expression dancing across her features.

"Dad spoke fondly of you." I leaned closer to her. "And if there's a problem with anyone here, please let me know." I nodded at her then strolled down the long hall, wondering whom she'd been referring to. Vincent would be my first guess.

My breath stuttered in my throat as I walked down the carpeted hallway, a growing sense of apprehension nagging at me. I had been there more times than I could count, waving at Dad's employees through the windows, but this time I stared straight ahead, stoic. I would address the staff later. First, I needed to make it behind closed doors before I broke down crying.

Phones rang, and the sound of people's chatter reached my ears as I arrived. Tears pricked the backs of my eyes while I scanned the room. With tentative steps, I walked to the wall of bookshelves and trailed my finger along the spine of a thick leather book. Pictures of our family lined the shelves.

"I miss you so much, Daddy," I whispered. I shoved the pain down and stuffed it into a little box. It wasn't the time or place to show emotion—not yet, anyway.

I placed my laptop bag on top of my desk, then sank into my seat and powered up my computer.

I turned around and stared out of the wall of windows that over-looked downtown Spokane. When I was younger, I would climb into that very chair, pick up Dad's phone, and bark out orders, like I'd heard him do a thousand times. A soft laugh escaped me at the memory. If I stilled myself, I could almost feel his hand on my shoulder.

The click of the door caught my ear, and I spun around to see who had invited themselves in without asking.

"Avery. You're looking very well." Vincent McCade smirked. "I thought I'd take a few minutes and welcome you." He shoved his hands into the pockets of his slacks. His burgundy shirt and black tie made his gray eyes appear more menacing. I wondered if he'd prac-ticed the sneer on his face in the mirror that morning.

I quirked an eyebrow and stood. My heels nearly placed me at eye level with that asshole. His brown hair had receded even more since I'd seen him last. I stifled a laugh. He didn't wear it well.

I promised Ramsey that I would pick my battles carefully, but I also knew I had to put Vincent in his place immediately. Even though I had barely buried Dad, I wasn't a weak little girl. I owned the majority share of the company, and he needed to understand who called the shots.

"Thank you." My tone was laced with steel.

Vincent's lustful leer traveled from my breasts, down my flat stomach, to my crotch. His tongue darted out over his bottom lip.

Inwardly, I shuddered, the memories of the rape assaulting my mind. He was trying to rattle me, but I refused to let him. If I gave him enough rope, he would hang himself, and his career would be over. I hoped like hell I would witness his fall from Eden too.

Vincent approached me, and I fought the impulse to halt him. He sat on the corner of my desk and folded his hands in his lap.

"What can I help you with? I have a lot to take care of this morning, so cut to it." I stared at him, my gaze unwavering and my heart beating so loudly that I was sure he could hear it.

"Just because Daddy left you the majority share of the company doesn't mean you know how to run it. I'll have you out of here before your nameplate arrives." A devious smile spread across his ugly mug.

I pursed my lips, carefully weighing the words that were forming on my tongue. "Mr. McCade, it's obvious that my father didn't keep you in the loop about his plans for me and this company. That's okay. Neither of us needs your permission to do … well, anything we want." I flashed a pitying smile at him. "Let's make this clear. Do. Not. Fuck. With. Me. Your days of harassing women and stealing from the company are over. I have everything I need to put you away for a long time," I said, hoping he couldn't see through my bravado.

Vincent blanched, the blood draining from his face.

"Dad found out you were embezzling money a few weeks before he passed away and shared the information with me. You have forty-eight hours to replace the thousands of dollars you siphoned, or I'm calling the cops."

Vincent hopped off the desk and waved his hands in the air. "No police. I swear you'll have it by the end of the day tomorrow."

"You had better hope so. As for the rape …" My eyes narrowed to slits. "I'm going to speak with every female employee, and if even one of them tells me you looked at them inappropriately, not only will there be charges brought against you, but I will also destroy your career, then bury you in the remains of it."

Vincent's bushy eyebrows shot up, and he took a few steps backward.

"You can take the rest of the day off. You have money to return." I waved him away as though he were a servant.

He and I both knew he would be out the door before the end of the week. I would buy him out at a reasonable price, or I would go to the board and present all of the evidence I had. Either way, I'd waited a long time for the opportunity, and it was almost in reach. He was nothing but a spineless, weak bastard who got off on hurting women. If he went to prison, he would understand how he'd made me feel that day when some burly man made him his little bitch.

I took a deep breath, my legs trembling. Sinking into the chair, I grinned. It had felt good to fuck with him and take my power back. I might not be able to stop him from preying on other women, but it sure as hell wouldn't happen at my company.

The morning went by without incident, and by three in the afternoon, I realized I hadn't eaten anything. My tummy growled, urging me to feed it.

I grabbed my cell phone and switched the ringer back on. Immediately, it chimed with missed calls. I tapped the screen and listened to the first one.

Avery, it's your mother. I'm home, and there's no food in the house. Can you pick up something for dinner on your way here? I'll have Gladys run to the store tomorrow.

I massaged my forehead. The queen was at the palace without any explanation of where she'd been or why she hadn't attended Dad's funeral. My nostrils flared in disgust. *Fuck her.* I would buy my own food and eat it in front of her. She could get her own food.

The next voicemail began to play, and a disguised voice blared through the speaker.

So sorry to hear about dear ol' daddy. One down and one to go. I thought the car accident would end you both, but that's okay. I love a good game of cat and mouse. Be careful, little girl. If you share this message with anyone, you'll seal your fate even sooner.

My phone clattered to the floor, and ice flowed through my veins, rendering me momentarily immobile. *Holy shit.* The car wreck wasn't an accident. Fear seized my throat, and I attempted to swallow. With trembling hands, I retrieved my cell and noted the time the threat had been left—eleven minutes after eight. I'd been driving to the office.

I clenched my jaw, grinding my teeth together as a thought teased the corner of my mind. Although I couldn't tell if the voice was male or female, I immediately considered Vincent. He was trying to scare me before I'd even shown up. *Sorry bastard. That was a super shitty move.* Anger swirled inside me, and I collected my laptop bag, then closed and locked the door behind me. I hurried down the hall and approached Janine. "Hey," I said. "Do you have a minute?"

"Anything you need."

Her bright smile calmed my violent mood. I wanted nothing more than to pummel Vincent McCade's sneer right off his face.

I leaned on the counter, then glanced around to see if anyone was lingering in the lobby. "I am assuming that you have access to Vincent's calendar, correct?"

"That's right. Let me pull it up for you." Her fingers flew across the keyboard.

"What does today look like?" I hesitated to give her a reason why I was asking. She didn't need to be in the middle of our war.

"He was here early this morning. There was a meeting with him and two other employees in the main conference room."

I caught myself before I frowned. "Was anyone else in the meeting, or was it a WebEx?" I asked quietly.

"Yes, Mr. Kleindale and Mr. Fitz from—"

"I know who they are. They own the NBA team the Hornets." I couldn't hide my frown that time. "Were they on time?"

"I was here at seven thirty and set up the conference area for them. At a quarter till eight, everyone settled into the room until nine thirty. It was a short meeting." She glanced at her screen again. "Afterward, Mr. McCade had a brief break before a conference call."

Fuck. That was about the time he had visited me. "Thank you, Janine. I'll be back tomorrow. If you need me, call my cell." I located a piece of paper near her phone, scribbled down my number, and handed it to her.

"Thank you, but I have it. I called you for your dad sometimes. By the way, your new business cards should arrive in a few more days."

"Perfect. I really appreciate it." I patted the top of the desk then left the office.

Hurrying down the hall, I assessed the situation and the probability that the call had been from Vincent. He could have briefly left the meeting in order to threaten me, excusing himself to use the restroom, then strolled back in without raising any suspicion. It would have been an excellent alibi.

The elevator doors whooshed open at the end of the hallway, and I picked up my pace to reach it in time. I jammed the lobby button and leaned against the wall as the elevator descended. *Who can I trust with this?* The voicemail had warned me I couldn't tell anyone. If it was Vincent, I could handle it. But the more I chewed on the information Janine had shared with me, I wasn't so sure. He might be a thief and a rapist, but I wasn't sure whether he was capable of killing someone.

I unlocked my dark-blue Bimmer and tossed my belongings onto the passenger seat. The leather squeaked as I settled in and started the car. Fear crept up my throat, and my heart pumped wildly. The voice from the message looped over and over in my mind. Dad's death wasn't an accident. "Oh my God," I whispered. Dad had been murdered. My head hung down, and panic ripped the air from my lungs.

I wasn't supposed to be alive. His letter had warned me someone might have been after him, and the threat had confirmed his suspicions. It was no longer speculation. It was a cold, hard reality. I'd been warned not to go to the cops either. *What in the hell am I going to do?*

Crying uncontrollably, I slammed the palm of my hand on the steering wheel. My stomach twisted into knots as it fully dawned on me that I was in a car and about to drive home. Maybe I was being watched or my BMW had a tracking or listening device.

An anguished cry slipped from my lips, and I covered my mouth in an attempt to muffle the sound. For the moment, I had to assume I wasn't safe, and neither was anyone else in my life.

My hand trembled as I shifted the car into drive, and I cautiously pulled out of the parking lot and headed toward the house. Until I figured out my next move, I needed to pretend nothing was wrong.

For the umpteenth time, I tossed my phone onto the bed. I wanted to call Tensley and tell her about the threat. Though I needed to talk to someone I trusted, my brain reminded me that my father was dead, and I couldn't risk my best friends too. I was giving myself serious whiplash from my indecision.

My thoughts returned to Dad's letter, and before I chickened out, I googled a phone number. Seconds later, I was listening to the line ring.

"Harrington and Associates. This is Katie. How can I assist you?"

"Hi, is Mr. Harrington available?" My voice sounded thick and foreign to my ears.

"He's in a meeting right now. I can take a message and have him return your call when he's finished, if you would like. What's your name?"

My pulse pounded in my head. "Avery. Avery Davenport," I replied quietly.

"Oh." A loud rustling filled the line. "Hang on, hon. I'll transfer you right away."

My brows knitted, and within seconds, my call was answered.

"This is Franklin Harrington."

I scrambled to find my voice. "This is Avery Davenport."

"Are you safe?"

Completely caught off guard by his question, I hesitated. "I don't think so. I was threatened. Dad told me to contact you if ... In a letter, he told me you were ..."

"Don't say any more. Can you meet with me?" Franklin cleared his throat and waited for my response.

"Yes." He was an attorney, and I suspected he knew how to hide his emotions well, but I didn't miss the hint of concern in his tone.

"Listen to me carefully. Buy a few burner phones and call me from one of them. I'll give you directions at that time."

Holy fuck. This is serious shit.

"Okay. I'll talk to you in a bit."

"Avery, don't stop anywhere except to purchase a phone. Do you understand? I'll explain everything when I see you."

"Yes." I ended the call, then stared at the mural on my bedroom wall. The ocean waves beckoned me, and all I wanted right then was to feel safe while I basked in the warmth of the sun rays on the beach. *What in God's name is happening? Did Dad participate in illegal activity?* Questions spun around in my mind like a weathervane caught in a tornado. I needed answers—immediately.

HALF AN HOUR LATER, I grabbed one of the burner phones I'd purchased at the convenience store and called Franklin again.

"Are you in your own car?"

"Yeah."

"Where are you now?" he asked, concern hinging on his words.

"I'm on Third Avenue."

"Perfect. You're only a mile or so away from Sam's Auto Shop. When you arrive, pull into a bay and tell them I sent you. They'll know what to do. Don't say anything else until you're out of the car."

"Do you want me to hang up?" I asked while I attempted to calm my galloping pulse.

"No. Stay with me," he said again.

I put the phone down, added the information into the car's GPS, and slowly drove out of the parking lot and turned left. It felt like a fucking nightmare, and I was struggling to keep a clear head.

Spotting Sam's Auto on my right, I pulled in, then I entered the bay like Franklin had instructed. I turned off the BMW, then quickly gathered my handbag and tossed the other phones into it.

I was greeted by a burly man that appeared to be in his forties. His blonde beard needed trimming, and so did his ragamuffin-like hair.

"Ma'am," he said. "What can we do ya for?"

"Franklin Harrington sent me." My voice shook with my words.

"Avery?" A bushy eyebrow arched as his beefy fingers ran over his stomach. He hooked a thumb on the bib of his overalls, while his other hand scratched his left ass cheek.

I nodded, ignoring his lack of manners. If Franklin trusted him, I would have to as well.

"I'm Tim. Franklin called me a few minutes ago. Let's get you taken care of." He limped toward the wall, then pushed a large red button. The garage doors began to close, screeching like fingernails on a chalkboard.

Panic rippled through me. "Franklin!" I whisper-yelled into the phone. "I think he locked me in here with him." My eyes widened with alarm while I attempted to find a way to escape.

"I'm here, Avery. You're safe. He's going to take you to his office where we can talk."

The guy waved me toward him, and my legs wobbled as I followed him.

"Take your time." He motioned to a seat in a small, cluttered room, then left me alone.

I checked the door handle and made sure I could lock it from the inside. As I closed the door, the smell of oil and car fumes assaulted my nose.

"What the hell is happening, Franklin?" I sank into the rickety plastic black chair, my senses hyperalert.

"I'm sorry. I didn't mean to scare you. Tim will check your car for tracking devices along with other items. Not only is he a mechanic, but he also works with Westbrook Security when he's needed. He looks scary, but he's a good man. You have my word."

I slumped in the seat, my nerves on edge.

"Take a few deep breaths. I'm having someone pick you up. I don't know if you're being tailed or what the situation is yet, so we want to take all the precautions necessary."

I nodded as though he could see me. "Who is picking me up?" I managed to ask.

"His name is Tad Murphy. He works for Westbrook Security. He will bring you to a safe place where we can speak openly. When we're done, Tim will have your vehicle ready to pick up, or Tad can take you wherever you'd like to go."

"Okay." *What choice do I have but to trust him?* "I received a phone message." I stood and paced across the small threadbare red carpet.

"Did you delete the voicemail, or do you still have it?" Franklin asked.

"I kept it." I placed my hand on my hip and looked at the sagging, water-stained ceiling. The place was the fucking pits.

"Tad should be there to get you any time. We're going to meet in person, then we can talk openly."

A soft rap on the door caught my attention, and I turned slowly.

"Avery?"

"A man with red hair, six two-ish, big shoulders, is here," I rattled off to Franklin.

"That's Tad. Why don't you let me talk to him for a minute?"

I held the burner phone out to the drool-worthy man standing in front of me. If he ever grew tired of working security, I bet Skyler would be happy to employ him at The Lily. Hell, I wouldn't mind breaking him in either. If he weren't staring at me, I would slap myself for thinking about sex at that moment, but my stress showed up in weird ways.

His ice-blue eyes stared at me while he spoke quietly with Franklin. "Here she is." Tad handed the burner back to me.

"Hi, it's Avery again."

"Do you want to stay on the line with me, or do you feel safe with Tad?" Franklin asked.

"I'm okay to hang up. I remember Tensley said you were really good to her when she needed you. You wouldn't send someone to hurt me."

"Call me if you need to. Otherwise, I'll see you in about thirty minutes."

"Thank you," I whispered, then I disconnected the conversation.

"Follow me," Tad said, ushering me forward.

He led me to a black Mercedes parked near the front of the building. Once we settled in, I tried to relax, but it was futile.

"Did anyone follow you here?" Tad asked.

"I don't know. Honestly, I wouldn't even have a clue of who to look for." I rubbed my forehead, realizing my head was pounding. "I've not eaten today."

"At all?" Tad asked, an eyebrow arching.

"I had a banana at seven this morning." As if on cue, my tummy growled loudly. "Sorry. Everything happened so fast. I was leaving work to grab some lunch when I received the threat."

"Is there any fast food that you like?" Tad asked, staring ahead while he drove.

"Arby's." I glanced out of the passenger window, wondering if whoever had left the message for me had seen me get into Tad's car.

9

Half an hour later, I peered through the windshield at my surroundings as Tad parked in front of a beautiful two-story home with numerous outdoor lights.

"Where are we?" I asked, opening the car door and stepping outside.

"Franklin's place. As you could tell from the ride here, it's very secluded. He has security here twenty-four seven, too."

"You're one of his employees, then?" Eyeing the beautiful Victorian home, I spotted the mother-in-law house down the hill.

"I am, but our assignments change a lot, so I'm not Franklin's permanent guy. Follow me." Tad strolled in through the front door, and we entered the foyer. Franklin's home was gorgeous. It had warm colors, and large decorative pillars marked the opening of a formal dining room to the left and a more casual living area to the right.

"This way." Tad strode with purpose past the stairs and down the hall. Pictures of who I assumed were Franklin's wife and kids covered the wall. My chest warmed, followed by a piercing ache. I would never be able to ski or sail with Dad again. All I had left were our memories. I clutched my purse against my tummy, focusing on the supple leather beneath my fingertips in order to maintain my composure.

"Avery." A handsome man stood, walked around his desk, and extended his hand to me. "I'm Franklin Harrington, a friend of your father's."

Law books filled the tall, dark shelves, and a stunning painting of the sun casting warm golden hues over the calm ocean hung on the wall. For an attorney's office, the room offered an inviting and cozy atmosphere. I suspected it had to do with the images that depicted a happy man with friends and family. I wondered if I would ever feel that way again—happy.

I peered up into kind, beautiful blue eyes as I shook his hand. "Hi. I don't recall seeing you at the funeral."

Franklin Harrington was a striking man. Streaks of gray threaded through his dark hair, and he'd been graced with perfect cheekbones and full lips. Confidence radiated off him in waves.

"Please, have a seat." He motioned to a black leather chair and smoothed his light-blue dress shirt. "I was there, but in the back of the room near the door. Unfortunately, I had a client emergency, so I left early. I'm sorry about your father, Avery."

"Me too," I whispered. "Do you always have clients in your home at … eight at night?" I cleared my throat as the reason why I was sitting there came rushing back, overwhelming my senses.

"Only if it's a necessity. Plus, I know we're safe here. If anyone followed you, we'll catch them on the security video. I can't imagine you're doing okay, so I won't ask if you are."

"I wanted to thank you for taking my call so quickly today."

"You can call anytime you need me. Your father and I go way back, and I promised him I would keep an eye on you if anything happened to him. He also mentioned that if you ever called, it would most likely be life or death. My receptionist was told to patch you through even if I was in a meeting." Franklin steepled his hands together then dropped them into his lap. "You stated you received a threat?"

I grabbed my purse, pulled my cell phone out, and tapped the screen. "Here's the message."

The disguised voice filled the room, and I bit my bottom lip. My stomach clenched as the caller admitted openly that the car accident had been intentional. The message ended, and a heavy silence hung in the air.

"Steven …" Franklin drummed his fingers on his desk, his expression filling with anguish. "I still can't believe he's gone," he said, his tone thick with emotion. Franklin ran his hand through his hair and sighed.

"Me either. I think I hear him downstairs in the mornings, then I remember …" My chin trembled, and I placed my hand over my mouth. I didn't want to break down crying in front of Franklin.

He cleared his throat and sat up straight. "Steven contacted me a few months ago. He was worried he had trusted the wrong people, and it was going to come back to haunt him. I think your call is supporting his concern."

"Was it a business deal gone bad?" I steeled myself for the answer. Dad had mentioned I would learn his secrets in the letter he'd left me, but I didn't want to. I wanted to hold on to who I knew he was—a kind, loving father, a devoted husband, and overall an honorable and trustworthy human being.

"Avery, no matter what you learn, your father loved you very much. He was a good man, but he got caught up in a bad situation." He leaned back, his chair creaking softly. "His business partner, now your business partner, got mixed up in some criminal activity. Your dad tried to intervene, but it was too late."

"Vincent?" I snorted. "He's a piece of—" I caught myself before I went any farther. "Honestly, I think he might have been behind the voicemail."

Franklin's eyebrow arched. "Why don't you tell me what you know."

"I … Vincent." My throat tightened, refusing to allow my words to surface. "I never told Dad, but Vincent raped me when I was seventeen. Since then, he's tried to bully me, but I put him in his place earlier today. When I heard the message, my first thought was that Vincent was behind it. I inherited the majority share of the company, and it would make sense that he wanted me out of the way."

Franklin shot out of his chair and shoved his hands into his pockets, the driving pulse in his neck becoming apparent. "Now I can finish your sentence. Vincent is a piece of shit. Any man who takes advantage of a woman deserves ..." He blew out a breath, his anger evident on his face. "Who else knows about the assault?" he asked, his voice gentle.

"Ramsey Goldman. Patrick and Olivia's son."

"I wish you had reported it, Avery. You along with every other woman that has been harmed deserves to see justice."

"Well, I need him taken care of now. If the message is true ... Dad was murdered, and I'm next." A cold shiver skated down my spine. "I'm not sure if it's true or if it's meant to scare me." I glanced up at Franklin. "Do you know anything?"

Franklin returned to his seat. "When Steven helped Vincent, he didn't know he owed a lot of money to a crime family in Seattle. I can't give you any more details than that. It's for your own safety. But your dad contacted me, and we discussed the situation at great length. When Steven told Vincent that he couldn't have the money to pay them back, Vincent stole it from the company."

"That's why he stole half a million dollars?" I asked, rubbing my arms in order to calm my nerves.

"Yes. And now you've inherited the problem."

"I don't understand why Dad was killed, though. And why would a crime family come after me?"

"Steven had proof of a sex-trafficking and money-laundering ring they were running. He went to the police but got nowhere. The crime family is very well protected, and they have a lot of cops on their payroll. My guess is that the crime family retaliated against him, but I'm not positive. If they are after you, Avery, I suspect it's because they think Steven confided in you about the illegal activity."

"Suspect?" My heart jumped into my throat.

"I was supposed to meet Steven for dinner on a Saturday evening. He said he had some new information he needed to discuss with me, but we never got the chance." Franklin's voice faltered.

He didn't need to say anything else. I understood. Dad and I had been hit by the truck.

"What now?" I asked. "Am I in danger, or is someone trying to scare me?"

"I understand this is a lot to process, but I always take something like this message seriously." Franklin opened a desk drawer, rummaged through it, then produced a business card for me. "You might consider hiring a bodyguard. These guys are the best I've ever dealt with."

"Thank you," I replied, taking the information from him. The gold-and-black Westbrook Security logo glimmered in the light. Their bodyguards had been at Tensley's adoption party. Michael and Marilyn, Benji's parents, were close to Franklin as well and had hired them to secure the area while some of the wealthiest people in the Northwest rubbed elbows.

Franklin's phone rang, nearly making me fly through the roof. My nerves were shot to hell. Although I still suspected Vincent was behind the voicemail, the idea of a crime family killing Dad had sent me into a mental tailspin.

"Hello?" Franklin asked. "That's great to hear. Thank you. I'll take care of the bill. You bet." Franklin disconnected his call and placed the iPhone on his desk. "Your vehicle is all clear. There were no bombs or tracking or listening devices. It's clean."

I blinked at him, attempting to wrap my head around the word *bomb*. It hadn't occurred to me that someone would plant one in my BMW. *Shit.*

"That's good news. Thank you for helping me."

"Avery, you can do what you feel is best, but I'd be extra cautious until we learn more. I don't think the threat is over. Call Pierce and talk to him about the situation and hire some protection for you and your mom. Everything you share with him or Sutton is confidential."

I nodded. "I'll be sure to park the car in the garage. I'll reach out to him tomorrow."

"Contact me if you need to. And Avery ... you were the entire world to Steven. He loved you more than anything else. He spoke highly of you every time we saw each other."

Tears welled in my eyes. "Thank you for sharing that with me. It means a lot." I stood and extended my hand to him. "I'll keep in touch, if that's okay."

"I'd like that." A warm smile slipped into place, and I wondered what he was like in court. He hadn't gotten to where he was by being a pushover.

"Tad will take you to your car, then follow you home or wherever you're going."

"That sounds good." And it did. I needed time to sift through the new information and make an informed decision. Dad had died, but something about the threatening message wasn't sitting well with me. It was obvious that someone was yanking my chain, but maybe that wasn't all. I chided myself for downplaying the situation. A part of me wanted proof before I admitted I was in danger, but Dad was gone. *What else do I need?* My pulse pounded in my ears as I followed Tad out of Franklin's house and into the car. For now, I desperately wanted some sleep. I would focus on the facts the next day.

1 0

A soft rain pattered against my bedroom window the next morning. I stretched, reveling in the good night's sleep I'd finally had. Life had been hell, and a clear brain to make some decisions would be helpful.

I sat up slowly, my thoughts returning to my conversation with Franklin. He was right. Regardless of whether someone was trying to scare me, Dad had died, and I had to watch my step.

I gathered clean clothes and headed toward the shower, toying with the facts in front of me. Dad and I had been hit on purpose. Even before the voicemail, I'd wondered if that was the case. The truck had sped out of nowhere, then it was gone in a blink of an eye. I shouldn't be standing there with hot water streaming over my body—I should have died along with my father.

Vincent McCade was wading into dangerous, shark-infested waters with vicious criminals and had sucked in my father as well. If the crime family was involved, I could only assume that they'd ordered a hit on Dad since he'd gone to the police about the illegal activity.

I huffed while I rinsed my hair clean of the vanilla-and-lavender shampoo that permeated the bathroom with its soft, relaxing fragrance. *Fuckers.* A surge of anger swelled inside me, simmering beneath the surface. *Focus, Avery.*

How will I find out if they were behind it? Or was it Vincent? Either would make sense. One thing was certain. I needed to deal with Vincent before he came after me. I was left with no other choice than to step up my game and finally put him in his place, not only for raping me, but I blamed Vincent for Dad's death. In a way, he was responsible. *Now, the motherfucker will pay.*

Gaining a little bit of relief, since I had a plan, and pieces of the information made sense, I finished my shower and dressed. I located the business card Franklin had handed me and left a message for Westbrook Security. Hopefully, I would hear back from someone soon. At least I'd parked my car in the garage and had set the security system the moment I stepped foot into the house. No bombs or tracking devices would have been planted without the system squawking.

For now, it was time for some stress relief.

AN HOUR LATER, I sauntered into The Lily. Once I'd decided to take Vincent McCade down for stealing and involving my father with a crime family, exhilaration traveled through me like a jolt of electricity. My mind was sharp, and a renewed energy had bubbled to life inside me. Maybe revenge suited me.

"Avery, it's so nice to see you again." Skyler looped her arm through mine and escorted me through the store. "We have some new designer jeans I'd love to show you." She winked at me. "They came in yesterday."

"Skyler, you know I can't resist a good pair of denim." I grinned at her as we approached two full racks of new items.

"How are you?" she asked softly, genuine concern flickering in her gaze.

"I'm all right. I'm more than ready for an afternoon romp," I whispered.

"After you're finished, I'd like to speak to you." Skyler's professional image was in place, but I knew by the small twitch of her upper lip that something wasn't right.

My brows furrowed. "Are you okay?" I asked, searching for a size two in the jeans.

"Yes and no. It's business. Personally, I'm fine. Thank you for asking."

Skyler was always polite and soft-spoken. It added to her natural beauty, but at times, I wondered what was beneath it. *What secrets is she protecting?*

"Of course. And I'll meet you in the lounge after my session." I selected a pair of jeans and strolled to the changing area, still chatting with Skyler. We stopped before we reached the area for the members. "I'll try these on, then see you later."

"Your ass is going to look amazing in them. I promise." Skyler patted my shoulder, then left me alone. I slipped into the dressing room and through the door behind the mirror. I would try the five-hundred-dollar denim on later. I had two men waiting for me.

Locating my room, I strolled inside, then I tucked my purse and jeans into the corner of the tidy area. It was staged like a kitchen with a sturdy table in the middle of the space. I bit my lip in anticipation of being bent over it and fucked senseless. However, I wouldn't put my blindfold into place until after I saw the guys who would take care of me and cater to my every whim.

Memories of my afternoon with Ramsey suddenly came rushing back—his touch and his mouth. I closed my eyes, shutting him out. He wasn't allowed in my head right then. Our session had been a freak incident. It was an accident, and I refused to give it any more thought.

I discarded my clothes, the air caressing my skin, and for the first time since the car wreck, I was content. Maybe it was an illusion, but I would take it, even if it were for only an afternoon.

When I spotted toys on the kitchen counter, I walked across the room to inspect them. A grin split my face as I ran my finger over the handcuffs, the blindfold, and the vibrators. One thing I appreciated about The Lily was that the toys were discarded after one use. Those were fresh out of the packaging. The thought of reusing sex toys, even after they'd been disinfected, disgusted me. I had no idea if it really happened or not, but I trusted Skyler to keep her agreements. She ran a top-notch business.

The door opened, and two men entered the room. Relief spread through me. I'd never seen either of them before.

"Hello," the tall blonde said while he discarded his robe, revealing a lean, muscular body.

"Hi," I said, assessing him. We never exchanged real names at The Lily, which worked for me. Everyone remained as anonymous as possible. It was also against policy to contact anyone outside of those walls. Once we walked out onto the busy sidewalk, all relationships were off-limits. *Except for Ramsey,* my thoughts whispered into my ear.

The dark-haired guy walked toward me, exuding power. My core clenched, waiting for him to take charge.

He circled me, his eyes scanning every inch of my naked body. He removed his white robe, revealing a thick, hard cock. I couldn't wait to run my tongue all over it, then suck him dry.

"Call me Tyler, and you can refer to him as Jeff." He nodded toward the blonde.

Jeff grinned at me as though he were about to indulge in an all-you-can-eat buffet. His long dick was erect and ready for the fun.

Tyler stood in front of me and spread his feet shoulder width apart. Jeff went straight for the handcuffs and secured my wrists behind me.

"Kneel," Tyler ordered.

I sank to my knees, then Tyler slipped my blindfold into place. A hand cupped my chin, tilting it upward. "You're going to look good with your pretty little mouth wrapped around my fat cock."

Chewing my lower lip in anticipation, I smiled. "I'm ready."

I wasn't sure whose thick shaft parted my lips and slid toward the back of my throat, but I didn't care. I ran my tongue around the width of it, sucking it as though it were the last lollipop on the planet. Fingers threaded through my hair and jerked my head back.

Another pair of hands cupped my tits and rolled my nipples. My senses heightened immediately. The blindfold kicked the playtime up several notches.

"Stand up."

Strong arms lifted me to my feet, and I was guided to the table, the only furniture in the room.

My ass hit the edge, then someone leaned me back against the hard surface and spread my legs apart. A mouth latched onto my tit, and I moaned in response. Teeth nipped my inner thigh, and I tilted my hips up, longing to be fucked and to forget everything that was happening in my life.

The sound of the vibrator filled the room and pushed at my core, entering my slick pussy. I leaned back as someone straddled my tits and rubbed his dick all over them.

I moaned, pleasure rippling through my entire body.

"Roll over." The still-running sex toy left me, allowing me to change my position.

Whoever was on top of me moved, and I rolled onto my stomach. Fingers wrapped around my ankles and tugged me to the edge of the table. My feet landed on the tile floor, my ass sticking in the air. A loud smack rang out, and pain shot through my butt cheek. My body jerked forward with each stinging slap against my skin. A smaller vibrator eased into my core, then pounded me fast and hard. Once it was slicked up with my juices, he removed it and pushed it into my puckered hole.

"Oh God," I moaned, pushing against it. The sound of a condom wrapper reached my ears, then a thick cock slid into me. I wasn't sure which guy was fucking my ass with the vibrator, and which was in me, and I didn't care.

"Harder." I panted. Raw, animalistic desire took over me. Suddenly, I wanted to see them. I needed to call the shots. "Stop," I commanded. "Take my blindfold off."

My body begged for more as the toy and the cock left me. "Remove the handcuffs." Once I was free and seeing again, I stood and smiled.

"Tyler, sit on the kitchen counter behind us," I ordered. "Jeff, join me on the table." I patted the hard surface next to me. "Lie down."

I straddled Jeff, my shaved pussy fully exposed to Tyler. I lowered myself over Jeff's full lips, then circled my fingers around his dick and stroked it. Flashes of Ramsey entered my brain without permission, and I shoved them to the side. *This is my time, dammit.*

I glanced over my shoulder at Tyler and grinned as I ground my hips against Jeff's mouth. "I want to watch you jack off while he buries his tongue inside me."

Tyler wrapped his hand around his thick shaft and stroked himself, his eyes never leaving my wet slit as Jeff licked and sucked my sensitive flesh. I whimpered while Jeff's cock jerked, and I grabbed it, pumping it fast and hard.

"Tyler, come here." Tyler hopped off the counter then circled around the table. I eased down Jeff's body and sat on his dick. I rocked against him as his hands dug into my hips. My tits bounced up and down the faster I fucked him.

Tyler's dark gaze remained on my chest.

"Come for me," I said, panting.

Tyler ran his hand up and down the length of his shaft, and I picked up my pace with Jeff as he slammed himself into me.

Growling, Tyler closed his eyes briefly as his come shot all over my stomach. I tilted my head back and released a low moan, the walls of my core clenching around Jeff's cock. An intense orgasm ripped through me while Ramsey's face flickered in and out of my mind again. *What the hell?*

My breath came in ragged gasps as I held onto the base of Jeff's condom-covered shaft, then lifted off him.

Spent from the delicious sexcapade, I collapsed onto the table. The sound of running water from the kitchen faucet caught my attention. Moments later, Jeff returned with a warm cloth and wiped off my tummy.

"Thank you. Both of you. I needed that." My voice cracked, a sudden blast of negative feelings robbing me of my contentment. *Why am I suddenly emotional about all of this?* I'd visited The Lily for months, and not once had an enjoyable romp left me moody.

Sitting up, I rubbed my forehead, and the guys slipped on their robes, said goodbye, and left me alone with the cold hard truth dangling in front of me.

I shook my head as though I were replying to someone's question rather than talking to myself. Hot tears slid down my cheeks, and before I knew it, I curled into a fetal position on the table and sobbed. I cried for my dad, I cried because of the threat, and I cried that the one person who might be able to help my heart heal wasn't next to me. I'd just fucked two strangers instead of admitting how I really felt. But I couldn't worry about my feelings right then. I had to meet Skyler.

Five minutes later, I was dressed and had touched up my makeup after my sob fest. I blew out a big breath. It would be the second time Skyler had seen me upset after a visit.

I grabbed a tissue from my purse and dabbed my cheeks. Catching my reflection in the mirror, I stared at a girl I no longer recognized. Dark circles shadowed my blank green eyes, and my skin appeared pale, even though my tan still lingered. My entire world had been flipped upside down with Dad's death, and I might or might not be in danger with Vincent.

I pulled my hair back and smoothed it down, attempting to soothe the pain that had reared its ugly head. It was useless, though. No amount of primping would cover up the fact that I'd lost my shit and broken down like a little kid.

I rummaged through my handbag and produced a small bottle of foundation to touch up my red, blotchy skin. I ran a brush through my hair and took a few deep breaths, then checked my phone, but I didn't have any messages or texts. *Thank God.* I was trying not to walk around paranoid, but I was still rattled after talking with Franklin.

Backing away from the mirror, I gave myself a once-over. Satisfied with my cover job, I tried on the jeans. As Skyler had suspected, they fit beautifully. I quickly dressed again, then I left the room and made my way to Skyler's office.

The door was open, and I cleared my throat loudly in order to gain her attention.

"Avery, come on in," Skyler said from behind her desk. "If you would close the door behind you, I'd appreciate it."

I set my purse down on the chaise lounge but remained standing. "I love the jeans. Thank you." I held them up, then set them on top of my handbag.

"I trust your session was enjoyable?" Skyler cocked her head to the right, assessing me. "You've been crying."

A soft laugh escaped me. "You don't miss anything, do you?" I gave her a quick smile, assuring her that I was okay. "With everything that's happened lately, I think I got a little emotional. Post-orgasm hormones." I waved it off as though it were nothing. There was no way I felt comfortable explaining that Ramsey kept popping into my head while I was with two other men.

"How are things with Ramsey?" Skyler folded her hands together in her lap, her well-shaped eyebrow briefly arching with her question.

Skyler was an exceptional manager. When she was with a client, no one and nothing else existed. I couldn't speak for any of the other women, but Skyler had a way of making me feel special and spoiled.

I sat on the edge of the chaise and tucked a stray piece of hair behind my ear. "We're good. I saw him an hour or so after we met upstairs. My dad passed away as we were fucking each other's brains out," I explained, my voice low as guilt clung to my words.

"That would explain why I've not seen you. I'm so sorry, Avery."

"Thank you." I blinked back tears while I peered into Skyler's concerned eyes. "I'm suddenly the majority owner of Davenport and McCade financials, so I have a lot on my plate."

"Yes, you do." Skyler stood and crossed the room. She extended her hand, then pulled me in for a hug. "I'm here for you, Avery. Anything you need at all, whether it's a sounding board or a few drinks with a friend."

We released each other, then she sat down in the chair across from me. "I'm going to apologize now. My timing is horrible." She ran her palms down her navy-blue slacks.

"What's the matter?" Skyler didn't realize it, but I needed to talk to someone else about the shit in their life. It gave me a break from mine. Maybe it was selfish, but at least I could return the favor and be there for her.

Skyler's shoulders tensed. "I'm afraid The Lily is going to close."

"What?" I shot out of my seat. "Why?"

"The owner is selling. She wants to retire and get out of the business. I don't know what I'm going to do after it closes. So many of the clients have become my friends. The men, too. We all work together. In some ways, they're family to me."

I paced back and forth, wearing a path in the carpet with my heels. "How much?"

"I'm sorry?" Skyler peered at me over the black rims of her glasses.

"How much is she selling it for?" I stared at her, an idea forming in my mind.

"A lot. I was hoping I could get a loan, but there's no way I'll be able to get one for that amount."

I chewed on my lower lip, deep in thought for a minute. "How much, Skyler?"

"A million, but it includes all the inventory and everything in the store. I would assume the rooms upstairs would also stay intact. I mean, I really don't know. As I said, I can't get a loan for that much."

"Is your credit good?" I sank onto the edge of the chaise.

"Impeccable."

"I need some time to consider it, but I can buy it. Of course, you would keep your job, and we would continue as normal."

Skyler's eyes widened. "Are you serious?"

"I think so. This place is amazing. Women of all shapes, sizes, colors, and religions come here for fun. No one is looked down on for having a sex drive or fantasies. No one is slut-shamed or condemned to hell. The ladies gain confidence in the bedroom and in themselves.

When we feel good about ourselves and our bodies, it affects every area of our lives." I paused, excitement growing in the pit of my stomach. "I wonder how many women have kicked an abusive asshole to the curb because of The Lily. They don't need a man for sex, which means they don't have to put up with the rotten ones in their lives, dictating to them how to behave or what's appropriate for them. One of my friends in high school wouldn't leave a guy who beat her because she was addicted to the sex. This place hands the keys of freedom to every woman here, giving them the ability to define their lives."

"Now that I think about it, one of our long-term members began visiting after her recovery with cancer. She'd lost her hair and was thin, and she said she no longer felt desirable." Tears brimmed in Skyler's eyes. "After a few sessions, she began to smile again, she gained some weight, and she exuded confidence. A year later, she continues to visit weekly. She also started her own interior design business, and she's still in remission. Once, when we had a drink together in the VIP lounge, she confided in me that The Lily saved her. It gave her the drive to live life again."

"That's exactly what I mean. It's not only about great sex. The Lily is so much more."

Skyler stood, and for the first time, I saw her fidget. Typically, she was calm and collected.

"What if I could buy in? I mean, I could get a loan for a fourth and put a fourth down. I would love to own The Lily with you. I've always dreamed of expanding it. Discreetly, of course. There are some rooms I would love to remodel, and we could add on a few more as well. It would provide the capacity to accept more clients too." Excitement danced across her beautiful features.

I stood in front of her. "I would consider it a pleasure to partner with you. Let's request the financials of the company before we make a decision. I need to know exactly what we're getting into. If the business is on track, we'll visit my attorney with a business plan. He can draw up the contracts, then we'll put in an offer."

Skyler threw her arms around me. "Oh my God, I'm so excited. Thank you!" She bounced up and down on her toes.

I couldn't help but laugh. I'd never seen her so animated, and it was amazing.

"I look forward to working together." I hugged her in return, nearly giddy myself at the thought of owning an upscale sex club.

"Oh goodness," Skyler stepped back and pushed her glasses up on her nose. "I'm sorry, I got a little carried away."

"Hey." I patted her arm. "We're going to get to know each other really well if we become partners. Don't think anything about it. I'll no longer be a client. We'll be equals."

She grinned at me. "I hope so. I'll talk to Sylvia tomorrow and tell her we'd like to look at the value of the business."

"Sounds great. I'll reach out in a few days."

Skyler and I said our goodbyes. I paid for the jeans, then made my way through the building and out the front doors.

I glanced around, my paranoia returning once I laid eyes on my car, but nothing looked suspicious or out of the ordinary. The downtown streets were busy with people walking and shopping. It would have been difficult for someone to tamper with my vehicle while parked on the street without being noticed. Still, I needed to be mindful.

When I reached my BMW, I pulled on the handle and watched the doors unlock. I settled in and blasted the heat. The early-evening temperature had dropped rapidly. My teeth chattered as I rubbed my arms, muttering to myself about how I should have remembered my jacket before I left the house.

The seat warmers kicked in, and I leaned back and checked my mirrors for any unusual activity around me, but I didn't see anything out of the ordinary.

I scrolled through my Spotify, selected a contemporary playlist, then powered on the stereo. *Holy crap.* If all went well, I was about to purchase The Lily. I wondered if it would make me a madam. I laughed softly. *Wait until Ramsey hears about this. Shit. Ramsey.* The idea of him sent my pulse racing. With a single thought, all of my complicated feelings for him appeared front and center. There was only one thing I could do.

I grabbed my phone, then tapped the screen and made a call.

"Hey. Are you busy? I need to talk." I drummed my fingernails against the steering wheel while I waited for a response. "Thanks. I'll be there in a few minutes.

The moment I rang the doorbell, the door flew open and Tensley pulled me in for a huge hug.

"Why do I feel like it's been years since I've seen you?" she asked against my hair.

"I know. So much has happened since Dad died. It's been hard to keep up with everything," I said, grateful for my best friend.

"Girl, let her come in the house before you assault her, for fuck's sake." Benji's lopsided grin popped up over Ten's shoulder.

I laughed. My besties were just what I needed.

Ten rolled her eyes at him, then stepped back while I entered the marble entrance and closed the heavy mahogany door behind me. The setting sun glistened off the chandelier from the window, casting glimmers of light in every direction.

"Hungry? The 'rents are gone on a business trip, so we have the house to ourselves." Benji wiggled his eyebrows at me.

"Yes, I'm starving. And drinks?"

"Always," Layne said, bounding down the stairs toward me, smiling widely. "It's good to see you."

"Hey!" I beamed at him and gave him a quick hug.

Tensley reset the door alarm and smirked. "You did say you needed to talk, right? Drinks and food go with the territory. If you get drunk, then stay the night."

"It's not like I have to report to anyone. Besides, this is what I need. Advice and some fun."

My heels clicked against the marble floor while I followed them. We entered the black-and-tan, granite-and-stone kitchen. As always, it was immaculate. The stainless-steel fridge hummed quietly in the background, and my gaze connected with Benji's.

"Mm-hm. You definitely have some serious shit on your mind. Take a breath, girl. The stress is rolling off you in waves." Benji's gaze ran up and down the length of my body. "Spill." He pointed at a chair. "I'll make us some strong-ass drinks while you start dishing."

Tensley grabbed my hand and dragged me toward the seats. She propped her elbows on the table and rested her chin on her hands.

"How do you know anything is going on other than the changes with my dad?" I quirked an eyebrow at him as he and Layne opened the cabinets and pulled down enough liquor for an army.

"Good grief, Benji," Tensley said, giggling and pointing at the five bottles of alcohol that he'd set on the counter. "We don't want to be sick tomorrow."

Benji spun around and wagged his finger to us. "Ladies, please. I'm making us huckleberry Long Islands. Keep your panties on."

"That sounds heavenly," I said, relieved.

"I've not tried it with the huckleberry yet." Layne winked at his fiancée.

"He makes them really strong, so drink slowly," Ten added, grinning.

"I remember." I placed my hands on the kitchen table, palms down. "I think …"

"I'm listening," Benji cupped his ear while he poured shots of vodka and triple sec into three tall glasses.

Tensley's lips pursed. "Benji, hush. Avery can't talk if you don't stop with all the chatter. Give the poor girl a minute."

I covered my mouth, snickering. "You two are definitely siblings. Maybe not by blood, but you act like it."

"You should live with them," Layne chimed in and shook his head, laughing. "It's nonstop entertainment."

Ten rolled her eyes and slumped down in her chair. "I wouldn't trade a single moment of our time together, or our relationship either."

Benji sighed. "Babe, you know it." He removed some straws from a drawer, plopped them in the drinks, picked up our glasses, and brought them to us. "When I thought I'd lost you, well ... it was a good reminder of what an amazing relationship we have." Benji tugged on a strand of Ten's hair and kissed the top of her head. "And you too." He kissed me on the forehead, then sauntered back to the counter and collected his drink.

Layne settled in next to Ten and took a long drink. "Damn, that's really good."

"Of course it is." Benji flashed us a grin as he pulled up a chair, flipped it around, and straddled it. "You have my unwavering attention."

I reached for his hand, then Ten's. "I ... I love you guys so much. Losing Dad has made me even more appreciative of all of you. You're my family. Layne ..." I focused on him. "I ... I've not said it, but your support means the world to me. My chest gets so tight sometimes that I don't know how I can breathe, then I remember that you understand exactly what I'm going through. Regardless of whether we discuss it or not, I know you're there, and it means the world to me. Thank you."

"I'm here day or night for you, Avery. The grief can gut you, but it will get better." Layne reached over and patted my hand, and I gave his fingers a quick squeeze before I let him go.

"We all are. You're not alone. Ever," Tensley said, smiling gently.

"And you know you're stuck with us. Like, you can't get rid of us." Benji chuckled, then took a long pull from the straw in his Long Island. "Mm. Layne's right. That's good." He smiled, obviously proud of himself.

I took a drink, savoring the flavors on my tongue. If I was about to confess to my friends, I needed some liquid courage.

"There's a lot going on. Some of it's business, so I can't really go into detail." I paused, Vincent's sneer looming in the background of my mind. "I think I have feelings for Ramsey." I slumped down in my seat and covered my face with my hands. I couldn't believe I'd said it. There was no turning back now.

"Hon, I know you have a lot on your plate, but do you want to tell us something Benji and I don't already know?" Ten asked.

"Really?" I asked, my focus bouncing between Ten, Layne, and Benji.

"It was obvious to us the last time he visited. You were with Justin, so I don't think you were aware of the slight touches or heated gazes between you and Ramsey." Benji cocked his head to the side. "Since we hadn't met him before … well, I thought you two had hooked up when you were teens, and he lit your vagina up like it was the Fourth of July."

A hearty laugh broke free from Layne, and a giggle erupted inside me, shaking my shoulders. Little did Benji know how right he was, but it had been a month ago instead of when we were teens. I would deny it since we weren't able to discuss The Lily.

Tensley threw her head back and laughed. "Oh my God, where do you come up with this stuff?"

I wiped the tears from my eyes. At least that time, I was crying from having fun. It was way overdue.

"Seriously, Avery. We all thought there was something between the two of you. I don't mean that you cheated on Justin or anything like that. It was … How do I say this? Raw chemistry." Ten arched an eyebrow at me.

"You saw that too?" I asked Benji and Layne.

"Girl, yes. You two sizzled," Benji said.

"I thought maybe you two had dated in the past, and it wasn't really over," Layne added.

"Shit. I had no idea. I mean, we've known each other since we were tiny. We spent every summer together in the Hamptons until I was seventeen, and he had a new girlfriend every week!"

Tensley cringed slightly. "Does he still?"

I shook my head. "I don't know. He's a football god where he's from, so there's never been a shortage of gorgeous girls rubbing their tits all over him." I bit my lower lip, wishing I could reel my words back in, especially since they'd spewed out of my mouth dripping with envy.

Benji jerked back as though my words had slapped him across the cheek. "Oh no. Jealousy is not a good color on you."

"Fuck that. I'd be jealous," Ten added, shooting Benji a knock-it-off look. "You would be, too, so behave."

"Thank you, Ten." I placed my head on the table and closed my eyes, wishing it all away. Even though Ramsey had said he cared about me as more than friends, I was terrified of admitting how I felt. *What if we lose each other?* Not to mention that guys I'd dated in the past had taken off running in the opposite direction after I'd admitted that I had feelings for them. Like Justin, except I'd caught him making out with another girl.

"I don't know how to handle this." I sat back up, my focus landing on my friends.

"Drink more for now." Ten nodded at my Long Island.

I took another drink, then another. Giggling, I slurped it down below the halfway mark. "Better."

Laughter filled the room, and I allowed the warmth of the alcohol to soothe my frayed nerves.

Tensley closed one eye and peered at me. My guess was she was feeling the liquor a little bit too. When Benji made drinks, they were for one purpose, and that was to get someone shitfaced.

"Has he ever said anything to you?" Ten drummed her fingers on the tabletop, assessing me. "You're hiding something."

Shit. Does she know we had mind-blowing sex?

"Like what?" I tilted my head to the side, waiting for her to respond. If they only knew about my threesome that afternoon, they wouldn't be so calm. I would be read the riot act for risky sex or paying for service.

Tensley took a drink, her blue eyes never leaving me. "Has he talked to you about his feelings?"

That wasn't the question I'd been anticipating, but I would take it. I gave a half-shrug, feigning innocence.

"That's a yes," Layne said, chuckling.

"He has?" Benji asked, his eyebrow arching. "Then what are you doing here and not at his place, feasting on that gorgeous man?"

"It's not like that. We talked the other night, but we were both emotional and exhausted. When someone dies, people tend to say things they wouldn't normally admit. Things they don't mean."

"Like what?" Benji folded his arms across his chest.

"He might have said that he loved me and that we belonged together." Before Ten and Benji could say a word, I tossed my hands up to halt them. "We were eleven. Okay? He was reminding me of what he said to me when we were kids. And just because he said it doesn't mean I'm ready to try a relationship with him. I mean … What if it doesn't work and I lose him forever? I can't handle it. I …" Hot tears streamed down my cheeks, and I brushed them away angrily.

"Hey, it's all right." The kitchen chair scraped across the wood floor as Tensley stood and walked around the table.

She wrapped her arms around me and I lost my shit. Maybe it was the alcohol playing with my unsettled emotions, but a sharp wail erupted from me, and I sobbed all over her shoulder. All the commotion from the voicemail, Vincent, Dad, and Ramsey smacked me full force like a tidal wave, pulling the sand out from beneath my feet and dragging me into the angry sea. I was drowning.

Tensley rubbed my back. "We're here, Avery. You're not alone," she whispered. A few minutes later, I sat up and reached for a tissue from the box that was suddenly sitting on the table.

"Thought you might need those, hon." Benji pushed the Kleenex toward me.

Silence hung in the air as I wiped my eyes and nose. Tensley sat on the floor in front of my chair and held my hand.

"Listen," Benji started. "You're a strong and beautiful woman. You have your shit together. Now, I understand you don't feel like you do right now, but you do." Benji's expression grew gentle. "Even strong women need to be loved. Strong women need friends. Sometimes strong women need help. There is nothing wrong with that. You don't have to prove your worth to anyone. It also takes more inner strength to allow people to show up for you. You don't have to do all of this on your own. If Ramsey wants to be there, let him. Let him in."

"He's right," Tensley said softly. "Layne helped heal me in a way no one else could have. His presence alone helped me feel safe and loved in a way I'd never experienced before. If Ramsey said you two belonged together, then I would speak to him. Tell him you have feelings for him, but you're scared of losing him." Ten's gaze drifted to Layne's, and they exchanged a silent moment between them.

"You won't lose him. He's known you all these years, seen you at your best and worst, and hasn't left you yet. He won't now either," Layne said.

I blew out a big breath. "Okay. I'll talk to him." I attempted a smile, but my stomach churned. We'd both lost my father, and Ramsey reminding me of his long-ago confession could have been to comfort me. It was another story when I admitted I was falling for him. It left me more vulnerable than I already was. Plus, we'd had sex, and I couldn't discredit my suspicions that Ramsey wasn't in love with me. His dick was.

My phone vibrated in my purse, and I rummaged through all of the shit in my handbag until I located it. An unrecognizable number flashed on the screen. My blood chilled, and I quickly silenced it. The last call from an unknown number had been a threat to my life. I would check my voicemail when I had a moment to myself.

AFTER ANOTHER HOUR of drinks and chatting with Tensley, Layne, and Benji, I excused myself to go to the restroom. I teetered slightly and grabbed the granite countertop, giggling. *Thank goodness I'm not navigating any stairs right now.*

Benji and Ten's laughter rang in my ears as I staggered toward the bathroom. I'd definitely had a lot to drink.

Closing the door behind me, I sat on the counter and rummaged through everything in my purse for my cell. My breath stuttered while I stared at the message icon. I closed my eyes, attempting to calm my galloping heart. There was only one way to find out if it was another threat. I tapped the screen and held the phone to my ear.

"Avery," came the deep voice of a man. "This is Pierce Westbrook returning your call. Franklin contacted me and explained your situation. I would like to help. Please call me back at your earliest convenience."

"Jesus," I said quietly, pressing my hand to my chest and sucking in a much-needed breath. I swallowed repeatedly, attempting to clear the lump in my throat. Before I had a chance to realize what I was doing, I tapped the screen and returned his call.

"Pierce Westbrook."

I inwardly groaned. "Hi, this is Avery," I said, praying like hell I wasn't slurring my words. "I'm going to apologize now in case I say something stupid. I'm at a friend's house … I'm with Tensley and Benji at Marilyn and Michael Parker's house. We've been drinking."

A soft chuckle carried through the phone. "At least you're safe there."

"I think so. I mean, I'm staying here tonight. I won't be driving, if that's what you mean." I frowned, slightly embarrassed that I was rambling.

"That's good, but what I meant is that Michael has a state-of-the-art security system, and as long as you stay in the house … if someone is following you, you'll be safe."

"Yeah. That too." I shifted on the counter, struggling with what to say.

"I talked to Franklin tonight," Pierce began.

"Good. I'm not sure where to start, honestly."

"I recommend a bodyguard. One of my men can keep an eye on you very discreetly. Do you have a security system in your house?"

"Yeah. Dad had it updated a few months before he …" My response lodged in my throat, unable to form on my lips.

"I'm very sorry, Avery. I met Steven a few times, and he seemed like a really good man."

"He was," I responded, my voice shaking as the sharp ache in my chest expanded.

"Good. I'm happy to take a look at it, if you want me to. I don't want to tip anyone off if you're being followed, though. My men drive black Mercedes. There's no logos or stickers anywhere on the vehicles, and they are bulletproof."

"I met Tad, so I know what his car looks like."

"They're all the same," Pierce explained. "Do you want me to assign someone to you?"

"Yeah. I don't want to admit it, but … I'm terrified. My brain is bouncing around like a ping-pong ball, one minute thinking that Vincent is screwing with me, then the next I analyze shit to death and think it's not him. Ugh. I'm sorry for my language. It's been a really long week."

"You're fine. Don't think anything about it. I've heard a lot worse, and said worse too."

I couldn't stop my smile. For a badass security guy, he was really kind.

"I'm going to send Vaughn Reddington over there tonight. He will keep an eye on the house and your car. Tomorrow, I'll assign Tad to you. Since you've already met him and know what he looks like, I think you'll feel better knowing who he is."

"Okay," I whispered, the gravity of the situation seeping into my bones and rocking me to my core. "Thank you."

"Other than Benji, Tensley, their parents, and Layne, who else can Tad expect to see you with?"

"Ramsey Goldman. We've been friends since we were born. His parents, Patrick and Olivia, visit often too. They're family to me. My mother, Davia, is around sometimes. She lives at the house."

"I'll let Tad know these people aren't a threat, then. Why don't you text pictures of everyone to me so we'll know what they look like."

"I will, and feel free to email me the bill, and I'll take care of it immediately."

"I'll send it in the morning. Franklin vouched for you. I'll have Vaughn there in thirty minutes."

"Thank you. I appreciate it."

"I'm only a call away, Avery. My clients are important to me. Your safety is important, so don't hesitate to pick up the phone if you have any concerns at all."

"I promise."

"Have a good night, and I'll touch base with you in a few days."

"I appreciate the help so quickly. I'll speak to you soon." I lowered the phone and ended the call as a shudder traveled through my body. I'd hired a bodyguard. I hoped like hell I wouldn't need him, but something deep inside me said otherwise.

After I'd peed and sent Pierce the pictures, I joined Tensley and Benji in the living room.

"You all right?" Ten asked, grabbing my arm as I walked past her.

I plopped onto the couch between them, stretching out my legs, and stifled a yawn. "Yeah. This is what I needed." As I placed a hand on Tensley's knee, warmth filled me. "I love you guys."

"We love you too." Ten patted my hand.

"Ditto." Benji grinned. "More drinks, ladies?"

1 2

The next few days passed without incident. Surprisingly, I rarely spotted Tad either. Pierce had been right. His men were incredibly discreet. If I knew Tad was there and had a difficult time seeing him, then other people wouldn't notice at all.

I glanced at the clock on my nightstand. It was nearly seven in the evening. Ramsey had football practice until six, so I figured by seven thirty he would be home and showered. Normally, I wouldn't arrive at someone's place unannounced, but I was reconsidering my plan to have a heart-to-heart conversation with him, so I hadn't made a commitment to show up on his steps. Mentally, I'd already backed out three or four times. I was a mess.

I smoothed my plum-colored top and wiped my clammy hands on my skinny jeans. Squaring my shoulders, I inhaled deeply, willing my frayed nerves to settle down.

"Now or never," I whispered to myself. I located my keys and my purse, then darted past my mother in the hall and rushed down the stairs.

"Where are you going?" she called.

"Don't wait up!" I slammed the utility room door behind me and hurried to my Bimmer in the spacious garage. I parked there religiously and set the alarm system the minute I stepped foot into the house.

I hesitated, my hand hovering over the car door handle as my attention landed on Dad's silver Range Rover. Tears pricked the backs of my eyes. No one had driven it since before the accident. Anytime I'd ridden in it with him, I had felt safe.

"Dad, I'm going to take yours tonight. I hope it's okay." A chill traveled down my spine, and my stomach soured. I realized he wouldn't answer me, but the worst part was that I would never hear his voice again.

I approached the vehicle, then hopped in. Closing the door, I sank into the plush, black leather seat. The woodsy scent of his cologne lingered in the closed space, and I gripped the steering wheel until my knuckles turned white in order to not start crying. I didn't want to show up at Ramsey's with swollen eyes and a red-tipped nose.

I started the car and connected the Bluetooth to my phone, and "5AM" by Amber Run began to play. Opening the garage door, I backed out. Bobbing my head to the beat of the music playing, I attempted to distract myself from what I was about to do.

A steady rain pattered against my windshield, and the wipers softly whooshed the drops away. As I left the house, my mind drifted to the letter Dad had written me, and I reminded myself that he had approved of Ramsey. I hoped like hell that I wasn't about to make an ass out of myself.

Memories of our afternoon together at The Lily came rushing back, and my body tingled. At least we were compatible sexually. I shook my head, still in a bit of shock that we'd connected there. *What are the chances?*

Ten minutes later, I pulled into Ramsey's apartment complex and parked. He was on the top floor, which gave me time to talk myself out of my confession once again. But I refused. I was a Davenport— strong and intelligent. We never backed away from a challenge, and Ramsey was mine. It still didn't stop my insecurities from marching front and center and blocking the gateway of my heart, though.

Taking two stairs at a time, I was grateful I'd opted for my comfy tennis shoes. Running up the steps in heels would not have worked well. I located his apartment number and knocked. My pulse rang in my ears, and I rubbed my arms while I waited for him to answer.

The click of the lock told me he was home, and I willed myself not to bolt. The door opened slowly, then a dripping-wet and shirtless Ramsey appeared in jeans that hugged every muscle in his long legs. My eyes widened as a bead of water trickled over his pec and down his six-pack. It took all my willpower not to drop to my knees and lick every droplet off his tanned, moist skin.

"Hey, Avery. Are you okay? I wasn't expecting you."

"Yeah … I …" I pursed my lips and closed the gap between us. "I needed to do this." Placing my hands on his chest, I pushed up on my tiptoes and kissed him gently. I backed away, allowing him a chance to respond.

"Who's at the door?" A pretty blonde asked behind him.

My mouth dropped open. "Shit. You're with someone." I shook my head at my stupidity. He hadn't been serious when he told me we belonged together. In fact, Ramsey was already hooking up with someone. *Why did I think I was special enough that he only wanted to be with me?* It was an emotional, fucked-up thing to say just because he was hurting about losing Dad.

Without another word, I rushed out into the pouring rain and down the flights of stairs.

"Avery, wait!" Ramsey called after me.

But I wasn't going to stop. I'd been a naïve idiot, and I should have known better. I was well aware that Ramsey had had flings since we were kids. He probably went through more girls in a month than he did toilet paper rolls. *Why did I think things might be different, or that I was special and important enough for him to only want to be with me?* Apparently, I'd lied to myself.

Rain streamed down my face, my long dark hair clinging to my cheeks as the plump drops fell fast and hard.

"Wait!" Ramsey's strong arms wrapped around me from behind and halted me in my tracks. "Avery." His minty breath tickled my ear. "It's not what you think. Please, let me explain."

"You don't owe me an explanation." Anger and embarrassment twisted my insides, and I struggled in his muscular arms, attempting to break free from his hold, but he was too strong.

A tall figure caught the corner of my eye. Tad was approaching us and fast. *Shit, he thinks Ramsey's hurting me.* He couldn't blow his cover. I shook my head adamantly, and he slowed but continued to keep tabs on us.

"I'm not letting you go. We can stand here all night in this crazy weather, but I'm not letting you walk away from me."

"Why? You're with someone, Ramsey. I should have called. I—"

"I'm not with her, Avery. It's not like that. If you'll come back upstairs, I'll explain everything."

I stopped fighting and relaxed against him. "You're not?" I asked, unable to hide the flicker of hope inside me.

"No." His response was followed by a rumble of thunder that rattled my teeth. A flash of lightning split through the inky blackness of the stormy sky, and I yelped. It was time to go indoors, whether it was my car or his place.

"Okay. We can talk."

Without any effort, he scooped me off the ground, his hard arms slipping under my knees and around my back. I clung to him while he ran through the downpour, puddles of water splashing behind him on the wet sidewalk.

He raced up the stairs, then bumped his apartment door open with his hip, and placed me down on the tile entryway.

"Oh wow. It's really raining out there. You two are soaked."

The blonde handed us each a plush white towel, and I minded my manners and thanked her while I internally scowled at her for being so gorgeous and knowing where his towels were. Hell, *I* didn't even know where they were.

"Thanks," Ramsey said, drying his brown hair and flinging water in every direction. "Avery, this is Callie. Callie, Avery."

"It's nice to meet you," she said, flashing me a warm smile.

I hated her already. Her shoulder-length blonde hair was thick and full, and her large brown eyes were framed by illegally long eyelashes. Even her teeth were perfect.

"Likewise." I busied myself with drying off to the best of my ability while Callie rambled on about rescheduling with Ramsey. Finally, she bounced over and gave Ramsey a hug and waved goodbye to me.

The second the door closed behind her, I ran my fingers through my hair and stared at Ramsey. "I'm sorry. I should have called."

Without a word, Ramsey took my hand in his strong, large one, led me through the apartment-sized living area, past the black-and-tan kitchen, and into his bedroom. A queen-sized bed with a navy-blue comforter was nestled into the corner of the small room. His thumb stroked my knuckles, then he opened the second drawer of his tall dresser. The walls were apartment white, and no pictures or posters were on them yet. It was a blank slate.

"Here, you'll need something dry to wear. I don't want you to get sick since it's cold out." He handed me a sweatshirt and frowned. "You're tiny, so nothing I have will fit you."

I held up the Denver Broncos hoodie and smiled. "This will probably reach my knees. I think I'll be all right."

"The bathroom is down the hall on your left. I can dry your wet clothes while we talk."

I took a step backward. "Sounds good."

"Avery." His gaze dropped to the floor, then came back to my face. "I'm glad you're here." His voice was low, sending delightful little goosebumps across my skin.

I nodded, then disappeared. I wasn't sure how to take his last statement. We'd been friends since birth, and we were always happy to see each other. This time I'd kissed him, though.

I closed the bathroom door, slipped out of my wet clothes, and removed my phone from my back pocket. I used the thick towel Callie had brought me to dry off the rest of my body before I slid his sweatshirt on. I bit my lip as the soft fleece caressed my naked skin. My nipples hardened in response to his scent, which clung to the fibers of his sweatshirt. I lifted it to my nose and inhaled deeply. If I stilled myself, I could almost feel his muscular arms wrapped around me again.

Shit. What am I doing? I wasn't even sure why I was still there. *Is it as a friend or potential-girlfriend status? Or...* I couldn't allow myself to consider the other possibility. I couldn't stand the thought of us not being in each other's lives. I slammed my eyes closed and willed my racing pulse to slow down. Grabbing the bottom of the sweatshirt, I gently tugged it over my hips and down my bare legs. I wrapped my jeans, shirt, bra, and thong into a ball and walked to the hall.

"The dryer is over here." Ramsey opened a closet and motioned for me to toss my wet clothes in.

He'd changed into gray sweatpants, which hung low on his hips, and I turned away quickly as my thoughts reminded me of what was beneath them.

"Thanks."

He leaned against the wall and crossed his arms over his bare chest, his biceps bulging. "You look good in my sweatshirt." His eyes darkened while they scanned over me, lingering on my legs.

A flush crept up my neck and ears as desire pooled deep inside me. From his expression, I guessed that he was thinking about our time together at The Lily. So was I, but it was a moot point until he explained about Callie. I couldn't assume that he wasn't interested in her.

Ramsey pushed off the wall, and I followed him into the living room.

Large boxes reached up to the ceiling and filled the corner. "It looks like you're still unpacking."

"Yeah." He plopped down on the tan leather couch and patted the seat next to him. I sat at the other end instead.

"You don't need to tell me why Callie was here," I started.

Ramsey stretched his arm out along the back of the sofa and stared at me. "I do, actually."

Shit. I was right. Something was going on between them. I braced myself for the news and shifted into fix-it mode. I needed to repair the awkward-kiss situation before it exploded and there was no coming back from it.

"First, I want to put your mind at ease. Callie is gay. She's not into me or any other guy, for that matter."

My eyebrows shot up. "Oh. I just thought ..." More relieved than I wanted to admit, I sank into my seat and shut my mouth so that Ramsey could continue.

"She's really friendly, so I know it probably looked like she was interested in me, but she's not." Ramsey hesitated, his gaze fixating on mine. "There is something I need to talk to you about, Avery." Ramsey leaned forward, placing his elbows on his knees and sighing heavily.

I willed myself not to fidget and readied myself for the blow, then I reminded myself that we would be okay. We would make it through. Our friendship was too deep to toss away over a misunderstanding— at least I hoped.

Ramsey shifted and faced me. "Callie is part of an organization, and I'm helping her with a protest in Idaho and several other states."

My brows knitted. "What kind of organization?"

"She's starting it, actually, and I've worked with her for a few months now. Even before I moved to Spokane, we worked together. It's fighting against conversion therapy for kids. We want to make it illegal across the U.S."

I shook my head in confusion. "I think that's fantastic. No one deserves to be brainwashed because they're gay. But why wouldn't you tell me?"

Ramsey rubbed his clean-shaven chin, then dropped his hand. "The same summer that Vincent ... hurt you." He paused, his jaw clenching with his words. "I never told you, but ... Tim and Danelle, my cousins, called Mom and Dad and asked if they could borrow some money. Their son, Rusty, had an opportunity to attend a football camp run by Eli Manning, and they couldn't afford it. At first, my parents weren't on board, but Rusty and I were close, so I talked them into paying for it. Begged them, actually. I wanted him to have the same opportunities that I had. He was talented." He swallowed and ran his fingers through his still-damp hair.

I tucked my legs beneath me and pulled his sweatshirt over my knees while I waited for him to continue.

"It wasn't football camp. It was conversion therapy treatment. They sent him away to get brainwashed because they found out he was gay. They had caught him kissing another guy and freaked. The treatment included electric shock, an exorcism, and he was drugged. They tortured him in a horrid attempt to change him because of his sexual preference. It was fucking sick."

My mouth opened and closed, the horror of the situation dawning on me. "Oh my god. Is he okay? Oh, Ramsey, that's horrible. No one should ever have to go through that." I reached for his hand, no longer thinking about how I felt or the kiss. I wanted to be there for my friend.

"Right before we left to meet you at the Hamptons, I got the call that Rusty had committed suicide. It's why we showed up a few days later than normal that summer."

"Ramsey." Tears slipped down my cheeks as I shook my head. "Why didn't you tell me?"

"I couldn't talk about it. I pushed my parents until they paid for that fucked-up—it was my fault. I should have asked more questions about where he would be or ..." Ramsey's shoulders slumped forward as he wiped the moisture from his eyes.

"This wasn't your fault. His parents made a choice to send him there. They lied to you and your family. This is all on them and that stupid camp," I spat, furious that people could do something so horrific in the name of religion or being narrowminded. Destroying an innocent person was never acceptable.

"I let Rusty down, Avery. I wasn't there for him. He was like a little brother to me, and I failed him. I had no idea that he was gay or was struggling with it." Ramsey's shoulders slouched in defeat.

I sat my phone on the arm of the couch, crawled over to him, and pulled him in for a hug. I stroked the back of his neck and placed a kiss on the top of his head. "It wasn't your fault," I whispered against his soft hair.

Ramsey wrapped his arms around me, his fingers clutching at my sweatshirt as he released his pain.

"I wish you'd told me. I'm sorry I wasn't there for you," I said softly.

Ramsey straightened, and his red-rimmed eyes landed on me. "Vincent had turned your world upside down. When you told me what happened, I put Rusty on the back burner so that I could be there for you." Pain flickered in his expression.

"You shouldn't have done that, Ramsey. I'm here now, though."

Ramsey leaned back in his seat, and I sat back down on my end of the couch.

"So that's why Callie was here? She's helping you stand up against these camps and therapy?"

"Yeah. She's a sweet girl, but we're just friends. She lost someone, too, so we connected. That's all." Ramsey scrubbed his face with his hands and blew out a breath. "Rusty's suicide still fucks me up. I suspect it always will." He placed his feet on the floor and stood. "I'm going to grab a beer. Do you want some wine? I picked up a few Rieslings for when you dropped by."

"That sounds great. Thank you."

Ramsey strolled into the kitchen, and I attempted to collect my thoughts. I wanted to support him, not add to the shit show.

"Here." Ramsey held out a glass to me a minute later. He took a long swallow from his beer, his Adam's apple bobbing and sat next to me. He slid his hand beneath my legs and extended them across his lap, then leaned his head against the back of the couch and stared at me.

Every fiber in my being warmed with his touch.

"About that kiss," he said.

13

"I shouldn't have done that." I attempted to look away from him, but I couldn't. His intense gaze held me captive and refused to let me go.

"Yeah, you should have." He leaned into me and stroked my cheek with the pad of his thumb.

Before I could respond, he pressed a kiss to the corner of my mouth. "I could do this all day long." His lips brushed against mine, and a soft whimper escaped me.

Dammit. I needed to talk to him first. "Ramsey, wait." I couldn't believe I was stopping him. "I want … I need to tell you some things."

He pulled back and laced his fingers through mine. "I'm listening."

The thump-thump of my clothes in the dryer was the only sound in the apartment.

I grabbed my phone from the arm of the couch. I needed something to keep my hands busy. "I have feelings for you. I … I think I'm realizing that I am in love with you. I know you said you loved me, but I wasn't clear if you were referring to us as friends or more."

Ramsey set his beer on the floor, his focus never leaving me. "Avery."

I placed my fingers to his mouth. "I need to share some information with you before you say anything."

He kissed my fingertips and held my hand. "Okay."

Ramsey had always been a good listener, even when he didn't want to be. It was one of the things I loved so much about him.

"I had to hire a bodyguard."

"What? Why?" Shock registered across his handsome features.

I chewed my bottom lip, grasping at the right words to explain it all to him. "I received a threatening voicemail. I don't know who it's from. The voice was disguised. But they admitted to killing Dad ..." My courage faltered, and tears streamed down my cheeks. "Dad was murdered, Ramsey. They meant to kill me, as well, and the message said they'd end me next."

Ramsey dropped my hand, lifted my legs off his lap, and jumped off the couch, his fists clenching and unclenching. "Goddammit, why am I just now hearing about this? When did this happen, Avery?"

"I only hired security a few days ago, Ramsey. I'm safe ... for now."

"They can't stop another car accident," Ramsey said, fear twisting his expression. "Jesus."

I fell silent, allowing him a moment to process what I'd told him. I was still trying to absorb the situation myself.

Finally, I couldn't take it any longer. "I'm putting you in jeopardy by being here, but ... my bodyguard is outside, keeping an eye on my car and your place. We're in good hands." Guilt from my actions crept into the depths of my soul. *What the hell is wrong with me?* If I really loved Ramsey like I believed I did, I would stay far away from him. "I'm so sorry. This was a horrible idea. I have no idea what I was thinking. I put my own desires above your safety." I placed my feet on the floor. "I should go."

Ramsey dropped to his knees in front of me and placed his warm hands against my outer thighs. "Avery, I have no problem with you being here. I'll feel better if I know where you are and that you're safe. I'll hire my own bodyguard if I need to."

I tipped his chin up with my fingers. "It's dangerous, Ramsey. I'm being selfish by wanting to be with you. I'm scared. Dad is gone, and if anything happened to you, I would never forgive myself."

"You can't make that decision for me, so let me help you with it so that you don't beat yourself up about it anymore." He paused, his eyes searching mine. "I want you. I want to be with you. I've waited for years to hear that you have feelings for me."

"Years?" I asked, a burning ache spreading through my chest. I couldn't even imagine how it would feel to love someone for so long and hope they might love you in return someday.

"So fucking long. I tried to get you out of my head, but my heart had other plans." He smiled warmly.

"What does this mean, then? What are we? Where do we go from here?"

Ramsey placed his palms on my cheeks. "It means I want to be with you and no one else. It means we're in love with each other, and we go anywhere this journey takes us. As long as you're next to me... that's all that matters, Avery. You're the most important thing to me."

If I could have melted into his couch, I would have. *How did I miss that he's been in front of me all this time?* Anxiety crept up my spine, and my breath caught in my chest. "Are you sure? Being with me puts you in danger too. Are you ready for that?"

"I'm positive, and we'll do everything possible to keep us safe. I promise. Besides, I suspect that whoever killed your dad knows I'm in your life already, along with Benji and Tensley. You've spent time with all of us since the accident. Let me help you through this." He shifted his weight and moved between my knees. Leaning forward, he hovered his mouth over mine. "Let me love you, Avery."

He placed his lips on mine, and I leaned into him. I threaded my hands through his hair as he kissed me.

"What if we don't work? How will we go back to being friends? Or worse ... what if I lose you all together?" I asked, my fear overriding any other emotions.

Ramsey stood and held his hand out to me and helped me off the couch. "If you think I'm ever going to let you go now that I finally have you, you're mistaken."

Without another word, he swept me up into his powerful arms and took me to his room. He gently placed me on his bed, his gaze sweeping over me. "You're so beautiful. Tell me you're mine, Avery."

The mattress dipped with his weight, and he hovered over me, his blue eyes sparking with desire.

"I'm yours, Ramsey." A fire ignited in my body as my heart beat with a new purpose, and the depth of my feelings for him bloomed to life.

Ramsey's palm cupped my cheek. "I love you. I love you so goddamned much. Thank you for not leaving tonight."

Tears welled in my eyes, and I wondered where I would be if I hadn't had the strength to stay. "I'm glad I'm here." I placed my hands on his hips and guided him down on top of me. "I have nothing on beneath your sweatshirt."

Ramsey moaned as he pressed his hard-on into my leg. "You have no idea what you do to me."

"Show me." I licked my lower lip, anticipating him inside me again.

Ramsey rolled onto his side and tugged at the sweatshirt. I pulled it over my head and flung it onto the floor. For the first time in a long while, I was nervous about having sex. I didn't think I was the only one, though. The chiseled lines of his face were etched with an abundance of feelings.

His fingertips traced down my neck, over my throat, and collar bone. He placed gentle kisses between my breasts and I arched up slightly. Butterflies ran rampant in my stomach as the warmth of his breath glided over my left breast, and his hand ran down my side and over my hip. My core throbbed, longing overtaking me.

Ramsey's tongue darted across my nipple, then his mouth captured my taut bud. My eyes fluttered closed, and I ran my hands up the muscular planes of his back. He lifted his head and groaned at the base of his throat before his lips crashed down on mine. His tongue expertly caressed mine, and I gave myself permission to relax and lose myself in his touch.

He trailed kisses down my tummy, and chills traveled up my spine as he hovered over my pussy. Ramsey glanced up at me, then slid down lower on the mattress and licked the inside of my thigh.

I grabbed a fistful of his comforter, bunching it in my hands while his tongue made contact with my throbbing core. The stubble from his chin scraped the sensitive flesh of my leg as I moved against him. He pushed two fingers deep into me, and with every lick and touch, I melted into him. Ramsey didn't waste any time while he made love to me with his mouth, leaving me breathless.

His piercing blue eyes peered up at me as my climax peaked, and I writhed beneath his caress.

He stood, dropped the remainder of his clothes, and rolled on a condom. His erection bobbed against his stomach, and he crawled back onto the bed, hovering over me. I reached up and touched his cheek.

"The condom broke the first time. I'm on the pill, and … have you been with anyone else after me at The Lily?" My heart beat wildly against my rib cage. Even though I'd had another appointment at the club, I wasn't sure I wanted to hear that he'd been with someone else. As far as I was concerned, he didn't owe me any details of his play-time, and neither did I. However, I needed to know if he was still clean or if there might be have been another condom issue.

"No. I couldn't even go back to work."

"Let's not worry about the condom. We've both been tested and are safe. I want you, Ramsey. All of you."

Ramsey sucked in a breath. "Are you sure?"

"I've never been so sure about anything in my life." I ran my thumb across his lower lip. "I love you, Ramsey. I think I have for a long time but didn't realize it." My pulse raced with my confession, and I wanted nothing more than to be with him.

He removed the condom and guided his cock to my entrance, then placed his hands on either side of my head. "Are you ready?" he asked with gentleness that momentarily caught me off guard.

"Yes," I replied.

He entered me slowly, our intense gazes locking while he filled me.

He remained still, his emotions running rampant in his expression. I'd never seen him so vulnerable and open.

"Ramsey," I moaned.

He pulled out and thrust into me. My nails dug into his comforter as he claimed me as his, and I willingly gave myself to him. My eyes closed, savoring the time with him.

"Are you all right?" he asked, slowing his pace.

I looked up at him. "Yes," I replied breathlessly.

Wrapping my legs around his waist, I lifted my hips. Our bodies were in perfect sync with each other. Waves of pleasure washed over me, and my core tightened around him while I grabbed his ass. I rocked up to meet his movements, my desire continuing to build.

His pace continued to pick up as he unlocked all the hidden places inside me that I'd sworn I would protect at all costs. That man owned me with every thrust, every touch, and every kiss. For the first time, I felt treasured. I didn't have to perform for Ramsey or prove to him I was worthy to be loved. He embraced me for all of my good and all of my ugly.

Tears welled in my eyes as every wall I'd erected to protect myself from hurting crumbled, and all of my fear dissolved.

"Ramsey," I moaned.

"This time, I want to see you come."

His rhythm picked up the pace, his cock reaching deep into me. My breath hitched, and I dug my nails into his flesh.

"That's it, babe," he whispered into my ear.

My core clenched around him, and delicious spasms rocked my body. My back arched off the mattress as he continued to slide in and out.

"That's it, Avery," Ramsey urged. His thrusts quickened, and he pushed into me a few more times before he came, his head buried in my neck and hair and his guttural groan muffled.

Breathless, we lay in each other's arms, relishing the intimate connection we had. Ramsey peppered my face with kisses, and a low chuckle rumbled through his chest. "I can't believe you're in my bed."

He pulled out of me, then he laid his head on the pillow next to mine, his attention focused on me.

I smiled at him and repositioned myself on my side. "I know. I'm wondering if I'm dreaming right now." I ran my fingers along his jawline and kissed him gently. "This was different from our time at The Lily, but I loved it even more."

"What you didn't realize was that you already owned my heart, but that day with you … Holy shit. I was completely whipped."

I pushed his shoulder. "Stop," I said, giggling.

His expression grew serious. "I've dated, and I've fucked around, but Avery … none of them were you. The sex was simply a physical release. At times, I thought I might be able to care about someone else, then a text from you would ping on my phone. No matter who I was with or what time of night it was, I always excused myself to speak to you."

"Ramsey!" My eyes popped open. "Those poor girls. You never had to sideline anyone to talk to me. We could have chatted after they were gone."

"I was an ass. I won't deny it. But they weren't you. I've wrestled with how much I love you for a long time. Maybe these feelings are new to you, but not me. There were times I thought it was going to break me, so I'd try to date someone. Anything to attempt to move on, but I couldn't."

"I'm sorry I put you through all of that while I figured out that I wanted you." I ran my fingernails down his chest, my attention following them. "With everything in my life turning upside down, I'm scared I'm going to wake up tomorrow and you'll tell me you got lost in the moment. It's easy to do when nothing is stable around you."

"Stop. Don't say anything like that again. This is real. I'm real. I'm right here. I won't regret a single second of our time together."

I swallowed, trying to trust that what we had was the real thing. I'd never doubted Ramsey before, which was an indicator that I was emotionally in way over my head.

"Okay."

"You should stay here tonight." Ramsey slipped his fingers between my thighs. He ran his finger along my wet slit, then massaged my bundle of nerves.

"I'd like that." I smiled at him and parted my legs, allowing him better access.

"Does this feel good?" His cock hardened as he continued to touch me.

"Yes," I whimpered in response.

He slid a finger into me, and he continued to rub my sensitive bud.

"Do you know how many nights I would lie awake and jerk off as I thought about licking your pussy or being inside of you?"

"Oh my god," I slammed my eyes closed while he told me how he wanted to bury his tongue inside me.

"Roll over on your back," he ordered.

I did as I was told.

"I saw your file at The Lily."

My eyes flew open. "What?"

"You didn't know the guys had access to your likes and dislikes?"

I shook my head.

"I know you love this." He grinned and pinched my clit. "And this." He curled his finger inside me. "I know your favorite position to have your pussy licked and sucked. The toys you like."

"You cheated," I said, panting, though I secretly loved the idea that I didn't need to train him in what I wanted.

"Promise me one thing, Avery." He leaned over me, his finger slick with my juices as he pumped me harder.

"What?" I gasped, rocking against his hand.

"Promise me …" He withdrew from me, and his gaze darkened. "Roll over."

I flipped onto my stomach, and he grabbed my hips and lifted me on all fours. "That this …" He ran his fingers over my slit. "Belongs to me."

He positioned himself behind me and rubbed his thick dick over my throbbing core.

"Promise me." He slammed into me, and I quickly placed my hand against his headboard in order to steady myself.

"Yes!" I cried.

"Say it." Ramsey tugged on my hair, forcing my head back.

I bit my lip, willing myself not to answer. If he had read my information, Ramsey already knew what to do next.

A sharp slap landed on my ass cheek, and I moaned. "More."

"Say it." Another smack.

I whimpered as he pulled out of me.

"No more until you tell me what I want to hear."

Silence filled the room, and I refused to give in to him, but my hormones had other ideas.

"You're so fucking wet that your juices are glistening on my cock. I know you want me to make you come. Tell me what I want to hear and I'll have you screaming my name in seconds."

I hid my smile. Ramsey had definitely read my information from the club and had played the game well.

"I promise," I whispered, and wondered if he'd even heard me.

He eased the tip of his dick into me and began to move slowly.

"Good girl." He ran his finger along my puckered hole and pushed against the opening. "You loved this that day at The Lily." A growl escaped him while he fucked me. "You're so tight, Avery. Tell me you're mine and that no one else will touch you."

Black dots floated across my vision as I gave my body to him. "I'm yours." My eyes slammed shut while pleasure ripped through me. "Ramsey!"

"Oh god, that sweet little pussy clenched my cock."

I bucked against him as I came. Seconds later, his roar reverberated through the room, and he emptied himself into me.

I collapsed backward with a huge smile on my face. "I don't know if I should be thrilled or disappointed that you already know what my tastes are. It's like you have the combination to my pussy, and you just do with it as you want."

Ramsey threw his head back and laughed. "I don't think I've ever met a female that would complain over a guy dialing in their fantasies."

My hand flew to my mouth, and I giggled. "I needed this. My

world is so fucked up right now that I just needed to relax and have some fun."

Ramsey's expression clouded as he lay down next to me. "It was more than fun for me."

I propped up on my elbows, my mood shifting immediately. "That's not what I mean. Ramsey, this was so much more than an orgasm or sex. It was even more intense with you because I love you. I love you so much." Tears pricked my eyes while I relaxed into the soft comforter.

"What's wrong, babe? I didn't mean to upset you." Ramsey smoothed my hair and pulled me to him.

I laid my head on his chest as he wrapped his arms around me, and my tears landed on his heated skin. "I'm an emotional mess. Maybe finally admitting my feelings for you and the harsh reality that Dad is gone and ..." I curled into him as the cries shook my body.

"We're going to get through this. You're not alone, babe. I'll always be here."

My phone chimed, and I peered over the edge of the bed and searched for it. Apparently, I'd dropped it while Ramsey was carrying me to his room. "There it is." I laughed and snatched it off the floor. The call stopped before I had a chance to answer it. I flopped back onto the pillow next to Ramsey and tapped the voicemail button and listened.

I shot off the bed and gasped.

"I'm coming for you, Avery. Now that Daddy is out of the way, you're next. And *tsk, tsk, tsk.* I told you not to tell anyone. I hope you've enjoyed your time with Ramsey, Benji, and Tensley. I'm going to rip everyone important away from you just like you did me. If you contact the police, you'll wish you had died along with your father."

"Babe, what's wrong?"

I shuddered, the disguised voice twisting my insides into knots as I staggered backward and onto the edge of his bed. I ended the call, my body trembling so violently that I nearly slipped off the mattress. "A message." I handed him my iPhone, pulled my knees up, and tucked them under my chin.

Ramsey replayed the message on speaker, the color draining from his cheeks while he listened. "Avery." He tossed the phone onto the nightstand and pulled me into his arms.

I placed my head beneath Ramsey's chin as he rubbed my back, my pulse ringing in my ears from the horror of the threat.

"Take a breath, babe." Ramsey smoothed my hair and rocked me gently. "I would like to meet with the firm you hired to see what we can do without alerting the cops. Plus, I know you don't want to, but we have to talk to Benji and Tensley. Michael and Marilyn will take care of them, but we all need security."

I nodded, my cheek brushing against the soft patch of hair on his chest. The steady beat of his heart began to calm my nerves.

"I'm sorry, Ramsey. I've put you all in danger."

Ramsey tilted my chin up with his fingers. "I chose to be by your side. Now let me."

I looped my arms around his neck. "Thank you. Thank you for loving me."

"Babe, you've got it all backward. I'm the one who should be thanking you."

I remained in the safety of his embrace until I stopped shaking.

"What time is it?" I asked softly.

"It's almost eight thirty. You're not leaving tonight. You have a change of clothes in the dryer. I need you next to me, Avery."

"Okay." I peered up at him through my eyelashes. "I need to call Franklin, though. I don't think it's too late."

I slipped off his lap and located his sweatshirt while he slipped back into his boxer briefs, then he sat next to me, and I pulled up Franklin's phone number. I placed it on speaker as it began to ring.

"This is Franklin."

"Franklin, this is Avery."

"Hi there."

"I apologize for calling at this hour. I got another voicemail." I could almost imagine Franklin leaning back in his office chair and frowning.

"Sir, this is Ramsey Goldman. We met briefly at Tensley and Benji's party at the bar when I was in town last."

"I remember you. You're a football player, right?"

The corner of my mouth twitched slightly. Ramsey was known and well respected in the NCAA. He had incredible potential to make the NFL if he wanted to.

"Yes. I'm here in Spokane now." Ramsey cleared his throat. "I was with Avery when the phone rang. She just didn't answer it fast enough. I've heard the message. She's in grave danger, but they also named Benji and Tensley, which also puts their parents, Michael and Marilyn, in jeopardy."

A heavy silence filled the line. "Are you both available to see me tomorrow at ten? I might change the time, but I want Michael and Marilyn along with the kids in this meeting. I'll help you talk to them, Avery. The first thing we need to do is add additional security. Michael and Marilyn know Pierce and his wife, Sutton, so I'll bring them in as well so that we can have a plan without tipping off the caller anymore. Try to remain calm and go to the places you normally do each day. But Avery … whoever it is, they know who's important to you. This is bigger than we thought."

I rubbed my face, wishing the nightmare weren't real. "I know. I'm scared."

Ramsey pulled me against him and kissed the top of my head.

"Avery is staying at my apartment tonight," Ramsey added. "She's safe next to me, and Tad is outside."

"Good. I'll reach out to everyone, then text you a confirmed time and place to meet tomorrow."

"Thank you," I said. "I appreciate it very much."

"You bet. You kids try to get some sleep."

"Good night," Ramsey and I said in unison.

14

The next morning, Ramsey and I met Franklin at Pierce Westbrook's home north of Spokane. It was a well-hidden log house surrounded by a brick wall with an iron gate.

Ramsey laced his fingers through mine as we were welcomed at the mahogany front door with a warm smile from Sutton, Pierce's wife. I'd seen her next to her husband at a large social gathering a few months ago, but I'd never met them.

"Thank you for inviting us," I said.

I'd been to a lot of expensive houses but never a log one. It was gorgeous. The light, shiny wood floors extended as far as I could see into the living and dining area and up the stairs. A gray stone fireplace stretched toward the vaulted ceiling, providing a beautiful contrast to the log walls. Fans circulated the air gently, keeping the room at a cozy temperature.

"You're welcome. Please come in. Everyone is here," Sutton said, leading us into her home, her bare feet slapping against the wood floors of the entryway and living area. "Please make yourself comfortable." Sutton motioned for us to take a seat.

My mouth gaped. Franklin wasn't kidding. Everyone was there, including Benji, Layne, and Tensley.

"Hi." Tensley hopped out of her seat and embraced me, then hugged Ramsey.

Benji was right behind her. Layne waited patiently until it was his turn.

Marilyn stood from her wingback chair and straightened her black slacks, her expression full of concern. Her shoulder-length dark hair was perfectly in place, but a flicker of fear flashed across her face. "Hi, hon." She wrapped her arms around me, her bracelets jingling as she lowered her hands.

"Thank you for being here," I said, kissing her on the cheek. Tears welled in my eyes, and my attention landed on Michael next. His burgundy button-down shirt was paired with black slacks and matching loafers. He and Marilyn had impeccable taste and rarely ever dressed down, even at home.

Michael and Dad had been hunting and fishing buddies for years. Michael gave me a fatherly kiss on the top of my head while he hugged me. A burning sensation spread across my chest. I missed Dad so much. Seeing his friends felt like a sharp two-edged knife. Although it helped me feel closer to Dad, it was also a reminder that he was gone.

Once we were settled in our seats, the official introductions began. Michael and Marilyn sat next to each other on the leather love seat. Tensley fidgeted in a recliner and flipped her long blonde hair behind her shoulder. Her soft purple sweater clung to her curves. I was so grateful she'd come out of her shell. Tensley was gorgeous. Benji stood next to Layne behind her and pushed up the long sleeves of his black polo shirt. No one had to say it, but everyone was on edge.

Pierce Westbrook stood next to his wife, and I recognized one of the bodyguards. It was difficult to forget someone with one brown eye and one blue eye. I offered a friendly smile at Vaughn.

Tad nodded at Ramsey and me as Pierce continued to introduce his employees, including Zayne, Jeffrey, and Jaxon. I'd seen most of them before, but a few of the men were new to me.

I'd not mentioned anything to Davia since she was rarely around and wouldn't have retained any of the information due to her drug addled brain anyway. She would be more of a liability, and I didn't have time to babysit her.

Franklin glanced at his watch and cleared his throat. "This won't be easy for any of us, but I wanted everyone to understand how dangerous the situation is." He slipped his hands into the front pockets of his khaki slacks.

Ramsey draped his arm around my shoulders, and I placed my hand on his knee. I didn't miss Tensley and Benji's approving nods. I hadn't had a chance to tell them Ramsey and I were together yet.

Questioning stares landed on me, and I chewed my bottom lip while Franklin continued to explain about Dad's murder and the threats. The room was filled with gasps and cries, but I just sat there numbly.

Franklin paused then said, "Avery, are you okay sharing the latest voicemail with everyone?"

I nodded and pulled my phone from my back pocket. My hand shook while I pulled up the message and played it. Closing my eyes, I slumped forward as shame washed over me. I'd put them all in jeopardy.

The message ended, and a thick silence filled the room. Ramsey kissed the side of my head. "It's okay, babe. Everyone is on your side."

I chanced a glance at everyone, but instead of animosity, all I saw was love and compassion. Anxiety seized me, and my leg bounced without my permission. I placed my palm on my knee in order to stop it.

Michael rubbed his hands together, nodded at me, then looked at Pierce. "It looks like we're hiring your men again."

"I think it's a good idea if everyone has an individual bodyguard," Franklin added.

"I agree," Ramsey chimed in. "I can't take any chances with Avery's life. Now that we're dating, at least we'll have two keeping an eye on us."

A hushed chatter filled the room while everyone discussed what they needed to do in order to help me.

"It's best if everyone continues as though nothing is wrong. Go to school, work, the gym, or wherever else you normally go. The caller already suspects that you've talked to your friends, Avery, but at this point, they're guessing. What we need to do is find out who this is and why they're coming after you," Pierce said.

"What about the crime family?" I asked Franklin. "Is that still a possibility?"

Franklin nodded. "It is."

"I'll gather the information from Franklin and do a bit of digging, if you're okay with that, Avery," Sutton said.

"Yes, please."

"Is there anyone you can think of that would want to hurt you?" Sutton asked, her tone full of kindness.

I shook my head. "No. I didn't even know Dad had enemies until the first voicemail." I shoved the ball of anger and grief back down. Later, I could scream and cry. For the moment, I needed to remain as calm and collected as possible.

Over the next half hour, security was assigned to Ramsey, Layne, Benji, Tensley, Marilyn, and Michael. A sick feeling twisted my stomach into knots as the harsh reality set in. It was no longer a phone call I could ignore. This shit was real.

"One quick question," I said before we finished. "Ramsey has his first football game on Saturday. Can I go? Is it safe?"

"You should go and try to have some fun," Pierce said.

"We'll be with her," Tensley added. "Benji and I … we're all going together."

"I'm sorry I can't make it. I have a previous commitment with my uncle. I'll make sure I'm at the next one," Layne explained.

I smiled at them, grateful they wanted to go with me. Ramsey's first game was important.

"Excellent, then everyone's bodyguards will be behind you and next to you while you're in the stands. Ramsey, you'll be on the field, so Jaxon will blend in on the sidelines with the coaches. I'm friends with the head coach, so I'll let him know some of the parents were concerned about a player's safety and hired some of my men. We've got it covered."

"Thank you," Ramsey said.

"I think that settles it. If any of you need anything or have additional concerns, contact Sutton or me. We all knew or had met Steven, and we all want justice for him as well as protection for Avery," Pierce stated.

I glanced at my watch and groaned inwardly. "I'm due at the office this afternoon, and I need to swing by my house and change clothes. I have to go."

Everyone stood, and once again, we all exchanged hugs.

Benji strolled over to me, his blue eyes flashing with worry. "Promise me you'll be careful."

"I will. Tad will follow me to work and be inside the building."

"Good. I remember what this is like, and if you need me, no matter what time of day or night it is, call me. I'm right there for you." Tensley took my hands in hers and squeezed them. "You're like a sister to me. I can't lose you." A tear slid down Tensley's cheek.

"You won't." I reached over and gave her a tight embrace. I released her and looped my arm through Ramsey's. "Where and what time do you want to get together for the game tomorrow?" I asked. I glanced up at Ramsey and smiled.

"Why don't we meet at the game at two. Then we can swing by the concession stand and find good seats," Benji suggested.

"That works. I'll see you guys there."

My head throbbed as I strolled into Davenport and McCade Financials.

"Hi, Avery," Janine said, smiling widely. "Happy Friday."

I returned her smile. "Hi, Janine, and thank you. I've got a lot on my schedule today, but I'll stop by and see how you're doing later." I hummed softly while I walked to my office, steadying myself for the challenge ahead.

As I slipped my computer bag onto my clean desk and stared out the wall of windows, my stomach plummeted to my toes. I had to talk to Vincent about the money while I was there. Either he had it, or I would be forced to turn him over to the cops.

Sinking into the leather executive chair, I powered up my laptop and immersed myself in my work. It was a welcome distraction. An hour later, my phone chimed. Rummaging through my bag, I finally located it. I couldn't stop my smile as I read Ramsey's text.

I miss you already. Looking forward to having you in my arms soon.

My fingernails clicked against the screen as I tapped out my reply.

Same. If you win tomorrow, I'll give you a surprise. I added a smiley face.

Seconds later, his reply came through.

Now I have to win. Lol

More dots flickered across my screen, indicating he was still typing.

I love you, Avery.

My chest warmed with his words.

I love you, too, Ramsey. I'll see you later tonight. As for tomorrow, I know you'll kick some ass, babe. I can't wait to cheer for you from the stands.

I waited for his reply, grinning like a teenager with their head in the clouds.

We can have our own pregame show tonight.

I laughed.

Game on. LOL

I placed my phone in my lap when my office door swung open, and Vincent strolled in as though he were on top of the world. I hoped it was a good indicator that he had made things right.

"Close the door behind you," I said, shutting my laptop. I stood, pretended to shut off my cell, and stared at him. "Have you replaced the money you stole?"

Vincent's eyes narrowed as though he were deep in thought, then he snapped his fingers. "About that."

"Yes or no, Vincent. There's nothing complicated about this."

Vincent approached me. His expression was unreadable. "No, I haven't, and you're not turning me in. In fact, you're not going to do shit to me."

I laughed. "And what makes you think I would let you continue to work here? You broke the law."

Vincent sat on the corner of my desk, his eyes darkening as his gaze swept over my body, and he massaged his crotch.

A cold sweat rippled over me, and my heart hammered, making me feel like I was going to faint.

"I still remember what it was like when I slid my cock into you."

Shocked, I stepped backward. "What in the hell is wrong with you?" I spat. If he was trying to unnerve me, it was working, but in the back of my mind, I wanted him to say more.

"You wanted it. You pranced in front of me with that perky little ass in the air." His tongue darted out across his lower lip as his dick grew harder beneath his gray slacks.

"I did not want it, Vincent. You raped me. I was seventeen years old. You pinned me down on your desk and raped me. How could you even look my father in the eye after that?" My pitch climbed with each word.

A malicious grin slipped over his face. "It was easy. In fact, I'd imagine you sucking my cock while I had business meetings with him."

"Get out." Rage pounded through me as I pointed at the door. "Not only did you rape me, but you also stole half a million dollars from the company. I hope you enjoy your prison cell."

Vincent laughed, and my nostrils flared. "Are you sure about that? If you press charges, I'll spill your daddy's secret like a gutted piñata."

"What secret?" My legs trembled. "I know about the crime family and that he was going to turn them in to the police." *Dammit, shut up, Avery.*

Vincent's bushy eyebrow arched. "Good for you, but that's not what I'm referring to. I would recommend that you start with your dear ol' mom."

Emotion punched my chest. Vincent obviously felt he had enough dirt on my family to threaten me. "What does she have to do with anything?"

He barked out an obnoxious laugh. Suddenly, I was floundering, and a silent scream built inside me.

"What do you know?" I asked him again, losing my patience with his bullshit games.

"You don't even realize who you are, do you?" His dark chuckle rumbled through the office.

I blanched and stumbled backward. "What kind of question is that?"

"A good one." He smirked and sauntered toward the door. "I look forward to having a long working relationship with you, Avery."

"Don't count on it. This isn't over."

My hands clenched into fists as I watched the sick bastard leave. Collapsing into my chair, I laid my head on the cool surface of the desk. I closed my eyes and dragged in deep gulps of air.

"Shit." I glanced at my phone and turned off the recorder. At least I'd had the frame of mind to record our conversation. Regardless of what he knew about my family, he was going down.

I collected my computer and my bag, then calmly left my office and walked down the hall as though nothing had happened. Mentally, I released a sigh of relief that Janine wasn't at the front desk. I would talk to her later, but at the moment, I needed a safe place to make a phone call.

THE DRIVE HOME had been uneventful, but I was well aware that someone could have easily been watching me. Aside from Tad. At least I hoped he was. I'd glanced in my rearview mirror several times, but I hadn't ever spotted him.

I activated the garage-open button, pulled in, and watched as the door slid shut again. Gathering my bag, I popped open the glove compartment and located the burner phone I'd stashed.

I hurried through the utility area and kitchen, then ran up the stairs. From what I could tell, the house was empty. The only safe place I knew of was my room. I closed and locked the door behind me, then sank onto the bed and willed my racing pulse to settle down. I rifled through my bag and located the information I needed. I placed the call and held my breath while it began to ring. I hoped like hell I was doing the right thing.

"Westbrook security. This is Sutton."

"Hi, this is Avery. I need your help." Relieved that she'd answered the phone, I rolled my shoulders in a vain attempt to release some of the stress.

"Hey there, I just hung up with Franklin. He was sharing the information with me concerning the crime family. I'm about to start digging in to see what I can find," Sutton said.

"I have more," I blurted.

"Are you all right?" she asked softly. "You sound scared."

"I am." I massaged my forehead. "Is our conversation confidential?"

"Yes and no. If this is about your case, then I have to share it with Pierce so that he knows how to protect you. Other than that, it can stay between us."

"I understand." A small cry slipped from my lips. "I don't know what's happening, Sutton. I don't know what to do or where to start."

"Talk to me, Avery. You're not alone. We're here to help. I promise that we're on your side."

I glanced around my room, and my attention landed on the mural I'd painted. Right then, I would have given anything to be on the ocean with Ramsey next to me. I returned my focus to Sutton and relayed my conversation with Vincent to her.

"I'm proud of you for recording his threats, Avery. At least you have proof that he hurt you, and also threatened you again. Men like him don't stop with one girl either. When are you going to use it against him?"

"Part of me wants to talk to the police now, but I know the crime family he's connected with have some cops on their payroll. I need to play my cards carefully. Plus, I have no idea how to start an investigation into him discreetly."

"I can help you with it, but first, what's your mom's full name and date of birth?" Sutton asked.

I could hear her fingers flying over the keyboard as I provided what she needed for the research. "Davia Marie Petersburg. She and Dad met here in Spokane through a mutual college friend, but I can't remember what his name was."

"Where was she born?"

I frowned, flipping through my mental Rolodex for the information. "Boston. Her date of birth is June seventh. She's forty-four."

"Has she worked anywhere or been home with you during the school years?"

"She's not worked a day in her life. Dad always took care of the financial responsibilities."

"I'm going to dig in. What number is good to reach you?"

I rattled off my cell number to her, then told her I had a burner phone to return her call so we could talk in case my phone was tapped.

"If I find anything tonight, I'll text you from an unknown number and confirm your hair appointment. That way, we won't raise any suspicions in case your phone is tapped. When's the last time you had it checked?"

"The night I met with Franklin. Maybe a week ago? I'm sorry, with so much happening, I can't remember for sure."

"I'll get a device to Tad that will detect any bugs on your cell or your car or in your house. Test every day, and don't leave your phone anywhere. Keep it on you at all times."

"I don't usually go anywhere without it, anyway."

"Try to have some fun at the game tomorrow. Not only will our guys be there, but large events have a lot of security as well."

"Thanks." I ended the call and flopped backward, exhausted. Before I fell asleep, I called Ramsey to let him know I was going to bed early so that he wouldn't worry about me, under the circumstances.

1 6

I stared at the clock on my nightstand and jumped off the bed. At some point the previous night, I'd fallen asleep and slept the majority of the day. Rubbing the sleep from my eyes, I realized I only had an hour before I had to meet Tensley and Benji. One of my superpowers was pulling myself together in a short amount of time, though. I loved a good challenge.

Ten minutes later, I eased my BMW out of my driveway and headed toward the school. At least the traffic wasn't bad yet, but it would be within the hour, so I opted for the back roads.

A huge grin split my face as I parked next to Benji's Lexus. He and Tensley waved, then Ten ran around to the driver's side and practically yanked me out of the car.

"I'm so happy to see you. We're going to hang out, watch your man win this game, and laugh." Her smile slowly faded. "We all need to laugh right now. No matter what has happened, Avery, we have each other. Those reminders and our fun times together got me through some shitty dark days. Even if it's only for a few hours, I want you to relax and be happy."

"I love you guys. I don't say it enough, but I really do."

"Same. Don't ever doubt it," Benji chimed in.

I pushed up on my tiptoes and gave him a kiss on his cheek and patted his butt and winked at him. "Don't tattle to Ramsey that I did that."

Benji rolled his eyes and laughed. "It doesn't count with you and Ten."

I checked my phone case and made sure my college ID and debit card were tucked safely into the secret compartment. Then I grabbed my Coach sunglasses and slid them into place. Although it was overcast, the moment the game started, the sun would push the clouds away, and I wouldn't be able to see anything. I inhaled a deep breath. The fresh air held the promise of autumn, and a hint of excitement sparked to life inside me. This year, the hours in front of the fireplace would be spent snuggled next to Ramsey. My heart quickened with the idea of holding hands and running through pumpkin patches, drinking spiced cider, and planning. *Oh my god. I want to plan a future with him.*

"How are you today?" Tensley asked, slinging her arm around my shoulders.

"I'm glad I'm with you guys. I'm also super excited to see Ramsey play today."

Benji slipped his arm through mine. "Girl, are you two official?"

I laughed, relieved to be discussing something other than everything that was going down.

"We are. As of Thursday night, actually."

"I'm so happy for you," Tensley said, leaning her head on my shoulder while we walked toward the entrance gate to purchase tickets.

The stadium lights flipped on, and the fans began to fill both sides of the stadium. "Blue Eyes Forever" by Charlotte OC reverberated through the speakers. A hum of excitement buzzed through me. I loved football, but more than that, it was *my* guy on the field, making the touchdowns. From what I'd seen on the news, Ramsey was one hell of a running back.

"I love this song," Ten said, bumping me with her hip as we entered the stadium. "When your life has settled down some, we should go dancing." Ten grinned at me.

"That sounds like so much fun. It's been too damned long. Plus, I love eating pancakes afterward. Ramsey and Layne haven't gone with us yet, so we should introduce them to our tradition." Benji adjusted his jacket, his attention roaming the football field and the seats. "We should sit on the visitor's side and scream for Ramsey at the top of our lungs." He wiggled his eyebrows at us.

"That would be funny, but I don't want to distract him. Maybe next time, though."

Ten, Benji, and I chatted about anything lighthearted. I loved them for attempting to keep the conversations focused on the positive. It was the distraction I needed.

Twenty minutes later, Ramsey and his teammates ran onto the field. The crowd roared and cheered, the energy sparking with excitement and anticipation.

After the players were introduced, the coin toss favored the Cobras, and they chose to start on defense. Our kicker lined up on the thirty-five-yard line and sent the ball sailing into the air. A blur of colors darted down the field to secure the ball.

"We're looking forward to a fantastic game today, and everyone in the NCAA is keeping a close eye on number twenty-two, Ramsey Goldman," the announcer said over the noisy crowd.

Tensley nudged me and grinned. "How does it feel to say he's your man?"

My nose wrinkled as my grin widened. "Good. Really good." I laughed.

"Interception! Look at him go, folks! What a way to start the first game!"

"Holy shit! Ramsey's got the ball." I jumped up and down, clapping madly with the rest of the fans. "Go, baby!" I cupped my hands around my mouth and screamed.

"Touchdown! Goldman puts the first points of the season on the board," the announcer boomed.

Cheers and stomps against the bleachers filled the stadium, and Ramsey's teammates high-fived him and slapped him on the ass.

"Excellent play," someone with a familiar, deep voice called from behind me.

I glanced over my shoulder and identified Tad two rows up. Pierce and Sutton sat next to Franklin in the section across from us. Scanning the area, I also spotted Vaughn with a beautiful blonde diagonal from us. I wasn't sure if Benji and Tensley had noticed them. If they had, no one had mentioned it.

With tears in my eyes, I exhaled, ridding my body of built-up anxiety. I was safe, surrounded by people who would protect me. Even if it was only for the next few hours, I gave myself permission to leave the grief and fear behind.

Ramsey continued to own the plays, as he scored two more touchdowns. He drove the ball up the field with a speed and agility I hadn't seen before. Whatever he was doing, he had upped his game. He expertly weaved between the opposing players and leaped over them as though it were the most natural thing he'd ever done. No wonder Dad had loved to watch him play. My throat tightened with emotion. Dad should be there with me, cheering loudly and losing his voice along with the rest of the crowd. At least I was able to remember all the fun he'd had talking smack with Ramsey's dad. They'd often rooted for opposite teams, except when it came to my boyfriend.

The Cobras had managed a two-point conversion, which had pissed off our coach to no end, even though we had a solid lead. He had a reputation for being a bit hot-headed. The game ended in our favor with a final score of forty-six to fifteen.

Patrick Droney's "The Wire" played through the speakers, drowning out the chatter while people filed out of the stadium.

"Man, I had no idea Ramsey was so good," Benji said as we entered the parking lot. "And good God, I have no idea why I've not been a football fan until now. So many gorgeous asses stuck up in the air. The view was beautiful today."

I barked out a laugh. "The view is always great." I nudged him on his shoulder with my hand and winked at him. "This was really good. Thank you, guys, for coming with me."

"Oh, I'll be there every home game now." Benji snickered behind his hand.

"Maybe next time Layne can join us too. He was helping his uncle with some projects at his house. I love that about him. Even though he really wanted to hang out with us, he honored his commitment. When he does that, it reminds me that I can trust him. It smooths away the fear and sharp edges from my past life a little more each time," Tensley said, a dreamy smile on her face.

"I wasn't sure about him at the beginning," I stated, remembering how rude I'd been when he first showed up.

"Neither was I," Benji added. "I mean, he was not good to Tensley in high school, but he redeemed himself. I hope I find someone that awesome one day too."

"You will," Tensley and I replied in unison.

"Besides, if anyone else ever treats you like Thomas did, they have to go through all four of us."

"Girl, please. No one will treat me like their bitch again." Benji placed his hand on his hip and smirked while we reached the entrance to Ramsey's locker room.

My nose wrinkled in disgust as the door flew open, a grotesque smell of body and foot odor nearly knocking me over. "Oh god. I hope he showers before he comes out."

Tensley tugged gently on my arm. "Why don't we wait a little farther away."

We burst into laughter as Benji practically ran in the other direction. She was right. There would be a ton of traffic while the guys filed out. Reaching the fence, I stopped. I could see Ramsey from there, even though we were a reasonable distance away.

A few minutes later, the door opened, and my breath hitched in my throat. Ramsey strolled out of the building along with another teammate. Ramsey's hair was still damp, a dark curl flopping over his forehead. His low-slung jeans hugged his muscular legs with every step he took. His fitted T-shirt announced every corded muscle in his chest and shoulders, and my body immediately responded to the sight of him. If there had been some privacy, I would have taken him around the corner for a ride. His smile lit up his bright-blue eyes as his laugh filled the air.

"Ramsey," a tall, thin brunette called and approached the guys.

"I'll catch you later, man," his friend said, leaving Ramsey alone with the chick, who immediately placed her hand on his biceps.

Ramsey flashed her a big grin and stopped to chat. The girl edged closer to him and ran her fingernail down his chest and his stomach.

"Oh shit," Benji muttered.

"Let's go." I whirled on my heel and stormed off. My fists clenched into tight balls as I considered marching up to Ramsey and punching him in the nose for allowing another girl to paw at him, but I refused to stoop to that level.

"Hey, wait up." Tensley double-timed her steps to catch up with me. "We have no idea what was said. Give him a chance to explain. Maybe he didn't realize you wanted to be exclusive."

I clamped my lips shut, and a sharp ache pierced my chest. "He was the one that wanted to be exclusive," I snapped. "Apparently, his football success comes with more than a possible offer to the NFL."

"I know it looked bad, but I'm with Ten. Ask him about it. You've known him for a long time, Avery." Benji shoved his hands into his pockets as we neared the parking lot.

I reached my Bimmer and whirled around. "You're right. I have known him for a long time, and Ramsey has always played around. He's been a total man whore since we were teenagers, so why should I think our situation is any different? I took him at face value the other night when he said he only wanted to be with me." I shook my head. "One of these days, I'll stop being so fucking stupid and see what's right in front of me."

"Avery, take some time, then talk to him," Ten offered, rubbing my arm. "Sometimes, things aren't how they appear." Ten walked back toward the locker room, and returned a minute later. "She's gone, Avery."

"Good, but I need to go." And I did need to, before I began crying and screaming like a two-year-old pissed off that Mommy wouldn't give me a shiny new toy. "I love you guys. I'll text you later."

Before they could say anything else, I started my car and pulled out of my space. My phone chimed, and a text message from Ramsey appeared on my screen.

Hey, babe, where are you? I can't find you anywhere. I thought we were going to meet after the game.

"Un-fucking-believable," I muttered. Approaching the highway, instead of turning left, I took a right and drove toward The Lily. I suspected that even though I didn't have an appointment, Skyler could squeeze me in. With the turn of events with Ramsey, I wasn't in the mood for a sweet little screw. I wanted the handcuffs, the blindfold, and the collar. The more guys, the better. I'd had two before, but three sounded sinful. With Dad dead and Ramsey a liar, I had no one to please except myself.

Another text came through from Ramsey, but I ignored it, planning my session instead. I parallel parked near The Lily, my emotions blazing inside me, which would leave me ruined when I experienced a release.

I hopped out of my car, locked it, and hurried to the sidewalk. Downtown Spokane's traffic was light. I suspected it was due to the game, but soon it would hustle and bustle with people celebrating or mourning the event.

Reaching the door of The Lily, I put my hand out to pull the handle, then hesitated. I stepped back, Ramsey's smile flashing across my mind's eye, followed by the brunette pawing at him. A small cry escaped me, and my hand flew to my mouth. *How could he have done that? Is that who he really is, and he didn't expect to get caught?* I couldn't be with a cheater. After Justin, I'd sworn to myself that I would never put up with it again. *But is this who I want to be?* Maybe I was using sex to soothe the pain that I didn't want to deal with. That didn't make me any better than my mother with her prescription drugs and alcohol.

I massaged my temples and slowly walked back to my car. I had no problem with my membership, but I wanted to let Ramsey know we had no chance. Otherwise, I would be following in his footsteps, and I wasn't willing to belittle myself and cross the line of becoming a cheater. I was better than that. I just wished Ramsey were too.

Intense pressure settled on my chest as I realized I needed to talk to him. Settling back into my car, I pushed the start button, then I tapped out a text to him. He responded in seconds.

Numbness wrapped around my heart, and I welcomed it. Unfortunately, I barely remembered the drive to his apartment, but suddenly, I knocked at his door.

It swung open, and he halted abruptly when he saw the expression on my face.

"Babe?" He reached toward me, but I backed away.

I felt hollow, a shell standing in front of him.

"What's wrong?" Confusion clouded his features, and he rubbed his jaw, obviously nervous.

"I've made a mistake, Ramsey. We can't be together."

"What? Avery, I don't understand. Please, come in so we can talk."

"We've been friends for years, and I'm okay with resuming that friendship, but I need some time away from you." My voice was calm, flat, and lifeless.

Pain slashed across his face, and a muscle clenched in his jaw as he visibly struggled to hold it together.

"I don't understand. What … what happened?"

"For some reason, I thought you only wanted to be with me."

"That's what I said, babe. Nothing's changed." He edged closer to me, and I raised my hand to halt him.

"The brunette with her hands all over you after the game said something different. I stopped by to tell you face-to-face that I can never be with a man that lies to me."

Ramsey's eyes slammed closed for a second, then his gaze found mine again. "It's not what you think, Avery."

"That's the second time you've said that in a week. I guess this part of you was easy to hide from me, since you lived in another state."

"I don't know what you think you saw, and yes, she put her hands on my chest. What you apparently missed was my removing them and telling her I was in a committed relationship with a girl I love with all of my heart. She left immediately. Word will spread fast that you and I are together, and most of the girls will back off. I will handle the rest of them. I swear. Avery, please believe me. I've always been open about my past. I've never hidden anything except Rusty's story, but that was because you'd been through hell."

Memories seized my brain as I recalled all of the open and honest conversations we'd had over the years. "And The Lily."

Ramsey ran his hand through his hair, fear flashing in his eyes. "I tried to call you a few times to tell you I was working there, but you never answered." His steady gaze bored into mine, and an uncomfortable silence descended over us. "My life seems upside down right now. I'm starting a new college with a new football team. My future is unclear, and I'm grieving the loss of your dad. But, Avery, you're the one thing I'm sure of. It's *always* been you."

He cupped my cheeks, worry flitting across his face. "Give me five minutes and let me show you something. If you don't want to be with me after that, then I won't stop you from walking away."

I shoved down the compulsion to kiss him. Everything inside me wanted to believe him, but the pain of losing Dad and opening myself to Ramsey had me raw and vulnerable like never before.

"Five minutes," I agreed.

Ramsey led me into the apartment and kicked the door closed with his foot. "Have a seat." He motioned to the couch. "I'll be right back."

I sat at one end, my back ramrod straight from the tension snaking through my shoulders and spine.

Ramsey returned and sat down, placing a square gold box between us. His eyes held mine, then he lifted the lid.

My forehead creased with confusion. I wasn't sure what I was looking at.

"This is the first seashell we found together. Our parents had decided we were old enough to play on the beach without supervision." He held it carefully in his palm with so much gentleness that it nearly overwhelmed me.

"We were eight," I whispered.

"This," he said, lifting a well-preserved, dried red rose from the box, "is the first flower I picked for you when you were thirteen. It was the first one that had bloomed at the vacation house. After it had wilted and you tossed it into the trash, I saved it. And this …" He lifted a photo out and handed it to me. "This was the next summer. We were fourteen, and I had a new camera. You were drawing, and the sun was setting. The soft-orange-and-gold rays surrounded you. I swear I fell in love with you that day. Your hair was in a ponytail, and you had your bare feet propped up on the white porch rail. I quietly watched you sketch in your pad, not wanting to interrupt, but my world had stopped the second my eyes landed on you. When we were eleven, I meant it when I said we belonged together, but when you were drawing, you reached into me and held my heart in your hand and never gave it back."

My breath hitched. "Why … why didn't you ever say anything, Ramsey?"

He closed his eyes, then opened them again. "I was too chicken. At the time, I thought it would be easier to keep you as a friend rather than lose you completely. It wasn't worth the risk of not being able to talk to you on the phone, text, and hang out with you. I'm not sure whether I could have handled it if I wasn't able to see your smile and hear the sound of your laugh."

"I understand." And I did, more than he would ever know. I'd never been so nervous to share my feelings with anyone before. Maybe the relationship with Justin had cut me deeper than I'd originally thought, leaving me vulnerable and unsure of myself.

Next, he removed a worn piece of paper with frayed edges. He carefully unfolded it and smoothed the creases before he passed it to me. "You mailed this to me after Dog died. I was fucking broken. Dog had been with us since I was two, fourteen years. Other than you, he was my best friend."

I sniffled, the memories of those times opening a dam of emotions I'd tried to contain.

"This …" He chuckled. "Was the envelope you sent me that held my sixteenth birthday card. "You were discovering new shades of lipstick and kissed the back of the envelope. As silly as it sounds …" A faint blush feathered his cheeks, and he cleared his throat. "I rushed off to my room and held your lip print against my mouth. It was the closest I thought I'd ever have to the real thing with you."

Tears slipped down my cheeks as I allowed the proof of his feelings to seep into me.

"These were a few of the moments when I realized how hard I'd fallen for you, Avery. I know that losing Steven has you reeling, not to mention there's some psycho after you and you're terrified. You're second-guessing everything and everyone, but I'm the real thing. I love you so much that it's nearly ripped me in two over the years. I swear to you I am making it clear to any girls that are flirting with me or asking me out that I'm not available. You're the only one I want."

"I'm sorry." My chin shook, a rush of emotion hitting me all at once.

"Don't be." Ramsey moved the box behind him and closed the gap between us. "I would have jumped to the same conclusions if it had been the other way around. Then I would have beat some stupid fucker into a pulp."

I giggled through my tears. "I need to tell you something. When I saw you with her … I took off in my car and drove to The Lily."

The color drained from Ramsey's cheeks. "Did you … were you with someone else?"

"No. I didn't even go inside. I'm going to cancel my membership. I don't want anyone else."

A heavy silence filled the space between us.

"Thank you for telling me. I'm relieved nothing happened. Let's put tonight behind us and move forward." Ramsey tucked a strand of hair behind my ear, his gaze full of understanding.

"I would like that."

"Can I kiss you now?" He leaned in, waiting for permission.

"Please."

His lips were soft and gentle, reassuring me of his feelings. I shifted, placing my left leg on the couch behind him and tugging him on top of me. The weight of his body on mine soothed my earlier fears. His tongue gently caressed mine, and I sighed with contentment. Ramsey's kiss grew more aggressive, and my hands roamed the muscled planes of his back and broad shoulders. His hand slipped beneath my light-gray Pirates football sweatshirt and danced across my skin. Electricity bolted over my body, and a moan escaped me as he pulled the cup of my bra to the side and rolled my hard nipple between the tips of his fingers.

"I love you, Avery." His whisper caressed the sensitive place on my neck directly below my ear, and I arched into him. "You're my first thought every morning when I wake up. My last when I drift off to sleep. You consume me."

He cupped my face, peering deep into my eyes. His expression was determined and sincere. "I don't want you to worry that I'm going to mess around on you. If you would have me, I would marry you tomorrow."

17

My mouth opened and closed as I recalled my earlier thought of planning our future days together.

"Are you proposing?"

His chest rumbled with laughter. "Not yet. Me laying on top of you, between your legs, isn't the way I have it planned out."

I pushed him off me and sat up, staring at him in disbelief. "You have a proposal planned?"

He ran both of his hands over his hair. "I'd hoped to be able to have a chance to ask you someday. I mean, now that you've told me you love me too."

"Holy shit. I had no idea. I thought … I … Over the past few days, when I finally admitted that I was in love with you, honestly, I started to think of what our future would look like. But I hadn't gotten that far."

He leaned toward me and brushed the pad of his thumb across my bottom lip. "Keep this conversation in the back of your mind for if you ever doubt my feelings for you again."

"I promise."

"Stay with me tonight." His eyes darkened with desire, and he pressed a gentle kiss to my lips. "We can finish what we started."

Ramsey stood and held his hand out to me. Smiling and relieved that we'd worked things out, I placed mine in his, then he led me to his bedroom, where he proved how much he loved me for the rest of the evening.

My phone rang at seven the next morning. I groaned and slapped my palm on Ramsey's nightstand until I located it.

"Hello?" I asked, my voice groggy.

Ramsey moved my hair and placed a gentle kiss on the back of my neck, sending delightful shivers down my naked body. Beneath the blankets, his hand traveled south along the curve of my side, over my hip, and to my ass. He cupped my butt cheek and released a soft moan.

"Avery, it's Sutton. Did I wake you? I know it's early, but I have some information for you."

"Hi, Sutton. It's okay. I was waking up. Let me call you right back, though."

"Okay, bye."

Ramsey stopped his foreplay, his breath fanning across my cheek as he waited for me to dig the burner phone out of my purse and return Sutton's call.

She answered on the first ring.

"Hey, it's Avery. I'm using disposable burner phones for any important conversations. If it's okay, I'm going to put you on speakerphone. Ramsey is next to me, so this will be easier than trying to relay anything new to him."

"Sure," she replied.

I put the phone on the bed between us and tapped the screen.

"Can you hear me okay?" I asked.

"Yeah. I know we spoke yesterday after Vincent said you should look into your mom."

Ramsey's eyebrows shot up in shock, then he frowned at me, obviously unhappy I hadn't filled him in on the conversation.

"I'll explain," I whispered to him, my eyes pleading with him not to be angry with me.

"Avery, your mom isn't your bio mother," Sutton explained, her tone filled with compassion.

"What?" I asked, scrambling into a sitting position. "Are you sure? I mean, this can't be right." I paused, my attention landing on Ramsey, whose mouth had gaped with her news.

"I'm so sorry, but your real mom died right after she delivered you. There were complications, and she didn't make it."

"I don't understand," I choked out, squeezing my hands into tight fists. "Dad wouldn't have ever lied to me. I mean … why would he have done that?"

"I don't know yet. You don't need to answer me right away, but do you want me to continue looking into what happened and why this was kept a secret?"

Ramsey sat completely still. I assumed he was too stunned to speak.

"Yes. Please."

"Are you open to a DNA test with your mom—"

"Davia," I said, my voice thick and strained with too many feelings to process.

I looked at Ramsey, and he nodded.

"We can get her toothbrush or hairbrush," he said, speaking for the first time in the conversation.

"Franklin knows a guy that can run a test and have results in less than a day. I can have Franklin call you."

"I'll go to the house this morning." I chewed on my bottom lip, holding back the tears that threatened to erupt. *Dad mentioned he had secrets, but this?* I needed more proof.

"I'll have Franklin set it up, then call you with where and when. In the meantime, I'll see what else I can find. What puzzles me is that I had to jump through a lot of hoops to even discover this much, but Vincent knew. Your dad must have confided in him."

"Thank you for your help," Ramsey said and took my hand and placed a kiss against my palm.

"Hang in there, Avery. And if you need to talk, give me a call," Sutton offered.

"Will do. Thanks." I ended the call and looked at the wall. A few tears escaped my eyes and dripped down my face, and I angrily swiped at them as rage overtook every other emotion. *How could Dad have lied to me about something like this?*

"Sutton doesn't seem like the kind of person that would provide you information before she was sure, but try not to jump to conclusions until the DNA results are back, babe." Ramsey smoothed my hair.

"I'll try, but it's going to be difficult. I'm sorry I didn't tell you about the exchange between Vincent and me. I was going to tell you about it, but I accidentally fell asleep. I slept the entire night and woke up in time for your football game. It fell to the wayside when I thought you were messing around with someone else."

I placed my feet on the floor as Ramsey got up and began to get dressed.

"He said he wasn't paying back the money, then he talked about how good it felt to rape me."

Rage flashed across Ramsey's face, and he balled his hands into fists. "I'm going to bury that goddamned son of a bitch!" Ramsey roared.

I shot off the bed and stared at him. It took a lot to piss him off, but when it did, everyone needed to watch the hell out. He came out swinging.

"I recorded it all on my phone. I'm going to turn him in, Ramsey."

In a few powerful strides, Ramsey stood in front of me. "Let me help you bury this bastard." His tone was full of venom and promise.

"I will. I swear."

Ramsey wrapped his arms around my waist and held me, his heart racing against my ear.

"As much as I want to stay here and hide from the world, I need to get … Mom's DNA." I pulled back. "Whether I like it or not, she's my mother until the DNA says differently."

"We can grab coffee and breakfast at Starbucks on the way to your house. I'll drive."

I tilted my chin up. "I love you, Ramsey Goldman."

"I love you, too, Avery Davenport."

An hour later, Ramsey pulled into my driveway. As a high school graduation gift, his parents had bought him a dark Sapphire Metallic Jaguar XJ three years ago. I was pretty sure he loved his car almost as much as he loved playing football.

Staring at the house, which no longer felt like home, I let out a heavy sigh. "So much has changed in a short amount of time." I kneaded my shoulders, hoping to loosen the tension knotting my muscles.

"I won't lie. My brain is spinning with everything that's happening. Thank god Franklin's helping you."

"I don't know what I'd do without him." My attention returned to the house and I pressed my lips into a tight line. "I have no idea whether she's home. If she is, she's most likely passed out and will never even know we're here."

I reached for the handle and opened the car door.

"Hey." Ramsey grabbed my hand. "I'm in this with you. If Sutton's correct, we'll find out what's going on. Regardless of what we learn, babe. I'm not going anywhere."

I leaned over and kissed him. "Thank you."

THE REST of the day was a complete blur. After Ramsey and I gathered the DNA, he drove me downtown for the test. I paid the doctor extra to speed up the results. I still wasn't expecting anything until the next day, but I could hope.

Ramsey attempted to keep me occupied, but our conversation continued to return to the possibility that Davia wasn't my biological mother. For years, she hadn't even been a decent fucking parent. She had rarely attended my track meets, my debate team competitions, or when my art had been showcased. In my senior year, I'd won the up-and-coming award, and my drawing was displayed for a month at a well-known gallery in downtown Seattle. Dad had never missed an event, especially for my art.

A sharp pang of regret stabbed me in the chest. "I miss drawing and painting," I said around a bite of Mongolian beef. We'd decided to grab dinner downtown at P.F. Chang's.

"When is the last time you drew anything?" Ramsey took a drink of his water then dug into his sweet and sour chicken.

"Honestly, I don't even remember." I frowned and speared a bite off his plate. "It always tastes better when it's on someone else's plate." I covered my mouth and giggled. It felt good, even if it was for a moment.

Ramsey chuckled. "You've done that since we were little. You'd sneak a French fry off my plate when you thought I wasn't looking."

I narrowed my eyes at him. "Are you telling me you knew about it?"

"Your ninja skills were a bit lacking, babe. But I would have given you anything you wanted. All you had to do was ask."

"Where's the fun in that?" I smiled and stole another bite of his dinner.

Ramsey's expression darkened as he laid his fork down. "What are you going to do if the results come back that you're not related to Davia?"

I slouched in my chair, a heavy weight suddenly pressing down hard on my chest. "Confront her. I want to know why. Then … then I want to find out more about my family on my biological mom's side." My statement slapped me full force in the face. "Fuck." I bit my bottom lip and leaned forward, my body pushing against the edge of table. "Ramsey, what do I even do with that? Do I want to meet them? Do I have grandparents? Siblings?" My hands trembled, and my knees bounced up and down, shaking the booth. "Sorry."

"Let's get out of here so we can talk." Ramsey signaled for the waiter.

Minutes later, we had the rest of our food in to-go boxes and headed to Ramsey's apartment. My thoughts swirled around like a twister, and I attempted to sift through the wreckage left behind.

"The waiting is the worst," Ramsey said, keeping his eyes on the road.

My burner phone chirped, and I dared a glance at Ramsey before I rummaged through my handbag and located it.

"Hello?" I answered.

"Avery, this is Dr. Albert Keene. I have your DNA results. Sutton is correct. Davia Davenport isn't your biological mother."

Bile burned the back of my throat, threatening to spill out. "Are you sure?" My voice sounded gruff, closed off even to me.

"I'm sorry, but there's no question. I'll have the report ready for you to pick up tomorrow. Feel free to swing by the front desk. It will be waiting for you."

"Thank you." I blew out a breath and ended the call.

I looked at Ramsey, my vision blurring from the tears collecting in my eyes as he parked his car in front of his apartment building. He turned the car off, released his seatbelt, and faced me.

"This doesn't change who you are," he whispered, cupping my cheeks in his warm, strong hands.

"This changes everything, Ramsey. If Dad lied to me about this, what else did he lie about?"

"I don't know. But for tonight, come upstairs with me, curl up in my lap, and let me love you. You have an answer. There's nothing else you need to do right now."

Panic bubbled inside me. "I might have an answer to my question, but now I have so many more. Ramsey, who am I?"

18

The following day, the early-afternoon sun warmed my back as I punched in the code and opened the heavy front door of my house. Ramsey had offered to come with me to confront Davia in case the situation became explosive, but it was something I had to do on my own.

The house appeared empty. But mom … Davia might have been passed out anywhere, including a closet.

Wrapping my fingers around the leather strap of my handbag, I dug my fingernails into the material. My palms grew clammy while I searched for her. The news that I wasn't her daughter played on repeat in my mind.

The only evidence that Davia had been home was an empty Johnny Walker Red bottle on the kitchen counter. I quietly made my way upstairs. If Davia were coherent, she would have heard the alarm system go off when I'd arrived.

Reaching her and Dad's bedroom, I turned the knob, then eased the door open enough for me to see inside. My nose immediately wrinkled, and I stepped backward as the stench of alcohol and body odor assaulted my nostrils. I massaged my aching temples, walked straight to the windows, and flung the heavy blackout curtains open.

The bright sunshine pierced the room, revealing a crumpled form of a human in the bed. I shook my head while tears burned my eyes. I hadn't been in there since Dad had left us.

I needed to have the housekeeper wash the sheets and drop off the burgundy-and-gold comforter at the dry cleaners. When I spotted one of Dad's watches on his nightstand next to a paperback, a lump formed in my throat. I'd always teased him about reading dry, boring books, but he chuckled and waved me off. I pushed my grief away and welcomed the anger simmering beneath it with open arms.

"Wake up ... Mom." I choked on the word, but I wanted the satisfaction of seeing the look on her face when I told her I knew she wasn't my mother. "Wake up!" I yelled at the top of my lungs.

Davia jerked straight up. Her eyes were bloodshot, and her once-beautiful dark hair was oily and matted to the side of her head. Her black nightgown had twisted around her body, exposing her too-thin frame and fake tits.

"Jesus," I said, approaching the bed and covering her back up. "You're disgusting, and you reek. When is the last time you took a shower?"

Davia wiped the drool from the corner of her mouth and peered at me through heavy lids.

Fuck, she's still wasted.

Folding my arms across my chest, I glared at her. "I know you're not my biological mother. I want answers." My tone was curt and unforgiving.

A sharp cackle escaped her as she flopped back onto her pillow. "You think you know so much." Her head lolled to the side, her unfocused gaze landing on me. "You don't understand shit," she slurred.

Hatred burned through my veins, and I stood over her. "Focus, for a change, and talk to me."

"Oh, Avery." She raised her arm, then it dropped to her side on the mattress. "So tired," she muttered. "Tired of all the lies."

I gritted my teeth as images of my hands around her scrawny little neck flashed through my mind. "What are you talking about?"

"I can't say a word." Davia held her finger against her lips. "Shh." She smiled, then giggled.

"Who was my real mother? Why did you and Dad lie to me all of these years?" My nostrils flared as I eyed something to throw and break. Not only would it make me feel better, but it also might snap her out of her drug-or-alcohol-induced stupor enough to answer me honestly. I spotted the vase Dad had bought her from their trip to Beijing. I wrapped my hand around the narrow neck and hurled it against the wall with all my strength. The high-pitched sound of shattering glass filled the room, and I covered my head with my arms as the shards sprayed in every direction.

"What the fuck?" Davia sat up, her eyes wide with fear.

"Why did Dad lie to me?" I asked again.

"Avery?" She rubbed her forehead, her attention bouncing between the pieces of broken glass and me.

"I know you're not my mother, Davia. Why did Dad lie to me for all of these years?" I placed my hands on my hips, my chest heaving from the escalation of fury rolling to a boil inside me.

Davia shook her head, her body trembling. "I … I can't."

I approached the bed, rested one knee on the side of the mattress, and leaned over her. "Pack your shit and get out of my house," I spat.

"You can't do that." Davia scrambled out from beneath the blankets and stumbled to the floor.

"I can. You're not my mother, and the house belongs to me. Dad made sure of it."

"I'm his wife. You can't kick me out," Davia sputtered.

"You have other homes he left you. Don't act like I'm treating you poorly." I turned away from her. The sight of her crawling on the floor, searching for who knew what disgusted me. Before I realized what I'd done, I hurried to her, jerked her up by her arm, and sat her down on the bed. "You're going into treatment, or I'll cut you off from every penny. You know Dad left me in charge of the finances. You have two houses and cars you can sell if you need to. I'm not watching you ruin your life anymore." I opened her closet, pulled out a suitcase, and tossed it onto the top of her dresser. "And while I have your attention, you were a pathetic excuse of a mother."

"Avery, no, please. Don't do this," she whined as she eyed the medication bottle on her nightstand.

I barked out a laugh and snatched up the pills. "Oh, I'm doing it, all right. You can take a shower before you go, or I will throw a robe around your shoulders and drag you down the stairs by your disgusting hair."

She patted her hair and frowned. "I'll get cleaned up."

"Excellent. You won't stink up my car, then. Hurry up. I have places to be."

I packed more of her items, a sense of calm hovering at the edge of my mind. I should have kicked her out the day she waltzed back into the house after missing Dad's funeral, but it had been too much to manage, and I wasn't sure how much more I could handle. At least I didn't have to deal with her anymore.

The sound of the shower running reached my ears, and I rummaged through every drawer, nook, and cranny of her bedroom for her stash of drugs and alcohol. By the time I was finished, twelve bottles of pills and a couple of eight balls of cocaine were scattered across her comforter. I shook my head, my stomach curdling. I grabbed her trash can and threw them all away, then hurried to my room, where I hid it in the closet. She didn't have the clarity of mind to look in there, which would allow me to safely dispose of it later.

I returned to her room and entered the bathroom. "Are you done?" I crossed my arms over my chest and leaned against the white counter.

"Can't a girl enjoy a little hot water?"

"For fuck's sake." I opened the shower door to find her curled up in the corner with her head leaning against the wall. It wasn't the only instance I'd had to clean her up. The first time was when I was twelve, and Dad had been away for a week on a business trip. She'd begged me not to tell him. I was too young to have realized I should have let him walk in on her so trashed that she couldn't stand up, but I hadn't. I was as guilty of covering our family secrets as he was.

Even though it was a futile move, I removed the showerhead from the base and tilted it away from me so I wouldn't get soaked while I cleaned her up.

What would Dad say if he could see us now? His note flashed through my mind. He'd said that no matter what I learned, he loved me. My throat tightened as I mentally scanned the contents of the pages again.

"Davia," I said, rinsing the shampoo from her hair. "Did you ever find a letter in Dad's office that was addressed to me?"

"Mm-hmm. He was going to tell you." She looked up at me through glassy eyes. "He would have ruined everything, if he had."

My hands dropped to my sides. Water from the spray had soaked my jeans and plastered them to my thighs. "Did you smudge it on purpose?" My voice hovered above a whisper.

"Nope. I spilled my drink on it." She giggled and reached out to touch me. "But I suspect you know now, so it doesn't matter. Your real mom is dead."

"What else?" I asked, hope that she might be sober enough to tell me more rising in my chest.

"Honey, you weren't the only one in the dark. Steven never told me the entire story. When we dated, he mentioned he had a daughter. You were only ten months old. I ..." She gulped, her eyes filling with an emotion I hadn't seen from her in years—love. "You were so beautiful." She reached out and touched my damp hair. "We had similar features, so it was easy to hide the fact that I hadn't given birth to you. You were... are still my daughter, Avery." She dropped her arm to her naked lap, then she curled into herself and sobbed.

BEFORE DAVIA and I left the house, I called Ramsey and updated him on my conversation with her. He'd wanted me to meet him at his place later, but I needed to clean up the mess I'd made in Dad's room, so we agreed that he would come over later. Plus, I wanted to sleep in my own bed that night.

After I dropped Davia off at a posh and discreet rehab center in Idaho, I wasn't sure whether my heart ached even more, or if I was relieved. At least I didn't have to deal with her for a while. Although she could check herself out, I had explained to her several times that she wouldn't receive any more money if she left. I doubted it had stuck in her addled brain, so I would have to tell her again when we spoke on the phone. For the first week, she could have no visitors or calls, which worked out well for me. I needed a break from babysitting.

At eight that evening, Ramsey rang the doorbell.

"Hey," I said, pulling him inside and wrapping my arms around his neck. "You're the best thing I've seen all day."

He pressed a kiss to my mouth, and I sighed.

"I'm glad you've hit the pause button with Davia, but I also hope she takes the help." He took my hand in his and led me to the kitchen.

"She was a fucking mess when I found her." I frowned as I recalled her drugged up and unable to hold a conversation. It shouldn't have bothered me. I'd seen it a thousand times before. But something in me had snapped.

Ramsey patted a barstool, and I sat down at the counter. "I'm making you a good stiff drink." He winked at me. "If it's all right, I'm going to join you."

"That sounds amazing." I stretched my arm across the cool-to-the-touch granite, then laid my head down and watched him. Since we had turned sixteen, he'd made drinks in that kitchen more times than I could count. The parents didn't care if we drank alcohol as long as we were with them. I was sure they realized we drank at parties and friend's houses, but they never said anything. We were careful not to come home sloppy drunk either.

"I can hear you thinking." Ramsey made a vodka and lemonade for me—well, mostly vodka with a splash of lemonade.

"I'm wondering if I'll end up a lush like Davia. Lately, I've drank because I can't handle my feelings." Tugging at my collar, I cleared my throat. "More than that, she said Dad kept her in the dark too."

"Babe, you're not going to end up like Davia. Cut yourself some slack." Ramsey placed the glass on the counter and sat down next to me. "Do you believe that she doesn't know about your Dad's past?"

I took a big drink before I responded. "I think she was as honest as she could be at the time. She was wasted, so her recollection of any events was hazy at best. I do suspect Dad shut her out. I don't understand why, though."

Ramsey rubbed my back, his brows knitting together. "I'm guessing she doesn't know any more than what she shared. Besides, she's used for so many years, who knows what's true or not? I think you can trust Sutton to find out who your bio mom is, then see if you want to reach out to that side of your family."

I took a long drink, allowing the liquid balm to seep into every nook and cranny of my being. I welcomed the hazy feeling along with a renewed sense of determination. "What would you do if you were in my position?"

Ramsey steepled his fingers together and held my gaze. "I would wait and see what Sutton learns, and afterward, I would consider whether I wanted to meet them. It's difficult to answer, until you know who they are. What if you have an aunt that's in prison for murder or some shit? I don't think you'd be rushing to visit her."

"Oh hell no." I tilted my glass back and drained it dry. "Damn, that felt good. If I tell you what a hottie you are and play with your penis, will you make me another one?" I gave him a sexy wink and laughed.

Ramsey laughed so hard that his chest shook, his eyes dancing with amusement. "I will make you another one, and you don't have to ask. My penis is yours whenever you want it."

"Oh my god. I'm really tipsy already. And what kind of word is penis?"

Ramsey flashed me a huge grin. "Vagina isn't any better."

"Oh no." I wagged my finger at him. "It's way worse."

Ramsey brought me another glass, and I immediately took a gulp. "I don't want to feel anything right now, Ramsey. Does the fact that I'm hiding behind the alcohol make me a bad person?"

"No. It means you're exhausted and need a break."

I leaned my forehead on the counter, then looked at him. "I hope

Sutton can find out more soon. I want to put this entire shit show behind me and move on." I snorted. "Move on." I propped my head on my fist. "How do you move on after your father has been murdered and you learn your mother isn't really your mother?"

"One step at a time, babe. For now, let's get you tucked in for the night. You're about to fall asleep."

"Are you staying with me?" I slipped off the chair, my body feeling like a limp noodle. After the day's events, I hadn't realized how exhausted I was until right then.

"I hoped I was." He gathered our glasses, rinsed them out, and loaded them in the dishwasher.

"I hate to say it, but my bed is so much better than yours." I snickered.

Ramsey's hand flew to his chest as he pretended that I'd insulted him. "Harsh words. Harsh words." He strolled toward me, then spun around and bent down. "Piggyback ride?"

"Yes!" I hopped onto his back, and he wrapped his arms around my legs. He took off running through the house, our laughter filling the air. Ramsey darted up the stairs, and I giggled into his ear. I couldn't remember the last time I'd laughed so hard.

Once we were in my room, he dumped me onto the bed and banged his chest as if it were a drum.

"Stop," I begged while another fit of giggles erupted from me. "Oh my god, I can't breathe."

Ramsey collapsed beside me, and we began to settle down. His gorgeous blue eyes searched my face and his expression grew serious. "You're so beautiful when you laugh."

I scrunched up my nose. "I sound like a hyena."

Ramsey chuckled. "I don't know where you got that idea, but I would have definitely given you shit about it if that were true."

"Yeah. You would have." I placed my hand on his arm and allowed myself to get lost in his gaze. "I love you, Ramsey."

He rolled onto his side and kissed me. "Every time you say it, my heart soars. Avery ..." His lips brushed across mine again. "Let's leave town for a few days. I can ask Dad when we can borrow the plane."

"That sounds like heaven, but I have classes and ... work." My stomach plummeted at the thought of seeing Vincent again at the office. Since I hadn't graduated yet, I wasn't at the business full time, but I wanted my presence to be known.

"You own the company. Call in and take a day off." He trailed feather-light kisses down my neck.

"What about football practice?" I moaned as he slid his hand beneath my shirt and cupped my breast.

"We finished two-a-days, and we're given a free weekend before normal training resumes. Let's go."

"You're not playing fair," I said, reaching for his jeans. Once I'd unbuttoned them, I didn't waste any time wrapping my fingers around his hard cock.

He ground his hips against my hold. "We can stay in bed all day and make love. I can bring you breakfast and eat you while you eat your eggs and bacon."

I laughed. "I doubt I would be focused on the food, unless you offered me a lollipop." I stroked him, emphasizing my meaning. "Maybe I should sample it now, though." I pushed his shoulder, and he rolled onto his back. I tugged his jeans down, and his erection bobbed free. I darted my tongue across my bottom lip as anticipation coursed through my body. "Relax," I said, my voice sultry.

Ramsey leaned his head back and placed his hands on my shoulders, and I rubbed his dick across my moistened lips. I licked the precum from the tip, then eased his entire length into my mouth. Stroking and sucking at the same time, I glanced up at him. He tilted his hips slightly as he threaded his fingers through my hair. I worshipped every inch of him, my desire growing stronger with his every moan and sigh.

"I need to taste you. Get naked and come here." He patted his chest.

I quickly discarded my clothes in the middle of the floor and joined him again. Before I realized it, Ramsey had turned me around and sat me on his face. I leaned over, my breasts grazing his stomach as I trailed kisses up and down his shaft.

"Mmm." I ran my tongue up and down the length of him while I rocked against him. In one quick move, I slid him between my teeth and to the back of my throat. Picking up the pace, I stroked him as my saliva slickened his skin. He bucked his hips, and I sucked harder, returning the same intensity he was showing my body.

I popped him out of my mouth and focused on his balls. His body tightened. My guy was close, but so was I. I wasn't sure how much longer I could hold out. He must have thought the same, because he pulled away from me and pushed on my hip. I faced him and eased him into me.

"Does it feel better without a condom?" I leaned over, riding him.

"You have no idea. You're so hot and goddammed wet." A low, guttural growl burst from his throat while he slammed into me, digging his fingers into the flesh of my ass cheeks.

I shifted my angle, and my hypersensitive clit rubbed against him as we found our rhythm.

With a few more deep thrusts, he poured himself into me, triggering my orgasm. My eyes shut as my body shuddered with intense pleasure.

I collapsed onto him, and his arms immediately encircled me.

"I could stay this way forever," he whispered, smoothing my hair.

"Me too." I relaxed against him, reveling in his touch. Seconds later, I sat up and placed my palms against his warm chest.

"Is something wrong?" he asked, still inside me.

"No, not at all, but I need to tell you something."

19

—————

I eased off of him and mentally debated how I should approach the conversation.

"I realize we've known each other our entire lives, but I'm a businesswoman. I definitely take after Dad." I stood and collected my shirt and jeans and dressed while I continued, thanking the universe once again that I didn't share DNA with Davia. At least I had a choice whether or not to have her in my life. We weren't related, so I no longer felt as though I owed her anything. Honestly, even if we had been related, I didn't owe her. Shit behavior didn't earn anyone a relationship with me. I didn't care who they were. I swatted away the thoughts concerning her. She was in rehab, and I had a life to figure out.

"An opportunity came up, and now that we're dating and planning a future together, I wanted to tell you about it." I placed my hands on my hips. "But make no mistake, Ramsey Goldman. I'm not asking your permission. I'm respecting you as the man I love and opening communication about it."

Ramsey sat up, his ab muscles rippling with each move and making me lose my train of thought. Instead of talking, I wanted to run my tongue across every valley and plane of his stomach.

"Understood." His forehead creased slightly. I suspected he was trying to assess the situation before I shared it with him.

I pinched the bridge of my nose and continued. "I'm going to buy The Lily." There, I'd said it.

Ramsey's mouth gaped, then closed. "What?" he asked, running his hand through his hair while his expression morphed from shock to utter confusion.

"It's going to close. The owner wants to sell it and retire, which I understand. Skyler and I are going to buy in as partners."

Ramsey narrowed his eyes slightly as he hopped out of bed and collected his clothes from the floor. Tugging on his sweatshirt and jeans, he remained silent. I knew him well enough to realize that he was collecting his thoughts before he opened his mouth. That was another thing I loved so much about him. He actually thought before he spoke the majority of the time.

"Are you leaving Davenport and McCade Financials?" He buttoned and zipped his pants, then folded his arms across his chest and leaned against the wall.

"Why would you think I would leave?" I sank onto the edge of the mattress. He was acting coy, and I wondered what his angle was.

"Have you considered that this would put not only you in jeopardy, but also the company? That if The Lily was ever investigated, you would go to prison?"

"You don't understand. Maybe most men wouldn't, but it's more than the sex for these women. I mean, that's one hell of a perk, but … the members gain confidence. They feel treasured, and they have the power to say no to a relationship if it's only about getting laid. Some of the women there have left abusive relationships. One member beat breast cancer, but she lost her hair and had reconstructive surgery. She was thin and didn't have any confidence left. The Lily gave her all of that back. Babe, it's so much more."

Ramsey walked toward me, then dropped to his knees and gazed up at me through his thick, dark eyelashes. "I love you so much."

My heart pitter-pattered against my ribcage. "I love you too."

He took my hands in his and brushed a soft kiss across my knuckles. "I love how special The Lily is to you. It certainly brought us together." He cracked a huge smile.

"It did." I flashed him a big grin, mentally revisiting that day with him.

"I need to ask you, though. Is it worth spending years of your life behind bars? You would be running an illegal operation, babe. You would also upend Davenport and McCade Financials. It would fall into the hands of Vincent. We wouldn't be together, and everything you've ever dreamed of would be lost."

An anxious, fluttery feeling descended on me. I didn't want The Lily to close, even though I was going to cancel my membership, since Ramsey and I were together.

"Is there anyone else that can buy it and keep it open?"

I gave him a half shrug, feeling defeated, but he had a point. I couldn't take a chance with my life and happiness. The risk was too high. "I could provide a business loan to Skyler. She really wants The Lily."

"You certainly have the means. Plus, you would only be loaning her the money for the women's clothing store. If she ever got caught, your name would be clear." He hesitated briefly. "Babe, I'm sorry. I want to be supportive, but I can't lose you. When it comes to having you in my life, I'm going to be selfish, so know that's how it's going to be. I don't mean you can't be the strong, independent woman I love, but don't buy The Lily. I also don't want to live our lives constantly looking over our shoulders. We're living that way right now, and it fucking sucks."

"Yes, it does. I'll see if Skyler is available for lunch to discuss everything. She needs to know that if The Lily ever got searched, I'm not going to acknowledge it or what the business loan was for. That's only fair. I guess with my emotions running high with Dad's death and my stalker, I wasn't thinking it all of the way through."

"I agree, but don't beat yourself up over it. We're partners, babe. This is why it's a good idea that we discuss big decisions, so we can offer each other different opinions." Ramsey stood and cupped my chin. "I will always be grateful for the part The Lily played in bringing us together. And you know I support the idea. Hell, I worked there for … one client." A sheepish smile slipped into place as he pulled me up and against him. "You turned me inside out, and I had to quit."

I gave him a playful smile. "You're mine now." I pushed up on my tiptoes and pressed a kiss to his mouth.

I STROLLED into the small but cozy Hometown Café a few minutes before two o'clock. One of the reasons I loved it there was the rustic décor, and Spokane and Washington's history was displayed on the walls with framed maps and information and stories about the first settlers. I scanned the room and selected a booth in the back corner, then I slid into the seat and faced the front of the restaurant.

Spotting Skyler enter, I waved to her.

"Do you ever look bad?" I laughed, standing to hug her.

She pushed her glasses up on her nose, then smoothed her designer bootcut jeans. "Thank you. That's super sweet of you."

"I don't think I've ever seen you in anything other than a dress or a skirt. I bet your ass looks fantastic in those." I wiggled my eyebrows at her.

She sank into the seat across from me and placed her purse next to her. "How are you? I'm sure it's difficult, trying to adjust after losing your dad." She reached out for my hand and squeezed it.

"I'm pretty lost without him." My gaze traveled to the picture window and down the street, where I spotted Tad talking on the phone. He blended in well in jeans and a long-sleeved button-down. His red hair was the only thing easy to identify. Most of the time, I didn't see him at all, and my stomach filled with dread. *Has he seen someone following me?*

"How is Ramsey doing?" Skyler asked.

My attention landed on her again. "He's grieving over Dad, but now that we're together …"

Skyler clapped, and her smile lit up her entire face. "I'm so thrilled to hear it."

A heated flush worked its way up my neck and across my cheeks. "It's amazing. I'm so happy with him. It all clicked when I finally admitted I might be in love with him. It was like the flood gates opened, and all of these intense feelings I had for him showed up."

"You deserve to be with someone who worships you. When he quit The Lily, I knew he only wanted to be with you."

"Really?" I asked, squirming and slightly giddy. I wondered if I would ever grow tired of hearing how much he loved me.

"Girl, yes."

Our waitress placed glasses of water in front of us, and I ordered a club sandwich and a soda. Skyler selected the Caesar salad.

"Listen, I need to talk some business with you." My tone was hushed, but we were alone in the back corner, so I wasn't very concerned that someone would overhear us.

"I have some paperwork for you." She dug around in her bag, then produced a manila envelope and slid it to me.

Regardless of whether I was a partner or provided the loan, I needed to see the financials. "Thank you." I pulled the papers out and fell silent as I reviewed the information, including the projections and growth. "Wow. These numbers are remarkable." I peeked up at Skyler.

"I agree. She's a multimillionaire off this alone."

"And a damned good businesswoman. This is very impressive." I finished reading the documents, then flipped them facedown onto the table.

The waitress delivered our food, and I made room for my plate. I hadn't realized how hungry I was until the smell of the mouthwatering carbs tickled my nose. Taking a bite of my sandwich, I took a moment to collect my thoughts. Although I didn't need the money, it was a fantastic investment, and my fingers twitched to sign papers that allowed me to be part owner.

"When we talked about being partners, Ramsey and I weren't together yet. This morning, I discussed the idea with him because it was the right thing to do."

Skyler's face fell, and she set her fork down. A piece of lettuce hung off a prong. "He doesn't want you to buy it, does he?" She grabbed a napkin and dabbed the corners of her mouth. "I understand, Avery. I do. It's amazing money, but it's a high-risk investment."

"He doesn't want us having to look over our shoulders. If anything … if, for any reason, there was suspicion of …" Even though we had some privacy, I didn't want to say it out loud. "I want to provide the business loan for you instead."

Skyler's eyebrows shot up to her hairline. "It would be all mine?"

"Yes. I think you'll do an amazing job too. But I can't be anywhere near it." I played with my straw. "The loan will be for the clothing store. If anything happens, I'll deny any knowledge of the upstairs activities," I said, my voice barely hovering above a whisper. "Those are the conditions."

Skyler assessed me with her big brown eyes before she spoke. "I would do the same, Avery. Besides, you have your dad's business now. You can't risk losing it."

A sigh of relief escaped my lips. "Are you sure? I thought you might be upset."

"Are you kidding? It would be mine. Oh my god, Avery, thank you so much!" Her hand fluttered to her chest. "I've always dreamed of owning it. Some things, I will keep the same, and others, I'll change."

I offered her a big smile. "I have no doubt in my mind that you will make it a huge success."

"Thank you … for believing in me. I realize that you won't be a member any longer. Well, I'm assuming now that you and Ramsey are together, you won't be. But one of the changes I want to make is offering our services to couples and not just women. It will be slightly different, but it will still offer a variety of rooms and scenarios with your partner. It would be an entirely separate part of the building from where the women book sessions. So once that's available, I'll give you a free membership, if you and Ramsey want to indulge."

"Oh, hell yes." I threw my head back and laughed. "I think it's an awesome idea."

Over the next hour, Skyler shared her vision with me. Deep down, I knew I'd made the right decision. She deserved an opportunity that not only would make her very wealthy, but was also something she believed in.

My phone buzzed with a text message from Ramsey. *Dad said we can have the plane to fly to the Hamptons this weekend. What do you think?*

"Ramsey wants to take me to the vacation house that our families share in the Hamptons. We have a lot of great memories there."

"That sounds lovely. I'm sure it would help you to have a change of scenery." She took a sip of her water and pushed her salad bowl to the side of the table.

"I think so, but this will be the first time I'll be there without Dad. It will be hard." I gulped over a sudden lump in my throat, grief threatening to push my emotions over the edge. "Losing Dad hits me out of nowhere sometimes. I think I'm doing all right, then it bull-dozes right over me, leaving me flailing, trying to find my footing again." My hand flew to my chest as a sharp pang stabbed me.

"Be good to yourself, Avery. It's going to take time. When you have those minutes or days that you're feeling good, don't beat yourself up about it. Embrace it."

"Thanks. I will." I checked the clock on my cell. "I have to go, but let's meet a few times a month to catch up."

"I would love to." Skyler slipped the strap of her purse onto her shoulder. "I'm only a phone call away if you need me."

"I appreciate it. My lawyer will draw up the loan papers this week, so contact the owner and make the offer." I paused. "And Skyler, I'm really proud of you for making The Lily such an amazing, safe place for women. More than that, I'm grateful for our friendship." I stood and smoothed my royal-blue blouse.

"That means so much to me." Skyler embraced me and we said our goodbyes as she excused herself to go to the ladies' room.

I exited the café, and the bright afternoon sunshine temporarily blinded me. I held my hand to my forehead, shading my eyes, then remembered I needed to respond to Ramsey, so I tapped out a quick text message asking for dates so I could clear my calendar.

Breathing in the crisp autumn air, I rubbed my arms against the brisk chill. I chided myself for not bringing a coat. I'd lived in Washington most of my life, and like clockwork, the beginning of October ushered in freezing temperatures at night and low fifties during the day.

"Excuse me, miss."

A tug on my fingers pulled my attention to a young boy in front of me. His tousled dark hair hung in his big brown eyes.

"Hi there. Are you lost?" I asked.

"No, my mom is in the store, waiting for me." He held up a long white envelope in his gloved hands. "I was told to give this to you."

I frowned, but accepted it. "Who asked you to give it to me?"

"I don't know. No one I knew, but they gave my mom some money."

An eerie feeling consumed me. There was nothing normal about the situation, and I intuitively knew it was my stalker. I glanced around us and noticed Tad was on the same side of the street as we were.

"Was it a man or a woman?" I asked, realizing it might be the first clue to who was after me.

"Can't say." The little boy swung his jacketed arms back and forth like a helicopter.

"You're good at keeping secrets, aren't you?" I knelt in order to make eye contact with him. "What can I give you to make you share with me. Candy?"

He giggled. "I love candy, but nope. Mom said if I told you, I would be sent straight to bed tonight without dinner."

I wrinkled my nose. "A growing boy like you definitely needs to eat. Can you take me to your mom?"

He twisted his cute little face up as he considered my question.

The Eastern Washington sun warmed me while I hoped and prayed that the young boy would help me. "What's your name?"

"Caden."

"Oh, I love that name. What do you think about taking me to meet your mom?" I held out my hand to him.

He backed away, shaking his head. "I have to go now." Before I could say another word, he took off running in the other direction.

Searching the crowded sidewalk for who the deliverer might be, I opened the letter.

I can get to you anywhere.

All the tiny hairs on the back of my neck lifted while I slid the note back inside the envelope. Pierce would need it as evidence. Sutton could look for fingerprints. Maybe my stalker and Dad's killer had just fucked up and delivered their DNA to me.

Son of a bitch. I shoved it into my purse as a wave of intense nausea swept over me. Doubling over with stomach cramps, I dropped to my knees on the unforgiving sidewalk. *What is happening?* A halo formed around my vision, and I squinted against the stabbing pain in my head.

"Coming through!" a deep voice boomed through the crowd.

"You got her?" Tad yelled.

I couldn't respond. I placed my hand on the concrete, willing my head to clear, but it was no use. Gasping, I felt my pulse kick into overdrive while fear wrapped its cold fingers around my throat.

"Help!" I gasped. My limbs refused to obey me any longer, growing more rigid by the minute.

"Avery," came a whisper at the edge of my mind called. "I'm Zayne. I'm one of Pierce's men. Tad called me an hour ago to help keep an eye on you from another direction in case our guy has caught onto him. Good thing he trusts his instincts. Tad is with us now, and he called 911. An ambulance is on the way."

An anguished cry pricked my eardrums—my cry.

A shrill siren filled the air as black dots floated across my vision. Somehow, I realized a crowd was gathering around us, but I couldn't decipher what anyone was saying. Warm arms wrapped around me, and I was hoisted onto a stretcher. My mind was suddenly plagued with memories of the car accident that had ripped my father away from me—the gurney, the hospital, my mother screaming at me, and my dad dying.

Agonizing pain shot through my body, and I cried out one more time before everything around me faded to black.

My eyes fluttered open to find three terrified faces staring at me. Rubbing my forehead, I attempted to adjust to the bright light that streamed through the picture window. I blinked rapidly, willing my blurry vision to clear.

"Babe, you're in the hospital. I'm right here along with Tensley and Benji. You're going to be okay, but you scared the shit out of us." Ramsey kissed the back of my hand. Fear was evident in his handsome features.

"What happened?" Dread seeped into my bones as I recalled the little boy talking to me, then doubling over in the worst pain I'd experienced in my life.

"The doctor said you were poisoned," someone with a deep voice interjected.

Benji and Tensley moved to the side and allowed Pierce Westbrook to approach me.

"Poisoned?" I asked, exhaustion suddenly taking over my body. My attention bounced to a policewoman and Franklin, who were standing at the foot of my bed.

"Yes. It was strychnine." Pierce's brows furrowed.

"Shit." I placed my palm against my forehead. "The envelope."

"What is he talking about?" Ramsey asked.

"How could I have been so fucking naïve?" Tears welled in my eyes as I realized that my stalker hadn't provided me with any clues of who they were. They'd tried to kill me, or at least make me seriously ill.

"A little boy brought me an envelope. He had gloves on, which I didn't think anything about. It's cold today, and I figured his mom had dressed him well. It's in my purse."

"I'm Officer Blakely, Avery. We'll gather your purse for evidence. Since the letter has poison on it, you won't get the handbag back."

"Okay. I have other purses at home. I just need my phone."

"I've got it, hon. It was in your back pocket." Ten held it up for me to see.

"Back to the little boy. What did he say to you?" Pierce folded his arms across his massive chest, a combination of anger and curiosity flickering in his expression.

Ramsey gently squeezed my fingers and stroked the back of my hand with the pad of his thumb, soothing my displeasure with myself.

"He said that someone asked him to give me the letter. I tried to get him to tell me who they were, but the little guy refused. For being so young, he knew how to keep his mouth shut."

"He was probably threatened that if he deviated from the plan, his sibling or parent would be harmed," Pierce explained. "It happens all the time."

"What did the note say?" Ramsey asked.

I shook my head, my level of my stupidity disgusting me. "It said, *I can get to you anywhere.*"

Silence fell between us. It was heavy and loud, or maybe it seemed that way.

"Avery, don't beat yourself up over this. Most people would have accepted an envelope from an adult they didn't know. No one would have suspected a young man."

I nodded, still struggling to process what had happened.

Pierce rubbed his slightly stubbled chin. "Avery, having security following you isn't enough anymore. Tad was discovered, and he real-ized it, so he called in Zayne to help. He was down the street in the opposite direction, keeping an eye on you. He got to you in time, but the fact that it was so easy … we're dealing with someone conniving. We have to step up our plan."

"So what do we need to do?" Ramsey asked, his voice shaking slightly.

"First, don't talk to anyone you don't know, and you need to stay put at your place. Call in sick to work, don't travel, and don't meet friends for lunch," Pierce said, his tone firm.

"What? I'm going to let this fucker win?" I scooted up in the bed, suddenly rejuvenated by the anger that was tearing me apart from the inside out. "They killed my father. I refuse to let them tear my world apart any more than it already is."

"If you don't want them to, then you need to listen to me. We'll have security around your house, and we'll make our presence known. The discreet route didn't pan out. Tad has a military background, and he's had to sneak up on the enemy plenty of times. He's highly trained. We all are, but since he was identified, it tells me your stalker knows what they're doing. We're not dealing with an amateur. This period won't last long, but it's necessary. If you're isolated it allows us to focus on finding the threat," Pierce said.

"Babe, I know you don't like it, but you can work from home as well as finish classes online. Please. You could stay with me, but I don't have a security system like you do at your house."

I collapsed onto the hard and lumpy hospital pillow. My jaw clenched while I analyzed my options. It didn't look like I had any if I wanted to be safe.

"Do this for me," Ramsey said, his beautiful blue eyes pleading with me.

Tensley and Benji stared at me, waiting for me to make the right choice. I realized they would all be worried sick about me if I didn't hole up in the house until everything was resolved, and I couldn't do that to them. Plus I didn't want to die, and the stalker had proved they could get to me easily. If I didn't do what Pierce was asking me to do, I might join my father sooner than I was ready to.

"Okay, but I've got to be able to get outside. I need some sunshine and fresh air at least." I pursed my lips.

"You have the swimming pool area," Ramsey suggested.

"Yeah. I can sit out there," I sighed, mentally admitting defeat.

"Is it closed in?" Pierce asked.

"No, it's an outdoor pool with a fence."

"When you're out there, one of my men will stand watch. You're going to have to get used to someone guarding the perimeter all the time." Pierce paused. "A minimum of two will be on the property."

"I won't be with her twenty-four, seven, but I'll be with her as much as I can." Ramsey squeezed my hand.

"We'll be in and out too," Benji added. "At least your guys know us already."

"Who else might be in and out of the house, Avery?" Pierce asked. "We need to know who to expect so that no one can slip past us."

"Davia, but I don't expect her for a while. She's in rehab." I searched my addled brain for anyone else. "Michael and Marilyn and Patrick and Olivia, Ramsey's parents, and Layne. I guess I can have food and groceries delivered to the house. I'll also give Gladys, our housekeeper, time off. I don't want her in the middle of this." I groaned and slapped my hands over my face. "I can't believe this is happening."

"Only for a little bit, but I swear we'll be visiting all the time. Besides, it's not like we can go long without seeing you," Tensley said, smiling.

"I'll have my men in place before you arrive home tonight. And Avery, I'm glad that you're okay. You gave us all a scare." Pierce shook hands with Ramsey, Benji, and Tensley before he left.

Before I could express my fear and frustration concerning the situation, Ramsey leaned over and pressed his mouth to mine. "I thought I'd lost you," he whispered, his minty breath fanning across my heated skin. "I know you hate this, but it will be over soon. Promise me that you won't try to sneak out on your own."

I placed my palm against his cheek. My pulse spiked at the thought of something happening and not being able to touch him or tell him I loved him again. "I promise. For you."

"We'll still visit the Hamptons after all of this is over. It will give us something to look forward to."

"That sounds fantastic. I can't wait."

Ramsey pulled me to him, and he rubbed my back with his large hands while he nuzzled his nose into my hair.

"I love you," I said softly.

"Love you, too, babe."

"Thank you, guys, for being here. If I'm honest, that was some scary shit. I don't want to ever experience that again."

⚜

It was nearly eleven that evening when Ramsey took me home. He'd left the hospital briefly in order to grab clean clothes and toiletries to keep at my place. My heart warmed with the thought of him having some of his belongings there.

After a hot shower, I slipped into one of Ramsey's soft T-shirts. I was ready for a good night's sleep next to him, but I wasn't sure my mind would stop spinning long enough to let me rest.

"I've not had a chance to ask you if you told your parents that we're together. Taking off for a few days to the vacation house isn't anything unusual. I mean, we've had trips with only the two of us before."

I turned down the blankets and slid beneath them, watching him undress and step into black sweatpants. Ramsey moved with a powerful grace, and I assumed it was all his years playing football.

He gave me a lopsided grin. "True, but all those were ploys to make you fall in love with me."

I laughed and snuggled underneath the covers. "It worked."

Ramsey placed a gentle kiss on my lips. "Yes, I told them. I hope that was all right."

"It is. Well, if they took it well, it is." To my surprise, I was nervous

172

about how they'd reacted to the news. "What did they say?" I bit my bottom lip, waiting impatiently.

"You don't want to know." His expression grew serious, his voice low.

"They're not okay with it?" My breath hitched. They were like parents to me, and since I no longer had any, I wanted and needed their approval. I was madly in love with their son, and it had never occurred to me they might have a problem with it.

"It's okay, babe. It's not changing my mind about you." He kissed my forehead, then my cheek. "They asked me when we were getting married," he whispered into my ear.

"Ramsey Goldman! You …" I smacked him on the arm as he threw his head back and laughed. "Dammit, you scared me."

"I'm sorry. I really wasn't sure you wanted to know what they said, but you immediately went to a dark place instead of them rushing us to the altar."

He rolled onto his back, then wrapped his arm around me. The warmth of his skin soothed me, scattering my fears concerning our future and the only family I had left.

"You're not screwing with me? They really asked when we were getting married?" I peered up at him.

"They asked me what took us so long to figure out what they'd seen since we were sixteen."

I propped up on my elbow. "Did you tell them it took mind-blowing sex at The Lily to bring us together?" I snickered, imagining the look of horror on Patrick and Olivia's faces.

Ramsey chuckled. "That would be a big hell no, but they're excited for us. They asked how you were doing, so I explained the stalker, that Steven's death wasn't an accident, and that you had full-time security, and so did I. They freaked, babe." Ramsey's gaze drifted away from me, then returned. "Mom and Dad offered to move in with us here, but I told them you needed some space to process everything, get some work done, and finish your classes. I realize I probably jumped to a conclusion, so I can call them back if you want them here."

I hesitated, thinking through my options. "No, you're right. I do need some downtime. The house is safe and quiet, and I've not had that in a while. I suspect I'll get some projects done and some deep cleaning, and maybe I'll sift through some of Dad's things to donate. I need to clean out the pool house too. Maybe I can talk you into taking them to Goodwill when I'm done."

"Yeah, I can do that. If you want me to help with Steven's things, I will. Otherwise, I'm going to give you some space, so you'll have to let me know what you need."

"Some days, I don't know what I need." I placed my head on his chest again and curled up next to him. "I'm just trying to survive at this point."

Ramsey rubbed my arm, soothing my anxiety and fear.

"Ramsey, I keep … I don't think Vincent is my stalker. He's an asshole, but I don't think it's him."

"I was thinking the same thing. What happened today didn't seem like something he would do. He would rather torment and scare you while you're in the office. He lives on that kind of drama, but not lacing a letter with poison and involving a little kid."

"I agree. It doesn't feel right. It's someone else. I can't help but think it's someone close to me. Maybe someone Dad pissed off, but why? What did Dad do that got him killed?"

Ramsey kissed the top of my head. "I don't know yet, but I suspect we're going to find out soon."

"Me too."

2 1

The following morning, Ramsey left for school, and I made a large pot of coffee and settled in at the kitchen table with my laptop and a different purse next to me. It never failed that I needed an item in my handbag when it was clear across the house.

My mind continued to play the envelope situation over and over. A niggling thought toyed with me, but it was in the back of my brain, and I couldn't figure out what I'd seen or what I was reaching for. For the moment, I had plenty to focus on and stay busy.

The doorbell chimed a little after ten. Frowning, I hopped up from my chair and hurried to answer it. No one would be able to go in or out without the security guys letting them in, so I assumed it was someone I knew. I pushed up on my tiptoes and peered through the peephole with one eye. A huge grin eased across my face as I smoothed my hair and adjusted my sweater and jeans. In order to continue good habits while homebound, I'd showered and applied makeup, like I would have if I were off to school or work.

I opened the door and waved Sutton into the house.

"I hope it's okay that I dropped by. I wanted to check on how things were working out." She patted me on the arm. "How are you feeling this morning?"

"I don't know, honestly. Physically, I'm fine, thanks to Zayne."

"Tad made a good call. I know we were in a difficult spot since we didn't want to tip off the stalker that you had contacted us for help, but it backfired."

"I don't think it did, Sutton. I might be dead already if they had known any sooner." I paused briefly. "What I don't understand is why they haven't hired a hit man … person. It's like they're enjoying tormenting me." I stared out the window, attempting to control an emotional outburst. "Would you like some coffee?" I asked.

"I would love some." She flipped her long blonde hair behind her shoulder and smiled. "By the way, while I'm here, I want to look at your phone and laptop for any listening devices or software. Since you'll be home for a bit, I'll just have Tad check it every so often. Don't click on any links you're not familiar with either. If something looks suspicious just call me."

"I won't. I'm always cautious about emails with links from people I don't know anyway." I reached into my purse and handed her my phone.

Within a few minutes, Sutton was finished. "All clear." She placed it on the table for me and leaned back in her seat.

"How did Tad realize he'd been spotted?" I led the way into the kitchen, then grabbed her a coffee cup. "Milk, creamer, sugar?"

"Is it flavored creamer?" Sutton asked, setting her tote bag and jacket on a barstool.

"Oh yeah. I love chocolate and caramel in my coffee."

"That sounds fantastic." She pulled out a chair at the table and sat down. "Tad wasn't sure whether he'd been spotted or not. He just had a sense of being watched.

"That's eerie." I joined her and set her drink down, then refilled mine.

"Pierce has trained the men to listen to their gut instincts. It has certainly saved all of us more times than I can count."

I sipped my steaming dark brew, recalling the events of the day before. "I don't know what it is, but something is bothering me. I mean, the entire thing is messed up, but … I'm not explaining this very well."

"I understand. My sister, Claire … it's a long story, but she was kidnapped and nearly shipped overseas to be sold as a sex slave."

"Oh my god. Please tell me she's okay." My hand flew to my mouth, the horror of the situation sending my emotions reeling.

"She is." Sutton took a drink of her coffee. "Pierce and I hadn't seen each other or talked in nine years when she'd been taken. He was in Portland unexpectedly, where I still lived at the time. I showed up unannounced and begged him to keep my family safe and help me find Claire. Multiple times, when we were searching for my sister, we had nothing to go on but our gut feeling, so don't ever ignore it. Today, she's happy and engaged to my best friend and one of Pierce's men, Vaughn. You've seen him. He's the guy with the mismatched eyes."

"That's amazing. It gives me some hope that everything will turn out all right." I gently tapped my fingernails against my ceramic mug.

"The insanity of Claire's situation … Well, it brought Pierce and me back together. We'd had some time to grow up and forgive each other for the mistakes we'd made when we were younger too."

"He seems like a good man, Sutton. I'm happy it worked out for both of you."

She smiled softly. "Me too. He was a bit of an asshole at first, but now I know it was because he was hurting and had blamed himself for the death of one of our best friends, Connor. That anger and pain had affected everyone around him. Guilt will do that, and the majority of the time, it's a waste of energy. Pierce wasn't responsible at all. In his mind, he thought he could have prevented Connor's death, but there was nothing he could have done."

"That's a lot for one person to carry."

"I agree. Just like I suspect it is for you concerning your dad."

Damn, she's good.

"I … I wonder why I survived, and he didn't." Tears welled in my eyes with my confession, and I quickly gazed out the back window and across the pool. A light wind had picked up, rippling over the water. I needed to have the pool drained and winterized soon. "When I look at the facts, I know I'm not responsible for his death, but inside … it rips me to shreds at night. It was my idea to go to lunch downtown. Dad wanted to head to Sandpoint for the day, but I talked him out of it. If I'd agreed to go …" I placed my face in my hands. "Maybe he'd still be alive," I choked out.

Sutton scraped her chair across the floor, then she set a box of tissues in front of me. "Whoever your stalker is … they would have followed you there too. You had nothing to do with his death, Avery. In no way are you responsible. I promise."

I dabbed the moisture from my cheeks and wiped my nose. "I'm sorry."

"Girl, please. You should have seen me when Claire was missing. I was a fucking wreck."

I snickered when she dropped the f-bomb. Sutton came across as highly sophisticated, and I had doubted she swore at all.

"I have a mouth on me." She laughed.

"Me too." I giggled. "Thank you for sharing. It's encouraging that my life can return to a … a new normal."

"It can."

Silence descended over us, then Sutton stood and collected her tote from the barstool. "I have some information for you about your biological mom."

"You do?" Just thinking about it had my shoulders pulling tight and added building pressure on my chest.

She pulled a thin manila file out of her bag and placed it on the table. "Her name was Cecile Carrigan. Avery, you look exactly like her." She flipped the folder open and waited.

"Holy shit," I whispered, picking up the eight-by-ten image of my biological mother. My heart beat frantically as I laid eyes on my mother for the first time in my life. "I always thought I took after dad, but Cecile … Mom …" My voice caught in my throat, and I gawked at the photo. She was tall, thin, and elegant. Her large green eyes stared back at me. Her long dark hair framed her narrow face, and a light dusting of freckles covered her nose and cheeks.

"She was pregnant with you in this picture." Sutton pointed to Mom's barely swollen tummy.

"Can I keep it?" My chin quivered.

"All of the contents in this file are for you, Avery."

I held the picture of my mom to my chest as a sob shook my body. After a few minutes, I pulled some more tissues from the box and wiped my cheeks. "Thank you. I can't explain how it feels to know who she is … where I came from."

"I can only imagine. Copies of her birth and death certificates are in there as well. After I found her, I was able to track down some of her friends who were close to her in high school. You might consider reaching out to them. They might be able to provide you with more information about who she was."

"That would be amazing."

"May I?" Sutton asked, nodding to the folder.

"Of course."

Sutton flipped through a few pages and pulled a piece of paper out. She placed it on top for me to read through it. "You have an uncle in Maine and an aunt in Texas. They each have three kids. Here are their addresses and telephone numbers, if you want to reach out."

"I have family left." My hand trembled while the truth dawned on me. "I thought I was the only one left. Dad didn't have any siblings, and Davia isn't my mother." I paused and glanced up at her. "It all happened so fast. Everything I knew about my life … The moment Dad died, the rug was pulled out from underneath me, and in no way did I land on my feet."

Sutton sat down again. "You have family, Avery. After this is all over, you can decide whether you want to reach out to them or not, but I wanted to let you know. I didn't dig any further for your relatives, but I suspect your aunt and uncle can help you with it."

Before I realized what I was doing, I'd pulled her in for a huge hug. "I can't thank you enough, Sutton."

She patted my back. "I'm happy I could help. You deserve something good in your life. You've been through a lot."

I released her and looked at the folder.

"Avery, there's one more thing."

Inwardly, I cringed. If she'd saved it for last, there was no way it was good news.

"What is it?" I tapped my fingers against the kitchen table, my anxiety climbing with each second that ticked by.

2 2

"Your dad wasn't legally married to Davia."

"What?" I gasped, my hand accidentally knocking my coffee cup over and spilling the creamy substance across the table and toward the papers.

Sutton snatched the folder, rescuing it before it got any damage. "I'll put this on the counter until we're done."

I jumped out of my chair to grab a dishtowel and mopped up the mess I'd made. Then I took the empty coffee cup and placed it in the sink along with the soaking-wet rag and washed the sticky goo from my fingers. Drying my hands on a paper towel, I inhaled a shaky breath.

"Are you okay?" Sutton asked, her expression full of compassion. "There's more."

"Of course there is. Dad warned me. He tried to tell me in a note he'd left that I would learn all of his secrets. But I don't understand the marriage." I shook my head, as though it might clear the fog from my overwhelmed brain.

"It took a lot of digging, but I found out your father's real name is Mariano. He's the son of Floris Russo, who is part of the crime family in Seattle that Vincent got in trouble with."

I barked out a laugh. "Are you kidding me? I'm related to a crime family? What the fuck!" I slapped my hands over my face, attempting not to lose my shit in front of Sutton. "I don't even know what to say, because I suspect you're going to tell me more."

"I'm sorry, Avery. Do you need a break, or do you want me to continue? We can take a walk and get some fresh air if you'd like. I'm fully capable of protecting you. I'm trained in martial arts, and I carry a gun. If you need some air, let's go."

Panic at the idea of what might be next consumed me and twisted me inside out. "I need to know. Just tell me everything now. I can pick up the pieces of my heart later."

Sutton returned to her tote and pulled out another file. "I have to give your dad major kudos. It took a lot of work to uncover this infor-mation." Her expression softened and she continued. "Avery, your dad ran and hid from his family, then met your mom, Cecile, in Maine. They fell in love, and around the time she became pregnant, your dad had reconstructive surgery. I suspect it was to protect you both from his family. He also changed his name to Steven Davenport." She placed the new manila folder on the counter next to the one that contained details on my mom. "There are pictures of him before his surgery, if you want to see them. It also has a few of him and your mom together."

I nodded, unable to form any coherent words that weren't profan-ity, so I kept my mouth shut.

"Your dad was trying to keep you and your mom safe, Avery. I know it's confusing, and I suspect that you're struggling with all of this, but he changed his identity to keep you hidden from his family. As far as his marriage to Davia, it was never officially recorded. Signed papers were never located or filed. However, he was specific in his will and trust, so legally, she still gets half of his estate."

"Maybe he was afraid that someone would learn his real identity if he filed the papers." I shook my head in disbelief. "Do you think he really loved my mom?"

"I think he fell head over heels for her and was willing to change his entire life in order for them to be together. He sacrificed everything for you both. Love doesn't get more real than that."

Tears spilled down my cheeks while I processed the information. "Why did he come back to Washington? If he were in danger, then why would he risk it?"

"I can't answer that, but if it were me, I would have done the same. Sometimes the best place to hide is right under someone's nose."

"Shit." My brows knitted as the pieces continued to fall into place. "They found Dad when Vincent screwed up and owed them money. They learned who he really was."

Sutton sat down at the kitchen table. "I don't have proof yet, but yes, we think they were behind his murder."

The world blurred, and my stomach churned while the harsh reality slapped me in the face. "Why would someone in the family want me dead? I had no idea they even existed."

"In their mind, they think that you're a threat somehow. When your dad turned in evidence against them, they assumed you knew about their illegal activities as well. By that time, someone had done their homework and learned you were going to take over Steven's business. Typically, in these situations, they not only remove the immediate threat, but they also tend to eliminate anyone else that might possibly be connected to the situation, which is you."

"Fucking Vincent." I squeezed my eyes shut, wishing like hell Ramsey were next to me. "Vincent needs to be stopped. Not only for raping me but also for putting my company in jeopardy with his actions."

"He's in deep, Avery. I won't go into the specifics I found out, but the smartest thing for him to do would be to disappear."

I quirked an eyebrow at her, seething beneath my calm exterior. "I'd love to serve him up to my family on a silver platter."

"I would, too, but it's safer if you stay out of it. My guess? Vincent will get what's coming to him."

I walked over to the file, my pulse kicking up a notch as I opened it and stared at an image of Dad before he'd had reconstructive facial surgery.

"You look like him in the eyes. Same shape, same eyebrows."

I traced my fingertips over the picture. "Even with everything I've learned today, I miss him so damned much." I closed the folder in order not to get tears on the images. "Is there anything else? Honestly, I'm not sure I can handle much more."

"Not today. It took me nearly a week to get my hands on this. It was buried deep and difficult to find." She sighed softly. "My gut tells me there's more, but I've not been able to find it yet. I promise that the second I find out what it is, I'll call you. Until then, you have security to keep you safe and friends who love you."

"Davia said that Dad had kept a lot of secrets from her too. She would have been in danger if she'd known the truth. Not to mention that she can't control her damned mouth when she's using."

"I feel like crap dumping all of this on you. Do you want me to stay until Ramsey or one of your friends comes over? I'm happy to hang out and keep you company, if that's what you want."

"I really appreciate the offer, but I think I need some time alone to look through the files and allow myself to fall apart. Because regardless of how all of this looks, I'm a Davenport, and I'll land on my feet, just like my daddy." I shoved the nearly debilitating heartache to the side.

"If you need anything, whether it's additional security or a friend, I'm only a phone call away. And when this is all over, I'd love to grab coffee sometime. Maybe we could hop over to the Hamptons or Paris together, have some drinks, and shop."

I smiled at her. "I'd love that. I'm ready to travel and relax after this is all over. Our families … Ramsey's family and I own a beautiful vacation home in the Hamptons."

"I think that would be a nice getaway." Sutton collected her tote bag and slipped the strap onto her shoulder. "Call me if you need anything." She gave me a brief hug, then let herself out.

As I stared at the folders on the counter, her footsteps faded, and the sound of the front door closing echoed through the house. I grabbed a bottle of vodka, my keys from my purse on the kitchen table, collected the files, and made my way to Dad's office. I eased the key in and unlocked the door. The scent of his cologne still hung in the air. Inhaling deeply, I imagined his arms around me. Every morning before I left for school, he would tell me how much he loved me and kiss the top of my head. No matter what his schedule was, he always made sure he had time for me before I started my day.

I placed the folders on his desk and walked toward the bookshelves, then twisted off the vodka lid and tipped the bottle back and took a swig, allowing the liquid to seep into every part of my being. I welcomed the hazy feeling that would soon follow. My feelings were spiraling out of control, and the only way to grab them by the tail and halt the disruption was to numb out. Ramsey wouldn't be here until around seven, which left me more than enough time to read the information and attempt to manage my thoughts, since it was almost one in the afternoon.

My attention landed on the shelf that Dad had always saved for me. His shelves were filled with leather-bound books that ranged from encyclopedias to a rare and expensive collection of literature. Dad's favorite was Edger Allen Poe. Oddly enough, he'd placed it next to an old, overpriced Holy Bible. Maybe it was his way of making peace with his dark past, the light of the Bible overshadowing Poe's demented and twisted thoughts.

Finally ready to look at my father's information, I sank into his office chair and took another long pull of vodka. I relaxed my shoulders and took a moment to allow the buzz to settle in. Then I replaced the lid and put the bottle on the edge of the desk and began sifting through all of the papers Sutton had brought me.

I wondered how Ramsey's day was going and how he would take all of it. As if he'd read my mind, my phone buzzed in my back pocket.

I love you. Be prepared to have your world rocked tonight when I get home.

No matter how bad of a mood I was in, he always brought a smile to my face. My fingers tapped the screen as I replied, *I'll be waiting.*

After a few more drinks, I dug into my past and where I'd really come from.

"HEY, AVERY."

I peeked an eye open and wiped the drool from the corner of my mouth. "Ramsey?" My voice was thick and heavy from the alcohol and tears I'd shed all afternoon.

"Babe, what's going on?"

I sat up, peeling my cheek off Dad's desk and wincing at the sharp pain that stabbed my neck. "I must have dozed off." I rubbed my face. "Shit. I'm still drunk." I snorted at the irony. "On the bright side, I'm not related to Davia, so her addictive personality isn't hereditary."

"You're not an alcoholic, by any means, but you're scaring me a little." Ramsey dropped his backpack onto the floor and pinned me with an intense gaze that burned right through me, setting my soul on fire.

I picked up the bottle and handed it to him. "You'll need a drink before I tell you about all of this." I motioned to the pictures and papers that were scattered across the desk.

Ramsey quirked an eyebrow at me and took a sip. "How many do I need?"

"More than that. And you'll need to sit down." I pointed at one of the leather chairs that lined the back wall.

Once he was settled, he looked at the contents. "Who is that?" he asked, pointing at the photos.

"Those are my parents." I tilted my head to the side, waiting for it to click with him.

Confusion flickered in his blue eyes. "Babe, that guy is not Steven. Are you sure you've not drunk too much?"

I barked out an obnoxious laugh. *Thank god Ramsey has already seen me at my worst.* We'd made it through our teen years together, which had included sudden tearful outbursts, braces, and acne on my part. Somehow, he'd managed to skip most of that. He was born gorgeous and emotionally steady.

"It's him, and that's my biological mom, Cecile. The picture is from before Dad had his face rearranged by a plastic surgeon in order to hide his identity from his parents, who are part of a crime family in Seattle. The very same ones that Vincent fucked over."

Ramsey's mouth gaped, his eyes nearly popping out of his head. "What the fuck?"

"Oh, just wait. There's more."

He stared at me, speechless, then offered me the bottle.

Over the next hour, I explained about my dad and mom to Ramsey as we passed the vodka back and forth. By the time I was finished updating him on the twisted tale of my family, I was pretty sure I was slurring my words.

"Jesus. Who else knows this?" He ran a hand through his thick hair.

"You and me. Oh, and Sutton. I would assume she shared everything with Pierce too."

"I think we should sit on this information until after we're married so that my parents don't shit themselves."

A fit of giggles bubbled up from out of nowhere. "Oh my god, we'd never be able to see each other again, and there's nothing funny about that. Like, at all!" I held my sides, unable to stop laughing.

Ramsey's chuckle filled the room, and the more I laughed, the more he did. By the time we'd settled back down, my stomach hurt, and I wondered if all of the drama in my life had finally drop-kicked me off the edge of sanity.

"Let's get something to eat. I'm starving, and I'm taking a guess that you've not eaten—"

"Today," I interrupted him. "Now that I think about it, I've not eaten at all. Huh, no wonder the vodka hit me so fast." I shrugged and hopped out of the chair.

"What do you have in the fridge?" Ramsey asked, leading me into the kitchen.

"Ice cream." I raised his hand to my lips and sucked on his finger. "We've never fucked when we've been drinking." I dropped his hand and pulled my sweater over my head and tossed it across the room.

Ramsey's gaze darkened as his focus landed on my lace bra. With one quick flick, I released the front clasp, then I slowly slid the straps off my shoulders. His palm moved to the wall over my shoulder, and his eyes scanned my face with a fierce intensity that made me weak in the knees.

I fumbled for the button and zipper on his jeans, then freed his erection. "Make me forget, Ramsey." I stroked him slowly. "Make me forget all the hell around me."

Without any effort, he scooped me up in his arms and placed me on the kitchen counter. My jeans and thong were off in record time, and Ramsey parted my legs. "You're already wet, babe."

"Stop talking and fuck me," I pleaded.

He grabbed his hard cock and shoved it into me, then stilled. He glanced up at me and back down at his dick as he pumped in and out of me, over and over again. My back arched off the granite, and with every touch and every thrust, Ramsey reminded me who I belonged to, who I was, and no matter what changed around me, that he loved me. He knew exactly what I needed.

23

The next morning, I woke with a pounding headache. I patted the space next to me, but I didn't find Ramsey. Scooting down farther in the bed, I tugged the comforter over my head. Maybe I could hide for a little bit longer.

"Hey, babe." The mattress dipped next to me as Ramsey sat down.

I peeked at him with one eye from beneath the covers.

"Are you all right? You were pretty wasted last night."

"I totally drank my feelings." I flung the blankets down, hair flying into my eyes, and huffed.

Ramsey chuckled, then smoothed the strands from my face. "You're allowed to sometimes. That was a lot to handle."

I sat up and stared at him. "I'm sorry you came home to a shit show. It might not be the last."

"Don't give it another thought. We've seen each other trashed plenty of times." He smiled at me. "I won't be over until really late tonight. Our practice is at a stadium in Idaho."

I pushed my lower lip out. There was nothing about that statement that I liked. At. All.

"It sucks, but our field is getting some work done. I'm going to swing by the apartment and grab a few more things to bring over, if that's okay."

"I'll be here. Maybe I'll see if Ten can hang out for a bit."

"I'm sure she would." Ramsey leaned over and brushed his lips against mine. "I love you."

"I love you too," I said, kissing him in return.

"Have a good day. I'll text later."

"Sounds good." I settled back against the headboard and watched him leave my room, taking my heart with him.

Groaning loudly, I forced myself to get up. The best thing for me was a hot shower. After some coffee, I would start organizing the pool house. At least it would give me something to do.

After breakfast, my head had cleared and I felt more human. Flinging open the front door, I waved to one of the security guards. Pierce must have swapped them out the previous night and forgot to tell me, because I didn't recognize him.

"I'm Graysen." He adjusted his Ray-Bans on his nose and nodded at me. He squared his broad, muscular shoulders and reached out to shake my hand. His dark hair was streaked with red highlights that glinted in the sun. Something about him made me wonder if he was an ex-Marine. Although I couldn't see the color of his eyes, the rest of him was as yummy as the other bodyguards. I could have sworn Pierce had plucked them right off the cover of *GQ Magazine*.

"Pierce didn't tell me he was rotating you guys out." I stepped out front and leaned against the wall, chewing on an imaginary hangnail.

"He left you a voicemail this morning."

Shit. I'd forgotten to check. "Okay, Graysen. I'm going to be out back. I have some projects that need my attention."

"Tad is at the back of the house, so let him know."

"Sounds good. Maybe I can talk him into helping me for a bit." I gave Graysen a small wave, then slipped back into the house and locked the front door. When I realized I'd left my iPhone in my room, I ran upstairs and grabbed it before I headed out back. Sure enough, Pierce had left me a message.

Puffy white clouds floated over the mid-morning sun, casting shadows across the pool. I would make a call that day and schedule an appointment to have it winterized. Since they wouldn't need to come inside the house, I suspected one of the guys could handle it for me.

"Good morning," Tad said, walking around the fence and through the gate.

"Morning. I'm not sure if it's in your job description, but I could use a little muscle in the pool house. Boxes are stacked everywhere. Maybe you could help me put a few outside so that I have some space to move around while I start cleaning up."

"I can help. By the way, I'm glad you're okay … after the poisoning." Tad stood rigid and alert.

"Me too. Thank you for calling Zayne for backup. He saved my life." I placed my hand on my hip. "And today, you'll be right next to me, so it's all good." I gave him an encouraging smile. It wasn't his fault my stalker had gotten to me. If a grown man had handed me an envelope, I wouldn't have taken it. It was in my nature to trust kids more than adults, which had left me a wide-open target.

"Did you secure the house?" Tad asked, staring at the entrance to the kitchen.

"I did."

I strolled over to the pool house and unlocked it. When I swung the door open, I was greeted by a musty smell and a whirlwind of dust that danced in the stream of light peeking through the curtains on the window. I coughed and fanned the air in front of me, hoping to clear away the particles.

"It's a little overwhelming, so try to prepare yourself. God only knows when anyone was in here last. Dad said he would take care of it, but that day never came." Tears welled in my eyes, and I quickly looked away from Tad. It was one thing to cry alone or with Ramsey and my friends, but not Tad.

He joined me, and we started hauling out boxes and stacking them near the side of the pool. Once a trail was cleared, we were able to maneuver inside the small house, and I started ripping the lids off the large plastic storage containers. Minutes turned into hours as Tad stood guard and helped with what he could. Not only did I appreciate the company, but he was tall and strong, which meant I didn't have to grab a ladder and hope I didn't fall off it while trying to move stuff.

A little after five, I'd filled the trash and the recycling bin with unwanted or broken pool items, toys, blankets, and pillows. I still had a lot of work to do, but we'd made a nice dent in it. For whatever reason, it made me feel better, as though I was making some forward progress in my life.

"I'm going to grab something for dinner and shower. Thank you for all your help today." I gathered my hair and put it in a ponytail, then held it in place while I assessed the rest of the work that still needed to be done.

"I'm glad I could help. Have a good evening," Tad said.

I brushed off the dust from my jeans and shirt before I walked into the kitchen. Not only was I starving, but I was also seriously thirsty. Half an hour later, I'd scarfed down a ham sandwich and a banana. I checked my cell phone for any calls or texts, but I had none. Ramsey must have been really busy.

I tapped out a quick message and sent it. *Miss and love you. Can't wait to see you tonight and hear about your day.*

Black dots filled my screen, and a smile eased across my face.

Sorry I've not been able to message sooner. Miss and love you too. See you soon.

I shoved my phone into the back pocket of my jeans and headed upstairs. At least I could get cleaned up and do some laundry before he got home. As I neared Davia and Dad's bedroom door, my footsteps slowed. Davia would most likely come back to pack before she moved out, which was fine, as long as she was sober. If not, I would have one of the bodyguards remove her, then I would put her things in the garage, where she could pick them up later. I'd already planned on changing all the locks, so she would no longer have access to my house. A sharp pang filled my chest. Dad should have handled her a long time ago, especially since they weren't legally married. I wondered whether she knew they weren't or if it even mattered to her.

My thoughts drifted to all the information that Sutton had shared with me the day before. I wasn't mad at Dad anymore, which was progress. It helped to know everything he did was to protect Cecile and me, exactly like he'd explained in the letter he had left for me.

I continued to the end of the hall and into my room. One of the things I'd loved about the house was the space between the bedrooms. We weren't stacked on top of each other. In fact, the house was built so well that I couldn't hear any sounds from Dad's room when he and Davia were in there. We all had a bit of privacy.

After flipping my bedroom light on, I strolled over to my dresser and began pulling out clean clothes. The floor creaked behind me, and the little hairs on my arms stood on end. I glanced up into the mirror, and my gaze connected with a cold, hard, lifeless stare. Before I could scream, I felt a sharp prick of my skin. The last thing I remembered was my knees buckling.

I opened my eyes, and panic ripped through me. My pulse raced, thundering in my ears while I tried to process what I was seeing.

"Hello, Avery. I'm Bexley. You've been knocked out for a few hours." She flashed me a big smile and sat on my bed. The silver buckle on her black boots caught the light when she crossed her legs.

I struggled to move, but my hands were bound behind my back. At some point, I'd been placed in a chair, and a rag had been stuffed into my mouth, rendering me speechless as I stared at a woman who looked exactly like me—my face, my height, and my hair. I shook my head and attempted to talk again. *Son of a bitch. I have a twin. An identical twin.* I slammed my eyes closed, hoping I would open them and be safe and sound in my room. Alone. My attention landed on her, and I mentally swore a blue streak.

"I have to say that you have the hottest bodyguards that I've ever seen!" She fanned herself and giggled. "They really are doing a fantastic job of protecting you. They're next to you every second, which made it difficult for me to get to you after that adorable little boy delivered the poisoned envelope." She paused, her green-eyed gaze assessing my room. "Speaking of, I was there and watched as the entire shit show went down." A laugh fell from her lips. "In fact, you looked right at me. Not that you would have recognized me. I wore a black baseball hat that covered my face, and my hair was tucked inside it."

Shit. I knew something had been bothering me. I'd seen her, and my brain was trying to tell me I'd witnessed someone or something out of place.

"I can't tell you how pleasantly shocked I was to find that your kitchen door was unlocked. I mean, you left it wide open for me and invited me right in. When you and the redheaded hottie were in the pool house, I slipped inside without being detected." She wagged her finger and literally looked down her nose at me. "I thought you were smarter than that."

Goddammit. I could have sworn I'd locked the door. Tad had even asked me before we started moving boxes.

"Ramsey won't be over for a while. He thinks you're sick. I needed to clear your schedule for a few days." She smirked, flipping her hair behind her shoulder. Her green eyes flashed with purpose—and revenge.

Whatever she'd used to knock me out had started to lift. I was clear-headed enough to hear her British accent as she continued to talk.

"I'm sure you have so many questions, and I'll admit that I'm looking forward to getting to know my long-lost twin. From the expression on your face right now, I'm guessing you had no idea I even existed."

I stared at her while I scrambled to put it all together. *Why didn't I know? Why wasn't Sutton able to uncover this huge piece of information?*

"*Tsk. Tsk.* I thought dear ol' Dad might have mentioned me but apparently not. Don't worry. We're about to get to know each other very well."

She hopped off the bed and stood in front of me. I shook my head, taking in every detail that we shared. If anyone saw her, and she didn't speak, they would think it was me. Her mannerisms were even the same.

"By the way, I love your taste in clothes. After watching you for several months, it was easy to buy some of the exact same jeans and shirts. Don't you think I look good?" She turned around and ran a hand over her ass, then smacked her butt cheek and laughed.

My nose twitched with disdain. Under any other circumstances, I would have been thrilled to learn about my twin, but she was obviously unstable. At times I was moody, but not fucking crazy.

"You're probably wondering why you're all tied up."

I nodded and pulled at the ropes that bound my wrists together.

"Well, first I want to get to know you a little bit better without you running off and blabbing to anyone about me. Next I'm going to literally step into your shoes and assume your life. Then I'm going to rip away everything you love and hold dear. The exciting part is that you'll get to watch and experience every devastating blow as it's delivered." Her voice was hard, and her eyes were tight with anger. "You were supposed to die along with Dad, but you had to be stubborn about it."

I blanched as my nostrils flared, and my stomach twisted into painful knots. The cold, hard truth crushed my lungs, and I struggled to catch my breath. My twin sister had murdered our father. *Jesus. How am I even supposed to wrap my head around that information?*

"Honestly, I think this will be so much more fun." She practically skipped across my room, humming a song I didn't recognize under her breath. "Oh." She held a finger up, blinked rapidly, then spoke again without even a hint of her accent. "Yes, I can and will assume your life. I must admit I can't wait to fuck Ramsey's brains out." She moaned his name.

Fire ignited inside me, and I jumped from the chair and charged her. My head connected with her stomach, and she went sailing backward and landed with a thud on the floor. Unfortunately, my balance was off with my hands tied behind my back, and I tumbled on top of her. Since I had no way to defend myself, she easily rolled on top of me and delivered multiple punches to my face. Blood oozed across my cheek as she sneered at me. "Nice try, lovely, and now you've done it. I'd hoped we could be civil to each other, but I guess I was mistaken."

She stood, brushing her hands off as though touching me had infected her with a deadly disease.

Bexley dug into a black backpack in the corner of my room and removed more rope. "I realize we just met, love, but you need to know something about me. Don't. Fucking. Piss. Me. Off." She sneered and looped the coarse material around my ankles. "That should do it."

Her gaze narrowed as she reached for a tissue from the box on my nightstand. Bexley forcefully wiped off my cheek. "That will do. I can't have blood on this gorgeous carpet." She leaned forward, inches away from my face. "Ramsey or your friends might ask questions."

Calculating my move, I reared and headbutted her as hard as I could. A sickening cracking sound filled the room, and Bexley lost her balance and rolled backward.

"You fucking bitch," she moaned, grabbing her forehead.

Dammit, I didn't knock her out. Nausea from the intense pain swam up my throat. My vision blurred, and I blinked repeatedly as I rolled toward the hallway. If I could tumble down the stairs while she was writhing around on the floor, I could kick at the front door and alert the guys. *Help me, Dad,* I mentally pleaded.

"Not so fast, Avery. Maybe you're smarter than I thought you were." She grinned, and a knot began forming on her head.

A muffled scream escaped me as she looped my long hair around her hand and dragged me toward my closet, then kicked me inside and slammed the door closed.

"Fucking bitch. I hope you enjoy your evening," Bexley spat.

The noise of a chair being placed beneath the doorknob reached my ears, and a lump formed in my throat. Crying wouldn't accomplish anything, though. I needed a plan.

At least I was conscious and could work on the ropes that bound my hands.

THE SOUND of the door opening woke me. I wasn't sure when I'd dozed off, but I was grateful for the small reprieve from the fucked-up situation I had landed in. I'd belittled myself for not paying attention concerning the kitchen door, but it wasn't helping me any. I needed to save my energy to outwit Bexley. So far, all I'd managed to do was piss her off, and she would expect me to fight her, so I had to back off and wait until she let her guard down.

"How's it going in there?" The overhead light glinted off the gun in her hand, and I trembled as I stared at her. "You're going to be a good sister and not give me any shit, or I'll put a bullet right between those pretty green eyes of yours. Got it?"

Unable to speak with the gag in place, I merely nodded.

Bexley positioned herself behind me, slid her arms around my chest, then dragged me out of the closet. Cringing from the light, I glanced at the clock. It was after eleven. Ramsey and I should be curled up together in bed, talking about our day, and making love.

"Up ya go," Bexley said, tossing me awkwardly onto the chair. "If you promise not to scream, I'll remove the gag. If you scream ..." She held the gun to my head. "I have a very nice silencer, so no one will even know I shot you dead."

I nodded again. Bexley jerked the gag out of my mouth and moved back, her gaze searching mine.

Closing my eyes briefly, I dragged in deep gulps of air. "Water?" I darted my parched tongue across my lower lip, which felt chapped from the rough material she'd shoved into my mouth hours ago.

Without a word, Bexley grabbed a bottle and opened it for me. She held it to my lips, and I gulped greedily.

"You're going to puke if you don't slow down." A flicker of compassion danced across her expression. "The only reason I care is that I'm the one who would have to clean it up." She removed the container and replaced the lid. "I'd love to chat, Avery. I know all of this is a bit extreme, but I'm happy to explain it. Why we never knew about each other until recently, and why you and Dad are on my shit list. Plus, I have questions for you too." She kicked off her boots, then sat on the end of the bed and tucked her legs beneath her.

"Why? What happened to you, Bexley? We're sisters. We're supposed to take care of each other, not … this."

"Right? That's what I've always said too. If I had a sister, we would be the best of friends. We would share all of our secrets, cover for each other when we were at a boyfriend's house instead of our girl-friends', and stumble in together past curfew, drunk off our asses." She shook her head. "It's a damned shame."

"How did you find out about me?" My voice trembled, betraying me and allowing her to see how scared I really was.

"Let's start from the beginning." Her gaze bored into mine, and a thick silence descended over us. "Mum died giving birth to us. Did you know that?"

"I found out a few weeks ago that Davia wasn't my mother and that my bio mom was dead."

"I'm sure that was a big surprise." Bexley quirked an eyebrow at me and tapped a manicured fingernail against her chin. "You really had no idea? Not even a teensy bit that the woman in your house wasn't your mum?"

"No." I figured the safest thing for me to do was to reply to her with short answers and not get myself in deeper shit than I already was. Plus, I didn't want to push her while the gun sat on the bed next to her, pointing straight at me.

"Imagine, if you will …" She raised her hands as though the words were written on a billboard announcing the newest movie. "A year ago, I was able to track down the nurse who was in the delivery room at the hospital in Maine. Her name is Freya. She explained that Mum had me first. In fact, little sis, I'm four minutes and sixteen seconds older than you are. From what I was told, Dad handed me to Freya. The doctor delivered you and placed you in Dad's arms. She said it was love at first sight, and he stood next to her, fussing about how beautiful we were. He kissed our foreheads, then mum started having complications. Something had ruptured or …" Bexley gave a half shrug. "I don't remember what Freya said. Medical terms aren't my thing. But basically, Mum bled out and died right on the table."

"Dad saw her die?" I asked, pain slamming into my chest. The horror of watching someone take their last breath was more than I could comprehend. It had torn my world apart when I had seen Dad after the car accident, and he had still been alive.

Bexley nodded. "One minute Mum was there, and the next she wasn't. Dad didn't have the means to raise us both on his own. From what I understand, he and Mum were broke. It wasn't until his early thirties that he became successful and began to build his empire. Anyway, I digress. He was devastated that Mum died, and he had no means to support us, so he contacted Mum's parents, our grandparents, and asked if they could raise me. I'm not sure how he chose which one of us he would keep, but I was shipped off to England like a bag of trash. My grandparents had a written agreement that he would never reach out to me and that he would let me get on with my life. Not only did they not like him, they were furious when he got their little girl knocked up. They doubted his parenting ability, and he felt guilty, so Dad held up his end of the deal."

I finally understood the accent. She hadn't been raised in the US like I had.

Bexley gulped and glanced away, and for the first time since I'd met her, I wondered if she had any normal emotions.

"I loved my grandparents. They were good people. When I was seven, they were killed by a drunk driver. Everything I'd ever known was ripped away from me." Bexley placed her hand over her chest. "I loved them so much." Tears welled in her eyes.

In a split second, a switch inside her flipped, and her entire expression morphed into something foreign. She sneered at me, her facial features completely void of any feeling.

A shudder traveled through me, causing me to pull against the ropes still snug around my wrists. "What happened after our grandparents died?"

"*My* grandparents!" she shrieked at me, standing quickly.

"Sorry. *Your* grandparents."

Bexley's chest heaved, anger and loathing flashing in her eyes. "My grandparents hadn't gotten around to making a will, so I was put into the foster system after that. No family. No grandparents. No father."

She spun on her heel and paced the room, shaking her head and muttering under her breath. Bexley rubbed her face with her hands and faced me again. "You had the life I was supposed to have. Stable. The shining star in Dad's eye. You were wealthy. *You* were wealthy, while I lived on the streets, searching in dumpsters for scraps of food to eat."

"I didn't know, Bexley. If Dad had known, he would have brought you here. I know he would have."

Bexley pointed at me. "Maybe, but he didn't. He never even tried to look for me. For nine years, I bounced from one shitty place to another. The foster care system was more broken than I was. As long as the check was delivered every month, the parents didn't care. Except ..." She placed her hands on her hips and stared at me. "Except when I turned twelve, I got tits." She grabbed her breasts and squeezed them. "Best thing that happened to me, because all of a sudden, I went from an ugly, scrawny kid to this." She ran her fingers down her sides.

"You're beautiful," I said softly, hoping that I might be able to stroke her ego and connect with her a little bit.

"After years of foster parents kicking me out for whatever reason, I landed in a gorgeous home. Ron and Bethany Holcomb. It was a dream come true. I had my own bedroom, and I wore nice clothes and showered every day. I never went hungry again."

"They really cared about you."

A harsh laugh bubbled up from Bexley. "Yes, they cared, all right. During those years, I learned all about the power of having a pussy."

I cringed, not wanting to believe that monsters like them had hurt her. But I knew firsthand they were everywhere.

"One night, when Bethany was sleeping, Ron took me downstairs. He didn't force me to do anything, Avery, so stop looking at me like that. The pity is dripping off you."

"I don't understand," I whispered.

"He gave me a choice. He would train me to be his plaything, and I could live there as long as I wanted. It wasn't rape, because it was completely consensual."

"Jesus, Bexley, don't you understand that what he did was the same thing? You could live on the streets or fuck him?"

A sharp sting landed on my right cheek. "Don't you dare speak about him like that. He loved me. Ron taught me how to please a man, but more than that, he gave me one delicious orgasm after another. The first night, he slid my nightgown up my thighs and my panties down my legs. He licked and sucked my pussy and showed me how amazing it felt. We didn't fuck for a long time. Ron never pressured me. Instead, it was secret meetings in the bathroom, where he'd bend me over and lap up my juices with his tongue until I nearly blacked out from the ecstasy. It was me that wanted more."

I bit my lip in order not to say anything else that might send her over the edge.

"Ron's room downstairs had a box of goodies in it. Blindfolds, ball gags, handcuffs … you name it, we used it. Every time we tried something new, he ravished me first. My needs were always met before his were. He was caring. Attentive."

"You were twelve for god's sake. That's rape, Bexley. What he did to you … he was a pedophile," I spat, not giving a shit about the consequences. Dad would have murdered Ron for touching his daughter.

"That's your opinion and certainly not a fact." She shifted, swinging her legs out in front of her like a little kid in a chair that was too big for her.

"What about Bethany? Did you ever tell her? She might have helped you."

Bexley flopped back onto the mattress and laughed. "That was the best part," she said finally, sitting up again and wiping the tears from her cheeks. "On my fourteenth birthday, Ron took me to his bed. I remember how terrified I was when I found Bethany waiting for us. I thought for sure my time there was up, and I would be scrounging through dumpsters for food again." Bexley's eyes cut over to me. "Apparently, Bethany knew all along about Ron and my activities." My sister groped her breasts, a small moan escaping her. "She wanted Ron to share me, and he did. I thought sex with Ron was amazing, but this … the feel of their hands and mouths all over my body. We only left the room to use the bathroom or for one of us bring up food and something to drink. Three days of lust-filled sex with them." Her hand eased between her jeaned thighs, and she rocked back and forth.

I stared at the floor. Watching my sister get herself off wasn't my idea of normal or acceptable. As soon as she'd started, she stopped again.

"Meh. I'm not in the mood. I just wanted to fuck with you." She snickered.

Pursing my lips, I waited for her to continue.

"When I was sixteen, they grew tired of me. I was interested in dating and exploring my options sexually. Once they caught me fucking a guy's brains out in the backyard at night, that was it. I suppose they wanted to trade me in for someone new, but before they could … a twist of fate happened." She held her pointer finger against her mouth. "But I'm tired, so we'll have to save it for another day."

My pulse kicked up. She wasn't done with me, which meant she wouldn't kill me … yet. But it was only a matter of time. I just had to stall her until I figured out how to get out of that nightmare.

"Stand." Bexley walked behind me and untied the ropes from my wrists and feet. "I'm going to let you go to the bathroom and shower, but make no mistake, little sis. I'll be with you, and so will Nellie."

"Who is Nellie?" I asked, rubbing my wrists and encouraging the blood flow to return.

"This," she said, picking up her gun from my bed and training it on me. "Get something clean to wear."

I did as she ordered, my brain once again scrambling to outwit her and reach the bodyguards that were right outside those walls. At least for the moment, I needed to follow along. Maybe a shower would help me think.

An hour later, I was clean, dressed in fresh clothes, and fed. Bexley stayed true to her word and never let her guard down, or the gun. A part of me wondered if it was even loaded, but one thing I knew for sure was that she was capable of murder.

Bexley bound my wrists behind my back again, but not my feet.

"Walk." She pushed the gun into my lower back, and the cold of the metal seeped through my thin shirt. "We're going to our father's room."

My breath hitched. *What is she up to?*

Bexley opened Dad's bedroom and shoved me inside. "I want you to see your new space." An evil grin spread across her face.

Dad and Davia's closet door was open, and she pushed me into it. I stumbled into the large space and spotted a kitchen chair in the middle of the floor along with a small TV that was mounted on the top shelf. Dad's side of the clothes and shoes was impeccably organized—suits, dress shirts, slacks, and jeans. Davia's side was a shit show, just like she was.

Dad's watch and cufflink drawer was open slightly, and the light bounced off one of the items. If Bexley had been after money, she would have raided his collection, but from what I could see, she hadn't picked through his belongings.

I wondered if seeing his clothes and smelling his cologne made Bexley miss the idea of him at all. It nearly broke me in two, but maybe in some strange way, I would find comfort in there. A whisper of his hugs before school every morning interrupted my thoughts. My chin shook as a rush of emotion hit me all at once.

"This is where you're going to watch as I take your life away from you. I added a few more cameras to the ones that were already in your house, and now they're connected to the TV."

I'd forgotten about the camera system because Dad had never used it unless we were out of town. He had access to view any area he wanted to from his phone or computer.

"You can have a front-row seat while I fuck your boyfriend and entertain your friends."

"You're sick. Don't you dare mess with Ramsey."

"Ah, jealousy doesn't look good on you, love." She shoved me into the chair, tied my ankles again, and replaced the gag." She checked the connectors on the TV, turned it on, then faced me. "This is all Dad's fault. If he'd only kept me ..." With that, she flicked off the light. "I'll tell Ramsey you said hello when he drops by tomorrow night. Thanks to some rest and Advil, I'm feeling much better." She shut the door behind her, leaving me alone once again.

Ramsey, I thought. *If he sleeps with her ...* Tears spilled down my cheeks as my sobs shook my shoulders, and I prayed to the universe that something would tip him off that Bexley wasn't me.

Ramsey's deep voice reached my ears through the TV in the closet before I actually saw him. I mentally screamed as he entered the house and hugged her. I struggled against the gag and attempted to rock the chair back and forth. If it fell, maybe he would come to investigate the noise. I leaned from side to side, but it didn't move. Bexley had secured it with a rope that extended from each individual leg to the wall.

When the hell did she tie the seat? The ties hadn't been there when she'd brought me in there. *Fuck.* She must have slipped something into my food and water to make me fall asleep hard.

What day is it, and how long have I been knocked out? I leaned closer to the TV and peered at the clock in the lower right-hand corner. I closed my eyes. It was a little after seven in the evening. I'd been out for nearly twenty-four hours.

Bexley's laugh pulled my attention back to the screen. She pushed up on her tiptoes and kissed Ramsey, her hands trailing over his chest and down his stomach.

"I'm so glad you're feeling better, babe."

"Me too. I think it was a combination of stress and exhaustion. I needed some sleep."

Bitch. She sounded exactly like me, and there was not a single hint of her accent. My nostrils flared as I witnessed my boyfriend make out with my sister. She'd taken things to a new level. When I got out of those ropes, I would wrap one around her neck.

Even though I knew it was futile, I screamed and screamed.

"I missed you," Bexley purred, easing a hand beneath his shirt.

"Me too. Don't hate me, babe, but I can't stay."

"What? Why?" She pushed her lower lip out, and I nearly gagged. Her performance was Oscar-worthy, and soon, she would have everyone fooled while I watched from a fucking closet, unable to do anything.

"It's Friday, remember?" Ramsey frowned. "Are you sure you're feeling okay?"

"Yes, I had just hoped your plans had changed."

"Babe, you know that every Friday night, we're at coach's house, discussing the game, eating, and preparing for tomorrow. We leave for Idaho at seven in the morning, and we won't be back until late. I want to be here with you, but I can't. I thought you were okay with my schedule."

Bexley huffed. "I am. Since I've been home, I've lost track of the days. Of course I understand. I have security right outside if I need anything." She patted his arm. "At least I got to see you for a few minutes."

"My weekends are packed, but I'll be here with you Monday. I'll make it up to you." Ramsey tipped her chin up and kissed her passionately.

I shut my eyes, refusing to watch as my sister and my boyfriend ripped my heart out and stomped all over it.

"I can't wait," Bexley said.

"I'll call you later tonight." He started to leave, then stopped and faced her again. "You're not going to be happy about this, but the vacation house in the Hamptons is undergoing some major repairs. Dad wasn't sure when it would be available again. I have no idea when we'll be able to go, but most likely not until after the new year."

My shoulders slumped forward as the tears started again. A rush of relief washed over me. My sister wouldn't be taking my place there, at least. We'd planned to relax and make love that weekend we were at the Hamptons.

"No, seriously? Ramsey, you know how much I need to get out of here."

Good job, Bexley. Turn on the whine. He hates that shit, and so do I. Although it was a slip on her part, I wasn't sure it was enough to make Ramsey think she wasn't me.

"I know, babe, but there's nothing I can do about it." He closed the gap between them and kissed her again before he left the house.

As soon as the door shut, she looked at the painting in the foyer and glared. "You forgot to mention the trip to the Hamptons." She seethed, her eyes shooting daggers at me through the TV. "Guess we need to talk some more, so I know what's on your schedule. Hang tight. I'll be there after I get some dinner." She laughed at her own joke and headed toward the kitchen.

I stared at the screen, realizing she had placed the cameras in every room and had accounted for every angle. There was nothing I wouldn't see.

With her back to the refrigerator, Bexley reached in her back pocket and produced a phone. Her thumbs flew across the keyboard, then she turned toward me, a devious grin lighting up her face.

"So sweet of Tensley to check in on you, but don't you worry, love. I told her you were doing great."

Bitch. It was *my* cell. I seethed while I stared at the TV and watched her every move.

An hour later, Bexley flung open the closet door, removed my gag, and untied the binding around my ankles. "It's a pain in my ass to drag you. Stand up." She patted the gun stuck in her waistband, reminding me I needed to behave.

I stood slowly and wiggled my toes in my shoes. "My legs are asleep."

"Tough shit. Turn around." She glared at me with an impatient expression on her face.

After a minute of finding my balance, I did as she said.

Bexley untied the rope from my wrists, and I shook my arms out. "Can I walk around a little bit while we talk? Please. I swear I won't pull anything."

"Sure, but watch your step. Sometimes I get trigger happy. It happens on occasion." Her tone was lifeless and matter-of-fact, like shooting someone was an everyday occurrence for her. Maybe it was.

I proceeded with caution, willing my legs to work as I left the closet and walked into the bedroom. Stretching my arms, I quietly stared at her, wondering what was going to fly out of her mouth next.

"Before I dive back in where we left off last night, I'll give you an update. Tad and Greyson have no fucking clue I'm me. It's not like we talk much, but it's enough to keep any suspicions down. You're definitely that friendly type that people love, so it would raise eyebrows if I were my rude self." Bexley folded her arms over her stomach and leaned against Dad's dresser. Davia's stench from the day I had shipped her off to rehab still lingered in the air. Too bad Bexley wouldn't crack a window.

"By the way, Sutton called."

I stopped stretching. "What did she say?" If anyone could figure out Bexley wasn't me, it was Sutton. At least I hoped.

"Nothing much. She wanted to see how it was going with Tad and Greyson and to see how you were doing from the other day when she dropped by."

Her smirk grew. "I admitted that all the information about Dad and Mom had hit me hard, but I was working through it."

My eyebrows shot up. "How did you know?"

Bexley rolled her eyes and pushed off the dresser. "While you've been sleeping your day away, I searched every nook and cranny of the downstairs. It's a huge house, so I haven't made my way up here yet. I gotta say it was a brilliant idea on my part, though. The files were on Dad's desk, and I found out so much about Mum and Dad. It was very touching. I continued to snoop and learned what your favorite color is, your childhood pet's name, and the address of the home in the Hamptons. Once, I returned to your … my bedroom and looked at the mural on your wall. I have to say that it took me a while to realize it was Ramsey you're sitting next to. So many juicy details that will help me step into your Prada heels."

Before she could see my reaction, I shut it down. I'd painted Ramsey next to me and hadn't even realized it was him. Even then, my subconscious had understood that I was in love with him. A sinking feeling consumed me. He was with the wrong girl.

"Are you going to tell me why you're doing all of this? Why you killed Dad?"

In a split second, Bexley's casual attitude twisted into hateful spite. "Weren't you listening last night, Avery?" She stepped toward me, her expression flashing with dark intentions. "He gave me up without a single thought and left me to rot on the streets while he pampered and loved you. He gave you everything that should have been mine, including the business. Now that he's out of the way, I can take what's rightfully mine."

Blood pumped rapidly through my veins and sweat trickled down my spine. "Why not just tell me who you were and let me make it right? I didn't support our dad's decisions, Bexley. I was a baby."

"You were." She put some space between us, her eyes assessing me. "Ever since I learned you existed, I wanted to meet you, but I never intended to share the spotlight with you. I would have always been the *other* sister, and that wouldn't have worked for me. I'm an all-or-nothing kind of girl."

I nodded, unclear of what to say. In a way, I understood. Dad was mine. I was his. Our bond was strong enough that it had pushed Davia into second place, even during times it shouldn't have.

Bexley strolled over to the window and opened the blackout curtains. A full moon hung in the sky and cast an orange glow in its wake.

"It's beautiful," I whispered, walking toward her.

Bexley wiggled her fingers, waving at one of the security guards. "Don't move," she said to me. "Dumbass," she muttered seconds later. "Your security guys are sexy as shit but as dumb as fucking stumps. They have no idea what's going on in here."

"That's because you see them and talk to them, Bexley. You're already taking my life away from me. They are good guys. They're smart and protective, but no one expected that I had an identical twin."

She remained silent and stared out the window. I wondered what twisted path her mind had just taken.

"So, Ron and Bethany." She flipped her long dark hair behind her shoulder. "They were nice enough to give me several thousand dollars, a suitcase stuffed with my clothes and toiletries, and my mail. I guess they figured I wouldn't turn them in for … as you said, raping an underaged girl for years." She gave a nonchalant half shrug before she continued.

"I headed to a cute little café that I loved so that I could figure out which direction I wanted to go. Once there, I ordered food and shuffled through my mail. To my surprise, there was another uncashed check to Ron and Bethany for my foster care. It was never about the money with them, at least." Bexley sighed and faced me. "One envelope caught my attention. It was addressed to me and was postmarked from the United States. My hands shook as I stared at it, wondering if Dad had finally reached out and wanted me to come home."

I sank down on the edge of the mattress, my legs wobbly from being tied up for so long.

"It wasn't him. Instead, it was his uncle. And suddenly an entirely new world opened up for me. I responded to Uncle Tim and Aunt Judy, and before I knew it, I'd landed at the Seattle airport and was picked up by a limo."

"That's their names? I've never met them. I had no idea they existed until a few days ago."

"Good. It was my turn to be the center of our family's attention. And man was I." Bexley laughed and slapped her leg. "Avery, these people are fucking crazy! Never in my lifetime would I have thought we were related to a crime family. Oh my god, it's so much fun."

I suddenly knew where the insanity had come from—Dad's relatives. Maybe he had fled and hidden while he was young enough that it didn't destroy him.

"I learned so much about money laundering, drugs, and sex trafficking. It was a business I could understand, and the money, Avery! Girl, the money I have now would make you look like a broke-ass bitch. For the last seven years, they've taught me everything I need to know to take over after Uncle Tim retires … or dies, whichever comes first." She shrugged, tossing her hands into the air as though she was fine with either one as long as she was able to step in and oversee the business.

Her words sat in my gut like sour milk, and I swallowed down the bile that swam up my throat. Bexley and I might have looked exactly alike, but I would never think her lifestyle was acceptable.

"One night, Uncle Tim told me I was going to Spokane with him and that he had a business deal to take care of."

"Vincent McCade," I whispered.

"Oh my god. You figured this part out!" She clapped and cheered, mocking me for fitting the puzzle piece together.

Fury surged through me, but I willed myself not to charge at her again. I didn't want to die. Somehow, I had figured it all out. Unfortunately, our family had bankrolled half the police department, so that wasn't a safe option for me to take the organization down. It was what had gotten Dad in trouble, or at least I thought.

"A friend of Uncle Tim's had recently sent him a photo of Dad, so we all knew his secret. He'd had plastic surgery. Crazily enough, Uncle Tim and I were sitting in his car when your … *our* father strolled out of the building and straight to that sweet little Porsche. No one had any clue he was here, and just like that, he dropped out of the sky and into our laps. Talk about luck."

I could feel the color draining from my face.

"Such a beautiful car. Well, it was before I drove that big-ass truck into it." She held her hands up and moved them together until they touched, indicating the result of the impact on the Porsche—a scrunched-up piece of fiberglass.

"You drove?" I hiccupped. "You didn't hire someone? *You* drove?" My pitch climbed an octave as my anxiety spiked to new levels. Clenching my fingers into fists, I flew at her, slamming her against the window. "You bitch!" I screamed, slapping her on the cheek. "You goddamned crazy bitch!" Tears blurred my vision while I punched her in the stomach, doubling her over, and I brought my knee up, smacking her chin. I grabbed her shirt and threw her to the floor.

I scrambled for my balance and hauled ass to the door. The click of Bexley's gun reached my ears as I scurried around the corner and into the hallway. Adrenaline coursed through my veins as I hopped onto the wood banister and slid down it like when I was a kid. As I landed, my socked feet slipped on the marble floor, causing me to land flat on my ass.

"Time's up, little sis."

I glanced up and stilled. This time Bexley wasn't smiling, not even a fucked up crazy-person grin. Even though she was at the top of the stairs and I was at the bottom, she had a straight shot, and the gun was aimed at my forehead. There was nothing for me to hide behind either.

"If this is how it's going down, then at least the marble will be easier to clean your blood off of. Much easier than the carpet." She descended the stairs, her weapon never wavering. "Enough exercise for tonight." She walked behind me and forced me up, jamming the gun into my back. "You're going back to the hidey-hole. I hope you enjoyed your time out. It won't happen again. You'll have food and get to take a piss once a day until I'm finished with you. Then … obviously, those needs will be a moot point."

My shoulders slumped with defeat as I climbed the stairs, and she escorted me to Dad's room again. Bexley allowed me to go to the bathroom and drink some water before I was bound again. She lifted the gag.

"Wait. What happened to Ron and Bethany?"

Bexley paused and dropped her hand while she laughed as though nothing insane had occurred between us a few minutes ago. "They're doing great."

Fear seized me while she chewed on a broken fingernail. "A few months after I had settled in with Uncle Tim and Aunt Judy, I told them everything I'd lived through. When Uncle Tim asked if I wanted to pay them a visit in England to 'thank them for all of their kindness,'

I agreed." She shook her head and smiled. "You should have seen their faces when they found us sitting in their kitchen. I don't know what little kid had replaced me, and I didn't want to know. I was sick and tired of everyone else taking what was mine."

She placed her hands on her hips and gave me a pointed look. "Anyway, I digress. At the stroke of midnight, we took Ron and Bethany to their basement. Uncle had called a few friends he knew in the area, and while I had been catching up with Ron and Bethany upstairs, the guys were digging graves."

My mouth gaped with horror.

"I have to admit, these dudes were powerhouses and had it done in no time." She snapped her fingers. "How do you all say it here? Oh, 'lickety-split.'" She shuffled her weight from one leg to the other. "Uncle tied their ankles and hands, then lined them up at the edges of their graves." Her hand fluttered to her chest. "I got to do the honors. I gave them each a hard shove backward and they flopped right in."

"Jesus," I muttered, terror ripping me in two from the inside out. She was beyond crazy.

"No, sis, he wasn't there. At all. Just goes to show how much reli-gion really helps people." She laughed at her own joke. "The best part was watching their eyes pop out of their fucking heads as the guys started to shovel dirt on top of them."

"You buried them alive?" My words caught in my throat, my stomach churning.

"In their own basement. It was sinfully fun." She tapped her finger against the tip of my nose, then stuffed the gag into my mouth. "Sweet dreams, sis."

Fear, grief, and anxiety crashed down on my chest, and I struggled to breathe. *How in the hell am I going to break out of this prison and escape with my life?*

2 6

If it weren't for the clock on the TV, I would have lost all track of time as I rotted away in the closet.

Ramsey's game would start soon, and I should be there, cheering for him from the stands. We should be celebrating and sleeping next to each other, but instead I was a hostage in my own home. Tears clouded my vision, and I wondered whether I would ever get to touch or kiss him again, or if our short time together had been all that we would have. *Will he be happy with Bexley, or will she grow tired of him and bury him as well?*

My moods cycled quickly from despair to hope. It was exhausting. Deep inside, I knew she would never let me walk away alive. She'd planned out everything to the last detail, and it disgusted me that it was working.

At one in the afternoon, the doorbell rang, and Bexley ran to the door and flung it open.

"Hey, gorgeous," Benji said, entering the house and embracing her.

Anxiety hummed beneath my skin while Tensley complimented her on her jeans and hugged her as well.

"How are you?" Ten asked, rubbing her arm.

When I'd first met Tensley, she wouldn't allow anyone to touch

215

her. It took a long time before she finally opened up about her past, but I was grateful she had. It had allowed Layne to come into her life, love her, and heal her heart.

"You said you have something exciting to tell me?" Bexley asked while she looped her arms through theirs and led them to the kitchen. I didn't miss her sly wink at one of the cameras.

Ten and Bexley pulled out barstools while Benji went straight to the liquor cabinet. I would have laughed if I'd had it in me.

A shy but beautiful smile eased across Ten's face. "Layne and I set a date."

My eyes widened. *No!* I shook my head in frustration. I would not miss my best friend's wedding. If anyone deserved a day filled with love, family, and friends, it was Tensley.

Bexley embraced her in a warm hug. "I'm so excited for you! When's the big day?"

"Thanks." Tensley glanced at Benji. "It's October twentieth, so a year from now."

"A fall wedding will be absolutely stunning. Have you picked out a dress yet?"

I growled. Bexley was playing it perfectly.

"I was hoping we could go together with Marilyn. We were going to shop in Seattle."

"I'd love to!" Bexley threw her arms around Ten again.

Benji carried the drinks over to them and grinned at Tensley. "Hurry up, girl, before I say it."

Bexley's expression clouded as her attention traveled between them. "Say what?"

"Will you be my maid of honor?" Tensley asked softly.

Bexley bounced out of the chair and nearly knocked Tensley over with her fake excitement.

I focused on taking slow and steady breaths. I could in no way allow her to take over my life. But I was at a loss. I'd fucked up two opportunities to escape already. If I botched another one, I would be dead right along with Dad.

"Cheers," Benji said and held up his glass. "To us. No matter how our lives change, we'll always be there to experience it together."

"Cheers," Ten and Bexley replied in unison.

For the rest of the afternoon, they chatted about dresses, possible wedding venues, flowers, and food. I tugged on the ropes that bound my wrists, hoping that over time I would be able to loosen them. If it worked, I would be ready to attack my fucked-up sister.

"I have a surprise for you today, love. There's been a change of plans." Bexley stretched her arms over her head and yawned, winking at the camera. She tossed the blankets off of her and slipped out of my bed.

I would give anything to sleep there again. My muscles ached, and my legs had started to cramp from the many hours in the chair. Maybe she would let me walk around a little bit.

Monday. Shit. Ramsey will be back. If she sleeps with him... I shook the thought out of my head. I had to stay focused and find an opening to take Bexley down. In order to occupy my time, I'd imagined shoving her out of the window and watching as she plummeted to her death. The minute I'd considered it, I cringed. I was no different from her if I was plotting her murder. The only scrap of solace I could scrounge up was that it was self-defense.

The closet door opened. "It's a big day today, Avery. Let's get you cleaned up for the afternoon action."

She removed the gag, and I took a deep breath through my mouth. My body was weak from lack of food and water, and my brain was numb, but I looked forward to a hot shower and standing.

Bexley was unusually quiet, which made me nervous as hell. She fed me and let me walk around my room for a few minutes, but she seemed mentally occupied.

For the first time, I wondered about Stockholm syndrome. *Could I learn to love her and depend on her if she continues to hold me captive much longer? Would her stealing my life from me leave me a hollow shell?*

Bexley glanced at my phone, then stuffed it into the back pocket of her jeans. She was adapting well. I hated her for it.

"Oh, it's almost showtime." She rubbed her hands together. "You're really going to like this." She threw her head back and laughed, and the sound made the hair on the back of my neck rise.

Once I was tucked away into my current living space and secured to the chair, the doorbell rang.

Bexley leaned over and whispered into my ear, "This one's for you, babe." The click of the lock notified me that she'd left. Her image appeared on the TV as she hurried down the stairs.

She slowly opened the front door and allowed Ramsey to enter. God, he looked good.

"Hey, babe." He wrapped his arms around my sister and stroked her hair. "I missed you so much. You were on my mind constantly, and I couldn't wait to get back to you." He leaned down and tilted her chin up with his fingers. He pressed a lingering kiss to her mouth, but instead of returning it, Bexley took his hand and stepped back. The chiseled lines of his face were etched with confusion. "Babe, what's wrong?"

"We should talk." Bexley guided him into the living room and sat on the leather sofa. Ramsey sat next to her, but allowed some space between them.

Bexley stared out of the large windows and massaged her forehead precisely like I would. "This isn't working, Ramsey."

My eyes widened, and my attention landed on Ramsey. Shock registered on his face as he stood slowly. "I don't understand, Avery. I love you. You love me. I … I…" He shook his head and ran his hand through his hair. "Are you mad about the Hamptons trip or my football schedule? You were on board when we got together."

I am on board, babe. You know I love watching you play. That's not me!

"It was fun while it lasted, but it's over. I'm sorry." Bexley stood and flipped her hair behind her shoulder.

Completely powerless, I witnessed pain and confusion rip through Ramsey. "Avery, don't say that. Please. Let's take a break for a while, but don't tell me it's over. If you're feeling overwhelmed, if we're moving too fast, or if you're still hurting too much over your dad to be in a relationship, then we can pull back or take a break." He closed the gap between them and reached out to touch her, but she jerked away.

"I've thought about this a lot, and we're simply not a good fit. The sooner you accept that, the sooner you can move on. I have."

Ramsey gawked at her. "There's someone else?"

Oh god, no. I would never cheat on him—never.

"Yes. I wasn't going to tell you, but since you're not taking no for an answer … there is someone else."

Ramsey's shoulders sagged with defeat, his emotions on his sleeve. He tossed his hands up in the air and took a few steps backward, his horror evident on his face. "If that's who will make you happy, then I'll go."

"That would be best. And don't call or come by to check on me. I have security until all this mess is over. Just … leave." She shooed him away as though he were a pesky fly in the house.

Tears welled in my eyes while he wiped his away. *Baby, it's not me.* I watched him quietly leave, my heart splintering into a thousand pieces. That was the last time I would see him, gaze into his beautiful blue eyes, or hear his deep voice, which sent shivers over my skin. I hiccupped through my tears, imagining how he must be feeling. As my cries quieted, several things began to sink in. I no longer had to watch him kiss my sister or her paw at him. He wouldn't have sex with her, thinking it was me. *Holy shit. She did me a favor.* A moment later, dread washed over me. She was getting him out of the way. Then it dawned on me that Bexley was nearly finished with me. Ice flowed through my veins. My time was running out.

2 8

The date-and-time stamp on the TV told me it was Tuesday morning. I hadn't been able to sleep at all, my thoughts bouncing between Ramsey and how long I had left to live. Even though he was devastated, I hoped Bexley's rejection would keep him safe from her. The farther away he was from her, the better.

I frowned when the doorbell rang at ten sharp. Bexley was waiting by the door, which told me she was expecting whoever was on the other side. She smoothed her short dress and flipped her hair behind her shoulder in anticipation.

If my mouth could have fallen open, I would have had to scoop it off the floor. Vincent McCade strolled into my house. *What the hell?*

"Thank you for coming over, Vincent. I really appreciate it." Bexley flashed him a sexy smile, and I nearly vomited.

"I'm a little surprised you wanted to see me alone." His gaze greedily raked over her, and he licked his lips.

"Well, I can't get to the office right now, so having you over made the most sense." Bexley stuck out her chest as she spoke. "Why don't we sit down in the kitchen. I've made us some coffee."

"That sounds great." Vincent kept his eyes on her ass while she walked in front of him.

Fucking bastard.

Bexley grabbed cups and filled them. "Creamer? Milk? Sugar?" She flashed him a charming smile.

"Creamer would be great."

She opened the fridge and bent over, her ass sticking in the air. "Here it is." She handed it to him, her fingers brushing his in the process. Bexley hopped up on the island and crossed her long, toned legs. "I miss seeing everyone in the office."

"Is that so?" Vincent's eyebrow arched as he placed his mug on the counter, his attention on her thighs.

"Mm-hm." Bexley uncrossed her legs and spread them open. "Oh gosh. I forgot to wear panties today. Silly me."

Vincent closed the gap between them. "I'm happy to see you've had a change of heart. You know I didn't rape you. You were begging for it."

Bexley flipped her skirt up. "And I want it right now too." She took his hand and placed it between her thighs. "Just so there's no mistake about what I want."

"You're so fucking wet for me."

"All for you." She rolled over and propped up on all fours for him.

Vincent's hand pulled back and slapped her hard on the ass. "That's for denying me."

"Oh, Vincent," Bexley moaned. "I promise I'll be good."

Smack. Smack. "I can't wait to fuck your tight little pussy again, but first ..."

I thanked God I didn't have a full view while Vincent dropped to his knees and buried his face between her legs. I flinched and looked away, reliving the rape in my mind. *That fucking bitch found out what he did to me, and this is her way of once again punishing me for having the life she wanted.* No way would I be able to approach the board of directors and have him removed after her disgusting behavior. Vincent thought he was with me.

Bexley moaned. "Oh, it's been so long. That's it, baby." Bexley continued to urge him on until she called his name.

The sound of shuffling and a zipper reached my ears, but I refused to look at the TV.

"I'm going to fuck you senseless," Vincent said.

"Oh, I hope so," Bexley purred.

The noise of grunting and bodies slapping together filled my small space. I attempted to think about Ramsey in order to distract myself, but it wasn't easy. I forced the bile back down my throat. As ill as Vincent and Bexley's show was making me, vomiting while gagged was dangerous.

"Oh yeah, you little bitch," Vincent said, panting. "You like it, don't you?"

"More, Vincent. Fuck me harder."

I shook my head, willing the X-rated movie to be over.

An eternity later, they finished. I chanced a peek at the screen. Vincent was lying on top of her, still groping her tits. Squeamish, I closed my eyes again and waited for the sound of Vincent's zipper and their conversation to begin again.

"My goodness, thank you. Now I can focus on business."

I returned my attention to the television as they finished adjusting their clothes. Bexley jumped off the island.

"Maybe we can do that again before I leave." Vincent smacked her on the ass and laughed.

Bexley whirled around. "Only if you're a very good boy. Maybe then I'll grab a blindfold and handcuffs." She gave him a wink.

"I'm going to use your restroom."

"You've been here plenty of times visiting Dad, so you know where everything is."

Vincent grinned at her before he disappeared down the hall.

Bexley picked up his cup and took a few drinks. She set it on the counter and busied herself with refilling it. After she replaced the coffee pot and removed a spoon from the drawer, Bexley stood still with her back to the camera.

"So, how can I help you with the business?" Vincent asked, returning to the kitchen.

"Let's sit." Bexley handed him his mug, then took a sip of her own.

She pulled out a chair for Vincent and settled into the one across from him. "I need some advice, and since you've been there and know everyone … Well, Vincent …" She reached across the table and took his hand in hers. "It will benefit us both if we're on the same side instead of enemies."

Vincent leaned back in his chair and took a few drinks, his attention never leaving her. "I like the way you think, but why now? You were a total bitch last week."

Bexley rolled her eyes. "Hormones. You know how we are. One minute we're fine, the next we're moody as hell." She giggled.

"You can say that again."

"There's one good thing about it, though." She leaned across the table and tugged the top of her dress down, exposing her breasts to him. "I'm horny as hell *all* the time."

Vincent reached out and pinched her nipple.

"Finish up your coffee like a good boy, then I'll let you fuck me from behind again."

In a few gulps, he'd downed his drink and placed the cup on the windowsill. He stood, walked to her side of the table, and unzipped his pants again. At least he hadn't removed his disgusting dick yet.

Bexley looked over her shoulder while he flipped her dress up.

Suddenly, Vincent staggered sideways and grabbed the chair for balance. He took several steps backward and clutched his chest.

Holy shit. I leaned closer to the TV, watching it all go down.

Bexley straightened herself and her dress, a malicious sneer sliding into place. Vincent collapsed to the floor, and she folded her arms across her chest and stared at him.

"Help me." He reached for her, but she sidestepped him.

"Vincent, Vincent, Vincent." She wagged her finger at him. "You don't honestly think I'm interested in you, do you?"

That time, I smirked.

"Help," he said again, his voice low and raspy.

"You're not going to last much longer, so I'd better get on with it. Tim Gambino said to tell you hello. He's Uncle Tim to me, and to you … he's the head of the crime family that you tried to double cross."

Bexley lowered her face closer to Vincent's, a devious grin slipping into place. "Want to know a little secret? I'm not Avery. I'm her identical twin, Bexley."

Vincent's eyes widened, fear twisting his typically smug face.

"That's right. I'm her sister and Tim's niece. It was very nice to meet you, by the way."

Vincent shook his head.

If he weren't dying, I would have laughed. Vincent had always pretended to be so smart, but not this time.

"You don't mess with my family and get away with it. I don't know why you never gave Uncle Tim's money back to him, but now we're even."

My brows furrowed. Vincent hadn't paid them back with the money he'd stolen from the company. My guess was that I would never learn the reason why either.

Vincent reached out to her again, his face beet red, then his arm dropped with a thud onto the kitchen floor, and I witnessed the life drain from his eyes.

Bexley looked up at the camera and sneered. "There's your lesson in poisoning 101." She walked around a lifeless Vincent, smoothed her hair, and squared her shoulders. "Showtime." A loud scream burst from her throat, and she ran to the front door. "Help! Something's wrong with my business partner!"

Greyson flew into the house while she followed, pretending to be hysterical. "I don't know what happened. He was fine one minute, then he clutched his chest and fell. Oh my god, is he okay?"

Greyson placed his fingers on Vincent's neck and removed his phone from his jeans pocket.

Over the next several hours, I watched the ambulance and police arrive. My house was full of people as the coroner removed the body. Bexley was a fountain of fake tears and uncontrollable trembles while the cops asked her a million questions.

Since Vincent was gone, Sutton wouldn't need to have him investigated for embezzlement, and Bexley had full control of the business.

I suspected that no one would ever realize Vincent was poisoned.

Bexley knew what she was doing, but worse than that, she was a cold-blooded murderer. I slammed my eyes shut as Vincent's dying in front of me played through my mind and the horror broke through my shock. *Fucking hell.*

My thoughts tormented me with different scenarios of how she planned to end my life. Somehow, I needed to convince her to let me shower and eat. Then I would make my move and pray like hell it worked that time.

"Wow, I'm exhausted," Bexley said, her accent returning as she entered the closet. "Was it a spectacular show from here?"

She jerked the gag out of my mouth and smiled. "I have to say that fucking him was a brilliant move on my part. At first, I contemplated allowing him to live so that I could force him out of the company. Then, with great pleasure, I would watch him fall into deep despair while I ripped everything away from him." She chewed her nail, appearing deep in thought. "But instead, I decided I didn't want to waste my time with all of that, even though it would have been fun. When he went to the bathroom, I slipped a little something extra into his coffee."

"I couldn't tell what you were doing, since your back was to me," I said quietly. It was vital that I not say anything that would set her off. In my gut, I knew it was my last chance to escape if I wanted to live.

"By design, sis. That way, no one had any proof. Not that they will find it in his system, but a girl has gotta cover her ass." She snickered. "Okay, let's walk you for a few minutes. I brought some food up, and since I had such a good day, I'll even let you get a shower."

My pulse rang in my ears as fear and hope intertwined inside me, making it nearly impossible to distinguish between the two. I had to stay alert for my opportunity.

Bexley jerked me to my feet and untied me. I shook my arms out and walked in place, allowing the feeling to return to my legs.

"No funny shit." She patted the gun in her waistband.

"Understood. I'm just grateful for a good meal and clean clothes." I wasn't lying. All of the small things I'd taken for granted had become special—valued and dreamed about.

She nudged me forward with her hand. "I think I'm going to miss you, Avery."

Chills shot down my spine, and I broke out in a cold sweat.

"I know our relationship has been unconventional, but I do have a heart. You *are* my sister. But rest assured, I'll think about you every day and all the good times we could have had … if only."

"How much longer do we have together?" I walked down the hallway and to my bedroom.

"I haven't decided exactly when, but soon. Since I like you and we're blood-related … twins. I've changed my mind. I'm not going to drag it out. Your death will be quick and painless."

My jaw clenched, and I willed myself not to cry. Beautiful images of Ramsey laughing and smiling raced through my head. My chest tightened with thoughts of the late nights we'd spent together as kids at the vacation home, and the way he touched me and made me feel loved and special. I held on to those, embracing them with everything inside me. He would be my last thought before I took my final breath. *His* name would be on my lips.

I glanced at the mural as we entered my room, hope flickering in my chest. *Daddy, help me.*

Bexley motioned to my dresser. "Hurry up and get your clothes." She paused, glancing at the painted picture. "Sis, I might as well tell you, not that it will do you any good, but Ramsey hasn't stopped trying to patch up our relationship. He really loves you. I might have to reconsider keeping him."

My nostrils flared, but I continued to search through my drawers for clean underwear and a bra in order to maintain my composure.

"He'll be good to you. He's a good man, Bexley. At least I know he wouldn't be alone when I'm gone."

Bexley's eyebrows shot up. "Are we having a sisterly moment?"

I turned toward her, forcing myself to say the opposite of what I felt. "I guess so. Ramsey and I grew up together. We have … you have a bond with him. He's your biggest supporter, and he's genuine. That's so hard to find. I think if you can settle down with him, it would be good for both of you." My voice came out confident despite the way I trembled inside.

Bexley's gaze held mine. She was probably trying to decide whether I was serious or not. Definitely not, but I needed to see if she had any humanity left deep inside her.

"I'll keep it in mind."

Bexley must have been in a good mood, because she allowed me to shower for a few minutes longer than usual before she told me to get out. As always, she handed me a towel the second that I finished and placed my foot on the bathmat.

"It's funny. We're identical twins, but there's one noticeable difference, if someone knew where to look."

"Really?" She had my interest.

She lowered her pants below her hip bone. "It's faint, but I have a birthmark. You don't. Honestly, it's why I couldn't stay with Ramsey. He would have noticed it and ruined my plan, and I would have had to kill him."

"Yeah, he would have." I ignored her comment about killing Ramsey. I was too afraid I might send her on a rampage. "I wondered if we had any small differences." I finished drying off and handed her the towel back, thanking God that Bexley's birthmark had saved Ramsey's life. I reached for my clothes, which were on the toilet, and took my time getting dressed. If they were my last minutes, I wanted to savor the feel of the denim on my legs, my lace bra against my breasts, and the silky cotton of my shirt against my skin.

Bexley nodded at the vanity and chair. "Sit. I'll dry your hair. We can pretend that we're close and discuss boys, shopping, and cars or some shit."

I caught myself before my eyes narrowed. "That would be nice. Do you have a guy in your life in Seattle?"

I sat down while Bexley picked up the hair dryer. "That's difficult to answer. I get bored and tend not to stay in a relationship for long." Sadness clouded her expression.

My sister was lonely. She'd had a tortured childhood, and even though she was out of that life, she was still trying to make people love her. My walls lowered a bit.

Over the next half hour, Bexley dried my hair. I watched her reflection in the mirror as she focused on me. An array of emotions danced across her face—anger, fear, and love. Whether Bexley admitted it or not, she cared a little about me. It was too bad I couldn't say the same.

"Your hair is so soft." She brushed it gently, then smoothed her hands down the long strands.

"I use a fantastic mask once a week. You should try it. It's in the third drawer.

"Oh, thanks! I mean, I saw it when I was familiarizing myself with my new things, but it means more when your sister gives you permission." She gave me a genuine smile. "Do you want me to do your makeup? I've always wanted to do that with someone."

My heart ached for her. She should have been able to have those moments with some of her friends. She really had entered into a pretend world with me, creating the experience she'd longed for over the years.

"I would love that."

Bexley opened up a bit about her life in Seattle and what our family was like while she applied foundation, eyeshadow, eyeliner, and mascara. Surprisingly, she was really good at it.

"Take a look." She chewed on her fingernail as I faced the mirror.

"Wow. Bexley, holy shit. You're amazing!" I tilted my head, examining my new look from every angle. Her work was stunning. "You're really talented."

A blush crept over her cheeks, and for a fleeting minute, I had a glimpse into the lost little girl in a woman's body. I wondered if I could find any way to reach her. Maybe I'd been approaching it all wrong.

I turned slowly and glanced up at her. "I would give anything to hug my sister. I've never been able to wrap my arms around you." My voice cracked with emotion. Within a short amount of time, I'd gone from hate to hope. Bexley was lowering her walls with me, and we were connecting on a deeper level.

Her gaze narrowed suspiciously. "I'll shoot you dead if you're messing with me."

"I'm not, Bexley. I ... if our time together is limited, I want to make the most of it. Let me hang out with you and learn more about those hidden talents. Let me hold my sister." Tears spilled down my cheeks.

Bexley's eyes glistened, and she wiped the moisture away with her hand. She pulled her gun out and gripped it tightly. "Fine."

I put my hands up and stood slowly, the backs of my knees brushing against the vanity seat. "It's okay. I promise."

She backed away, then stopped. "No one has hugged me since my grandparents died. Unless they wanted sex."

My throat tightened. "I'm so sorry." Before she could back out, I wrapped my arms around her and held her. "I'm so fucking sorry you went through all of that. We should have been together and the best of friends." My shoulders shook with my cries as I grieved for her, for me, and for everything we'd both lost.

Bexley embraced me, her fingers clutching the soft fabric of my shirt while her tears flowed freely. "I'm sorry too," she whispered in my ear.

We clung to each other, the anger and hate softening between us. Finally, I slowly released her. "What do you think about popping some popcorn and talking all night?"

Her arms dropped to her sides. I didn't miss her finger slipping on and off the trigger while she contemplated my offer.

"Maybe." She urged me forward into my room. She sat on the bed, her gun still tightly in her grip.

I leaned against the wall and folded my hands over my chest a few feet away from her.

Her gaze drifted to the floor, and silence filled the space between us. "You were outstanding in there." Her head snapped up, her crazy smile in place once again. "Avery, man. You had me for a minute. I really thought you might love me. Just a little bit. But how? I killed your Dad. I've held you hostage in your own home and stolen your life." She hopped up, her hands trembling as she raised the gun and trained it on my heart. "I almost bought it, Avery! I almost thought you loved me!"

A loud crack exploded in the room, followed by a piercing scream —*my* scream.

3 0

My body shook violently as I stared at the scene before me, unable to comprehend what had happened.

Someone wrapped their arms around me. "It's okay. I'm here, honey."

My wails pierced my soul while I looked at my dead sister, her dark blood soaking my lavender comforter. Davia had shot her in the forehead. I sank to my knees and clung to Davia.

Shouts filled the house, and footsteps thundered down the hall.

"In here!" Davia called, her voice shaking while we held each other tightly.

"Holy shit," Tad said, lowering his gun when he saw Bexley sprawled out on the bed. "Avery?"

"I'm Avery," I choked out.

Greyson's voice carried through the hall as he called 911 as he entered the room.

Tad knelt, and I peered at him through swollen eyes. "C-C-Call Ramsey."

He nodded. Even in my shocked state, I knew security had my friend's phone numbers in case there was an emergency.

His voice faded into the background while my sobs ebbed and

233

flowed. Davia rocked me and smoothed my hair, soothing me as if I were a small child and terrified after a nightmare.

"She … she killed Dad," I said, my voice sounding foreign to my ears.

"I heard her. When I came up the hall to tell you I was here, I saw her. At first, I thought it was you, but then she admitted … she admitted to killing Steven." Davia choked on the words, her sobs shaking her body.

In minutes, the house was filled with police and EMTs. Davia and I leaned against the wall and held hands, watching the flurry of activity around us.

"Is she dead? Goddammit, someone, please tell me, is Avery dead?"

"Ramsey!" I scrambled up from the floor and bolted for the door. "Ramsey! Ramsey!" I tore down the hall, frantically searching through the people that had gathered downstairs.

"He's with me!" I pleaded to one of the detectives I hadn't met yet.

The detective nodded, waved Ramsey through, and returned to his conversation.

"Avery!" Ramsey took the stairs two at a time, his expression filled with fear and agony.

"Ramsey!" I threw myself into his arms. "It wasn't me. She wasn't me. She was my twin." I tried to explain between my sobs. "I love you. Please don't ever let me go."

"Oh, baby. Oh god." His hand rested on the back of my head while he held me. "I'm right here, babe."

"Avery, we need you back in here, please."

I stepped away from Ramsey, then kissed him hard. "Will you come with me? The crime scene is in my bedroom … and so is Davia. The detective already allowed you up here with me, so as long as we're careful, it should be okay."

I led him down the hall, but before we entered, another detective stopped us.

"I'm Detective Maxwell Scott. I can't let you in." He gave us a pinched smile.

"Please," I begged. "We'll sit against the far wall and stay put. You have my word."

"You're Avery, correct?"

I nodded, silently pleading with him.

He placed a hand on his slender hip. "Are you the football star everyone is talking about? The one from Montana that just moved to Spokane?"

"Yes, sir," Ramsey replied.

Detective Scott ran his fingers over his bald head, then waved us in. "Stay out of the way until we need to talk to you. In a few minutes, this room will be sectioned off as a crime scene, anyway."

Ramsey gulped, his Adam's apple bobbing. He took my hand in his and nodded.

Silently, we walked into my room, the flash of the camera catching my eye as the investigation continued.

"Fuck," Ramsey said, his attention landing on Bexley. He gawked at her, before he stared at me. "Identical twin." The color drained from his face.

I could only imagine what was going through his head—how he'd kissed her thinking it was me, how he'd almost fucked her, and how he'd missed the slightest clues that something was horribly wrong.

I placed my hands on his cheeks. "I'm not upset that you kissed her. It's over. I'll explain as soon as I can, but I know everything that happened between the two of you. I want you back. I didn't break up with you. I love you, and I want to pick up the pieces and ..." I closed my eyes, then opened them again. "I want to spend the rest of my life with you. The days I was her hostage, I had time to think about what I wanted. You."

Ramsey stroked my cheek with the pad of his thumb. "I love you. I love you so fucking much." Tears welled in his eyes, then he pressed his lips to mine.

I turned to Davia, who was still sitting against the wall. "Davia saved me, Ramsey. She shot Bexley right before Bexley was about to pull the trigger and kill me. She needs us, and ... I need her." My hand flew to my mouth, muffling my cries.

Ramsey slipped his arm around my waist and guided me toward her. "Hey, Davia." He held his hand out to her and pulled her up into a hug. "Thank you for saving the love of my life." He placed a kiss on the top of her head, then we all embraced each other and cried.

I'd taken so much for granted. I'd lost everything that was important to me within such a short amount of time—Dad, Ramsey, and nearly my own life. There were so many things that I wanted to do differently, but for the moment, I wanted to cherish the two people standing next to me and let their love dissolve the remnants of the nightmare I was walking away from.

"Avery!"

I released my family and whirled around, searching for the familiar voice.

"Sutton!"

We rushed to each other and hugged.

"I'm so happy to see you."

"When Tad called to tell us that a shot had been fired, it scared the shit out of me. When he saw that you were alive, he let us know. All the way here, Pierce and I tried to figure out how someone had gotten to you. It wasn't until we arrived and Pierce spoke to the cops that we learned you had an identical twin." She released me and wiped my tears away. "I'm so sorry. I kept digging to find out more about your family, but I didn't uncover it in time."

"It's not your fault. Her grandparents raised her in England. It didn't sound as though there was a paper trail like there would have been if she'd been adopted. They took her straight home from the hospital."

"I couldn't find any birth records other than yours. I suspect Steven covered it up to keep her safe from his family. It's over, though. You're safe now, Avery."

I nodded, struggling for the right words, but there were none. I was exhausted mentally and physically.

"Ms. Davenport, we'll need to take your statement."

"Her attorney is on the way," Sutton interrupted, placing herself between the officer and me. "She and Mrs. Davenport will be happy to speak with you as soon as he arrives." Sutton's tone was firm. She wasn't taking no for an answer.

"Come on." Sutton led me to the corner with Ramsey and Davia. "We're about to be moved downstairs for questioning."

My attention landed on Bexley again, and my chest ached with an abundance of emotions. "I need a new bed," I whispered, peering up at Ramsey.

"You're not staying here. The second this is over, you're coming home with me."

"That sounds really nice." I attempted a smile.

The rest of the day was a blur. Franklin arrived, and we all moved to the kitchen for the questioning. Sutton brewed a fresh pot of coffee, and Pierce joined us along with Tad.

It took a while before they removed Bexley's body. The image of her with a bullet in her head had burned itself into my memory. No matter how hard I tried, I doubted I would ever be able to get rid of it. I had basically seen myself dead.

The police asked a ton of questions in a million different ways, but they received the same answers over and over again. Ramsey held my hand, giving me constant reassurance. I explained how Bexley had slipped into the kitchen when Tad and I had been cleaning out the pool house. I looked over at Tad. His shoulders sagged, and his expression was filled with regret. I shook my head. In no way was it his fault. It was mine. I'd made the mistake of not double-checking that I'd locked the door.

When I explained that I'd been tied to a chair and gagged, Ramsey's hand began to tremble. "There are cameras all over the house. Everything that happened was recorded ... except for Dad's closet, where I was kept."

Ramsey pressed his lips together in a tight line, his eyes reddening. We were going to have to talk it through. He couldn't have known I had a twin. It wasn't his fault, but I knew him well enough to realize that he blamed himself.

Finally, after I'd finished with the detective, it was Davia's turn. I reached for her hand, and we exchanged meaningful looks. It took me a minute before I realized that Davia wasn't high or drunk. Her eyes were clear for the first time in years.

"Mrs. Davenport? When did you realize there was a threat?" Detective Scott asked.

Franklin nodded at her and continued to listen intently.

Davia squeezed my hand so tightly that the blood flow was restricted, but I didn't care. She was terrified. I had been the victim, but Davia had pulled the trigger and ended Bexley's life.

"I came home … to pack." She glanced at me, then returned her gaze to the investigator. "I was quiet and secretly hoping that Avery wasn't here. I was … It's not important now." She took a shaky breath. "I heard a voice, so I walked toward Avery's room. The girl was talking about how she killed Steven." She gasped, covering her mouth. "I pressed myself against the wall in order not to gain attention, and it was then that I saw Avery. I have a concealed-carry permit, so I removed my gun from the secret compartment in my handbag." She shook her head. "Avery used the girl's name, so my suspicion that Bexley wasn't Avery was confirmed. When Bexley stood and pointed her gun at Avery, I fired."

"What happened next?" The detective's pen stopped midscribble while he stared at her.

"Bexley fell backward onto the bed, and I rushed over to Avery."

The detective looked at her, then me. I wondered if he was trying to unnerve us, but we were already spooked.

"Do you have everything you need, gentlemen?" Franklin asked.

Even though he was asking, he was letting them know it was enough for one night. Detective Scott put his little notebook into his jacket along with his pen. "We'll take the tapes, of course. If it supports everything that was said today, no charges will be brought against Mrs. Davenport."

"I will view them with you in order to make sure nothing is tampered with." Franklin shoved his hand into his pocket and pinned the detective with an intense gaze. "I've already made a call to Chief Watson, and he's agreed to it."

The detective nodded, then he and the rest of the cops and investigators left. Tad followed them and locked the door as the last person walked out of the house. He poked his head back in the kitchen. "Avery, I need you to set the alarm."

"I'll be right back." I stood, the harsh sound of the chair scraping across the floor shocking me. I stopped near Pierce. "Can I have a word, please?"

"Of course." He fell in behind me and lingered in the foyer with Tad while I punched in the code.

"I'll never forget to lock a door or set the alarm again in my life." I wrapped my arms around myself as though I could hold myself together.

"Pierce, I wanted to say this to Tad in front of you. This in no way is your fault, Tad. It was mine. You asked if I'd locked the kitchen entrance, and I honestly thought I had. You did your job." My attention bounced between the men before I continued. "Tad, Bexley was my identical twin that no one knew existed. You saw her and even talked to her when she was outside. She always kept it brief in order not to tip you guys off. She was smart, cunning, and terrifying. She killed …" My body went rigid with tension as my mind recalled her murdering Vincent. "Vincent McCade. She murdered him in my kitchen. The cameras recorded everything." I massaged my forehead as exhaustion crept in. "The cops will see that she turned her back to the camera. You can't see her slip the poison into his coffee, but she admitted it to me. She said it was one that was hardly traceable."

Pierce rubbed his chin. "Did she mention what she used?"

"No, just that it was difficult to detect."

"That's a start, at least," Tad said, speaking up for the first time.

"Thank you for all your help. I'd like to keep Tad and Greyson on for a while, Pierce."

"Are you sure? I can give you different men, if you want."

"I'm sure," I answered.

Pierce patted Tad on the back. "I'm going to locate my wife, and we're going to head out, unless you need anything else, Avery. I mean anything. If you want us all to stay here with you, we'll."

"Thank you. I'm going to head over to Ramsey's tonight, though.

I'll have Tad and Greyson, so that will work. No matter how much security I have, I won't feel safe for a long time."

"I know you have friends, but Sutton really took to you. I'll have her call you, and you two can go out for lunch or drinks once a week. It would be really good for her too. She works a lot."

"I'd really like that." I offered an exhausted smile.

3 1

It was nearly two in the morning when we arrived at Ramsey's apartment. Tad was stationed outside the door, and Greyson guarded the stairwell.

Ramsey flipped the dead bolt and slipped the chain into place. He set my suitcase on the floor, then took my hand and led me into the kitchen. "I know it's late, but you need to eat. I'll get you a drink too."

"Please. I'm exhausted and wired all at the same time." I slid my butt onto the barstool and placed my head on the island.

Ramsey poured me a supersized glass of white wine, and I took a few long drinks, looking forward to when it began to soothe my frayed nerves.

He was quiet as he made us some sandwiches and removed a bag of chips from the cabinet, then he plunked down on the seat next to me.

I popped a chip into my mouth and savored the BBQ flavor when it hit my tongue. "I never thought chips could taste so good."

Ramsey stared at me, his face clouding. "I'm so sorry, Avery." Heavy guilt hung on every syllable.

The pain in his expression wrecked me. "No more. I mean it. Maybe this conversation would be different if you'd slept with her, but it didn't happen. You thought she was me." My voice trailed off. "It tore my heart out to see you with her, Ramsey, but sitting alone in the closet allowed me to process it. During those days, I realized how much I love you." Tears clouded my vision. "I promised myself that if I walked away from her alive, I'd never let you go."

"I love you," Ramsey whispered, the pad of his thumb stroking my cheek.

"I love you too. She did you a huge favor when she broke up with you." As much as I tried to comfort him, I couldn't keep from crying again.

"It fucking gutted me. I've never felt pain like that before. I couldn't … I should have known then that something was off." He rubbed his face.

"Me too. I cried as I watched it on the TV, gagged and tied up in the closet. I love you so much, Ramsey. That's all that matters. The fact that we're sitting here eating together is a miracle. If Davia hadn't come home … I'd be gone, too, and you would never have learned the truth."

Ramsey stood and pulled me off my seat.

I wrapped my arms around his waist and pressed my head against his chest. The warmth of his body calmed me.

"I love you, Avery. From this day on, I swear to protect you with my own life."

A knock on the door nearly sent me skittering backward. Ramsey frowned at me. "Stay here," he ordered.

My head pounded while he opened it slowly.

Relief washed over me as I spotted Davia. She was a mess.

Ramsey stepped back, allowing her inside.

"I'm so sorry to drop in like this. I realize we have a lot to discuss, but can I stay with you and Avery tonight? I can't be alone in that house. I'm afraid I'll drink."

Her hands fidgeted until Ramsey draped his arm around her shoulders. "I have a guest room that has your name on it."

"Really?" Davia looked at me for permission.

"Really. We were just eating. Are you hungry?" I smiled at her. No matter what happened between us in the future, she would forever hold a special place in my heart for saving my life. I hoped she would stay sober, and we could build a new relationship.

"That would be lovely. Can I use your bathroom first?" she asked.

Ramsey pointed toward the second room on the left and took her overnight bag. The second she disappeared, I grabbed my wine and Ramsey's beer and hightailed it to his bedroom. I hid them on his nightstand by placing a picture in front of them. She was newly sober, and the last thing I wanted was for her to drink that night.

"Shit." I bolted back down the hall, past Ramsey, and to the fridge. "Help me." I waved him over and handed him his six-pack, then I collected the remaining wine. "Hide it. She doesn't need temptation tonight."

"Crap." In three long strides, Ramsey reached the sliding door and flung it open. He disappeared onto the balcony, then motioned for me to hand him my bottles.

"Hurry, she's coming," I whisper-yelled.

"Is everything all right?" Davia asked as Ramsey returned.

"Yeah, I was showing Avery the little outdoor space. The sun will be coming up soon, and if she's not asleep, I thought it would be awesome to snuggle up and watch it together. She deserves to see something beautiful." He locked the door, then kissed me on the forehead.

Nice save.

After we ate and helped Davia settle into the guest room, Ramsey and I crawled into bed.

I snuggled up to him and traced his stomach muscles with the tips of my fingers. "I wondered if I would ever get to do this again." I peered up at him through my eyelashes. "Or this." I reached up and kissed him gently. "Make love to me," I whispered.

Ramsey's eyes darkened with desire as he pressed his lips against mine. "I feel like my heart was given back to me tonight. I don't ever want to lose you again."

"You won't. Just please forgive yourself." I gave him an exhausted smile.

I slid into the warmth of his blankets and brought his mouth to mine. His kiss grew more aggressive as his touch began to soothe my shattered soul. I had questioned so many things over the last week with Bexley, wondering why all of it had happened and how I would put the pieces of my life back together if I survived. I wasn't sure I would ever have the answers to those questions, but the one thing I was sure of was the man next to me. I had no doubt in my mind that he was the love of my life.

3 2

Over the next three weeks, additional information came in concerning Bexley. The fact that she had been admitted into a mental hospital during her teen years while in England had helped our case. I wasn't told why she had been treated, but I'd had first-hand experience with her lack of conscience and mood swings. I didn't need to know anything else.

Davia was rapidly cleared of any wrongdoing as well. I was aware that Franklin had powerful connections. Plus, he had reviewed the recordings firsthand. After that, the case wrapped up quickly. We were all relieved.

I'd offered to let Davia stay at my place, but she declined. She said she wanted to visit the lake house and reflect on how she wanted to live her life. Before she left, we sat down and had a long talk. My heart softened even more toward her when I realized she had no idea the marriage to Dad had never been finalized. We speculated about why he never filed the license, but all we came up with was that he was trying to protect us. Just like everyone else on the planet, Dad had made some terrible decisions. Besides, it no longer mattered. To us, she was still his wife, and I had no doubt that she truly loved Dad.

Davia also admitted that Dad hadn't shared his past with her other than the fact that Cecile had died during childbirth. She'd been as stunned as I was when she learned I had a twin.

Through a stream of tears, Davia admitted that as much as she loved me, she resented coming in second place. At first, she'd dabbled with the drugs because she was lonely, and before she realized it, she'd found herself in the middle of a full-blown addiction. What still bothered me was the fact that Dad had never done anything about it. My best guess was that he had carried so much guilt for lying about Bexley that he ignored it. Dad was sharp and never missed anything in the business world. But outside of that arena, he was in denial and just like an ostrich. He stuck his head into the sand and showed his ass.

She was full of apologies for being out of her head instead of being the mom that I needed. We had certainly taken a step in the right direction, but it would take time for me to forgive her. The longer she stayed clean and sober, the more I could trust her. At least she had shown up when I needed her the most, and I was still alive. Only time would tell, but it sounded as though treatment had helped Davia. I was even looking forward to getting to know who she was when she was clean and sober. She had my full support.

I'd talked at length with Ramsey about contacting Cecile's side of the family. As much as I wanted to, Bexley had broken a part of me. After days and days of struggling with it, I finally gave myself permission not to contact them. I needed to heal, and it would take me a while to trust strangers again.

Sutton had called to see how I was doing, and we scheduled lunch. I admired Sutton's quiet strength. Even though she was only five years older than I was, I suspected I could learn a lot from her. It would also be nice to spend time with her outside of a crisis.

Patrick and Olivia had talked to me at great length about therapy. At the beginning, I was reluctant because I didn't want to relive the hell I'd barely survived, but once the chaos was over, I was left alone with the horror of the events. I didn't have a clue of how to process any of it. I'd only been six times, but I was learning some tools to use when the PTSD shredded me to pieces. Ramsey went with me the first few sessions as well. I was a bit surprised when he offered, but I knew he still wrestled with his own guilt. He also wanted to know how to help me when I had nightmares or found myself rigid with fear, unable to realize that I was safe. And in the back of my mind, I wondered if I ever would be. After all, Bexley was related to a crime family. Hell, I was related to them, too, and if I were lucky, maybe it would save my life instead of putting me in danger.

Since Vincent was gone, I wasn't worried about the business falling into corrupt hands, and I took some time to meet with Larry Townsend, the attorney Dad had lined up for me to assist with the company financials. He was a kind, older man with a sharp mind. I was grateful Dad had connected us.

Thoughts of my Dad filled my head every day. My heart ached to hear his voice and pick his brain about the business. I didn't have a doubt in my mind that he had been with me the whole time Bexley had held me hostage. I could almost feel his presence and see his smile in my mind's eye. Those times had kept me going. As the days went by, I also found myself angry with him for the secrets that had nearly cost me my life. *How could he not have reached out to Bexley after she turned eighteen?* I had to remind myself that he was a human being and was under immense pressure. From what I'd learned, most of his decisions had been to protect us, and that was what I chose to hold on to.

I had also spent a lot of time with Tensley, Layne, and Benji. One afternoon, I was finally ready to tell them everything, and we all gathered at their place. After I'd shared the full story with them, we all held each other and cried. Tensley begged my forgiveness for asking my crazy-ass twin to be her maid of honor. I rolled my eyes at her, cupped her beautiful face in my palms, and kissed her square on the lips. Benji nearly wet his pants from laughing so hard while Ramsey raised an eyebrow at me, then winked. Layne's chuckle rumbled through his chest.

"What was that for?" Ten sputtered, wiping her mouth.

"Because I love you."

Tensley stared at me, then giggled. "That was my first kiss with a girl." Her cheeks burned crimson as she glanced at Layne. "I hope you enjoyed it. I didn't really like it."

Laughter and playfulness filled the air. I stood rooted in place, overwhelmed with love for my family. They were all that I needed—not the money, not the business, and not a ton of houses and cars. All I really longed for was right in front of me.

LATER THAT EVENING, I curled up against Ramsey on the couch at his apartment.

"I'm excited about your game this weekend. You guys are undefeated, which puts you in the spotlight with the NFL."

He kissed the top of my head. "If I'm drafted, that will change our future, babe. How do you feel about that?"

I gazed into the most beautiful eyes I'd ever seen and sighed. "I will go wherever we need to go."

"Really?" he placed his palm against my stomach, and my body quivered with desire.

"Yeah. I will oversee the business and fly back and forth, but I don't see why it can't work."

"I have a confession," he admitted.

"What is it?" A twinge of fear nipped at me. I used to love surprises, but the last few months had changed me.

"If you didn't want to move or be married to someone in the NFL, I would decline an offer."

I twisted my upper body around so I could look him square in the eye. "Don't you dare. This is your dream. It's not about the money. We already have more than we know what to do with. I'm happy as long as you're in my life. Your dreams are important to me. Don't give them up for me."

"I would, Avery. Nothing is more essential to me than you. Yes, I want to play professionally if there's an offer on the table, but not if I lose you in the process."

"You won't. Unless …"

"Unless?" he asked, worry clouding his expression.

"Unless you fuck around on me, then you'll wish you'd never met me." I smiled. "So just don't do it."

"You're it for me." His kiss confirmed it.

I peeked out from the bedroom of the vacation house. Instead of Ramsey and me escaping for a weekend, we had invited everyone—Tensley, Layne, Benji, Michael, Marilyn, Davia, Patrick, and Olivia—to join us. They were all gathered downstairs, laughing and reminiscing while flames crackled in the fireplace. My heart swelled as I spotted Ramsey next to Davia. He'd stuck close to her after she had gone to rehab. I was grateful that he wanted to support her too.

"Oh my god. I'm so fucking nervous." I wiped my clammy palms on my form-fitting black dress. Tensley and I had spent a day in Seattle, shopping for a wedding gown for her, when I realized I wanted something special for myself.

"Girl, what are you doing? Don't wipe your hands on that gorgeous dress." Benji handed me a Kleenex and kissed my cheek.

"Dammit, you're right. I'm just a jitterbug right now." I inhaled slowly.

"You're going to be amazing. He has no idea." Benji winked at me.

"You look stunning. I'm going to record the entire thing," Tensley said, nearly giddy.

"Okay, hon. We're going to join everyone else." Ten gave me a kiss on the cheek, then slipped out the door.

Benji paused. "I don't think I've ever told you that one of the reasons I love you so much is that you're fierce. And … and behind that strength is a beautiful person who loves deeply. Girl, you make me so fucking proud."

"Benji," I whispered, tears welling in my eyes. "I can't ruin my makeup."

His chest rumbled, and he pulled me in for a long hug. "We're all here with you. Take a breath, and just be you." He placed a kiss on the top of my head, then left me alone with my thoughts.

My hand shook as I pressed it against my chest, my pulse pounding double time.

"I'm a Davenport," I said to myself. "Daddy, this one is for you." I looked skyward and blew him a kiss.

I was scared shitless, but descended the stairs with purpose. Ramsey glanced up, and his eyes grew wide while his gaze connected with mine. He stood and strode across the room, shoving his hand in his pocket, his gaze never leaving mine. Everyone grew quiet as my heels clicked against the hardwood floor of the living room, and I stopped in front of Ramsey.

"You're stunning," Ramsey said softly.

"Thank you." I quickly scanned all of the expectant faces, and Ten and Benji gave me a thumbs-up while Layne nodded and grinned.

I took one of Ramsey's hands in mine, then sank down to one knee. My chin trembled as my emotions overwhelmed me. A hush fell over everyone as he stared at me, speechless.

"Ramsey … words can never express how much I love you. You're the beat of my heart. I don't know where life will take us, what challenges we'll endure, or what victories we'll have, but I know I don't want to experience any of them without you." I sniffled. "Would you make me the happiest woman on earth and marry me?"

Ramsey shook his head, a huge grin splitting his handsome face. "Stand up, babe." Confused, I allowed him to help me.

Is he not going to accept my proposal? Oh shit. What have I done? My legs threatened to collapse. *This isn't good.*

Ramsey removed his hand from his pocket. "Only if you'll agree to be my wife." He flipped a little Tiffany Blue Box open and revealed the most stunning diamond ring I'd seen in my life.

My fingers flew to my mouth. "You were going to propose to me this weekend?"

"Yeah. I was."

I nodded. "Yes. Yes. Yes."

Ramsey slipped the ring onto my finger, tossed the box to Benji, then dipped me backward and placed a searing kiss on my lips in front of the entire family.

The entire room broke out in cheers and claps as Ramsey straightened us back up.

"Looks like we'll both be planning a wedding," he said to Layne and Tensley.

"I'd like to say something." Davia stood and smoothed her jeans and sweater. "I realize that I'm not your biological mother, but I always looked at you as my daughter, Avery. All the years of drugs messed everything up. I'm so sorry. I'd like to make it up to you and help you plan the wedding. Your dad would want me to pay for it too. So you choose anything you want. I'm—"

I bolted across the room to her and threw my arms around her. "Thank you, but ..." I dropped my arms from around her neck and held her gaze. It was amazing to see her clean and sober. "I want you to give me away."

"Really?" Shock registered on her beautiful face.

"Really. You know the one thing I ask, though. Stay sober."

"I will." She nodded empathically. "This will give me something to help you with as well. It will help keep me clean and sober one day at a time."

"On the days that you're struggling, do it for me—for your daughter."

Tears streamed down our cheeks, and we embraced again.

Everyone congratulated us, then we popped open bottles of non-alcoholic champagne.

A few minutes after midnight, everyone said good night and went their separate ways. The house had seven guest rooms, which housed my family comfortably.

Ramsey opened our bedroom door, and I hurried to where I'd hidden a bottle of real champagne and two glasses. I giggled. "Just in case you said yes."

"About that." Ramsey took the items from my hands and placed them on the dresser. "I never got to officially propose." He dropped to his knee and kissed the back of my hand. His blue eyes filled with so much love that it stole my breath.

"Since we were little kids and played in the sand together, I have dreamed about this moment. As hard as I tried, no one could fill your place in my heart. I've always belonged to you, Avery Davenport. Now that we're grown, I still dream of you. I dream about waking up with you every morning, making love to you, buying our first house together, and hopefully, someday, placing kisses all over your swollen belly as it protects and nurtures our first baby. I've never loved anyone else. It's always been you. I want it to always be you. Marry me, Avery, and make my dreams come true." He kissed my ring and smiled, then he stood and slipped his arms around my waist. "Thank you for being the strong, courageous, beautiful soul that makes mine complete."

"I love you," I whispered. "Thank you for waiting for me."

Ramsey pulled me against him and kissed me slowly and passionately. "I will always wait for you. Always."

***

Want more of the hot and mysterious bodyguard, Pierce? Don't miss Love & Corruption!

DEAR READERS, you might have questions concerning Avery and Bexley's crime family. Stay tuned for more.

Enjoy giveaways, the inside scoop about J.A. Owenby, and never miss a new release again! Sign up today at
https://www.authorjaowenby.com/newsletter

LET'S GET IN TOUCH! Connect with me here:
    Author J.A. Owenby Website
    Join my Newsletter
    Follow me on Facebook
    Join my Facebook Group
    Follow me on Amazon
    Join me on Goodreads
    Follow me on BookBub
    Follow me on Twitter
    Follow me on Instagram
    Join me on Pinterest

ALSO BY J.A. OWENBY

OTHER BOOKS BY INTERNATIONAL BESTSELLING J.A. OWENBY

Romance

The Love & Ruin Series

Love & Ruin

Love & Deception

Love & Redemption

Love & Consequences, a standalone novel

Love & Corruption, a standalone novel

Love & Revelations, a novella

Love & Seduction, a standalone novel

Love & Vengeance, coming 2021

Love & Retaliation, coming 2021

Romantic Suspense

The Wicked Intentions Series

Dark Intentions, a romantic thriller standalone

Fractured Intentions, a romantic thriller standalone

Standalone Novels

Where I'll Find You

Coming of Age

The Torn Series

Fading into Her, a prequel novella

Torn

Captured

Freed

CONNECT WITH ME

I appreciate your help in spreading the word online as well as telling a friend. Reviews help readers find books they love, so please leave a review on your favorite book site.

You can also join my Facebook group, J.A. Owenby's One Page At A Time, for exclusive giveaways and sneak peeks of future books.

Fractured Intentions

J.A. OWENBY

Edited by: Adept Editing

Cover Art by: Iheartcoverdesigns

Photographer: Wander Aguiar

First Edition

ISBN-13: 978-1-949414-40-0

Dear Readers,

If you have experienced sexual assault or physical abuse, there is free confidential help. Please visit:

Website: https://www.rainn.org/
Phone: 800-656-4673

ABOUT THE AUTHOR

J.A. Owenby lives in the beautiful Pacific Northwest with her husband and cat.

She also runs her own business as a professional resume writer and interview coach—she helps people find jobs they love.

J.A. is an avid reader of thrillers, romance, new adult, and young adult novels. She loves music, movies, and good wine. And call her crazy, but she loves the rainy Pacific Northwest; she gets her best story ideas while listening to the rain pattering against the windows in front of the fireplace.

You can follow the progress of her upcoming novel on Facebook at Author J.A. Owenby and on Twitter @jaowenby.

Sign up for J.A. Owenby's Newsletter:
   BookHip.com/CTZMWZ

Like J.A. Owenby's Facebook:
   https://www.facebook.com/JAOwenby

J.A. Owenby's One Page At A Time reader group:
   https://www.facebook.com/groups/JAOwenby